Saxon Sword

Saxon Sword

Book 10 in the Wolf Warrior Series
By
Griff Hosker

Saxon Sword

Cover by Design for Writers

Published by Sword Books Ltd 2018
Copyright © Griff Hosker First Edition

The author has asserted their moral right under the Copyright, Designs and Patents Act, 1988, to be identified as the author of this work.

All Rights reserved. No part of this publication may be reproduced, copied, stored in a retrieval system, or transmitted, in any form or by any means, without the prior written consent of the copyright holder, nor be otherwise circulated in any form of binding or cover other than that in which it is published and without a similar condition being imposed on the subsequent purchaser.
A CIP catalogue record for this title is available from the British Library.

Dedicated to all my US Marine fans! Semper Fi!

Saxon Sword

Contents

Saxon Sword 1
Chapter 1 10
Chapter 2 30
Chapter 3 42
Chapter 4 56
Chapter 5 74
Chapter 6 89
Chapter 7 98
Chapter 8 112
Chapter 9 125
Chapter 10 146
Chapter 11 161
Chapter 12 171
Chapter 13 182
Chapter 14 194
Chapter 15 208
Epilogue 217
Glossary 220
Historical note 225
Other books by Griff Hosker 233

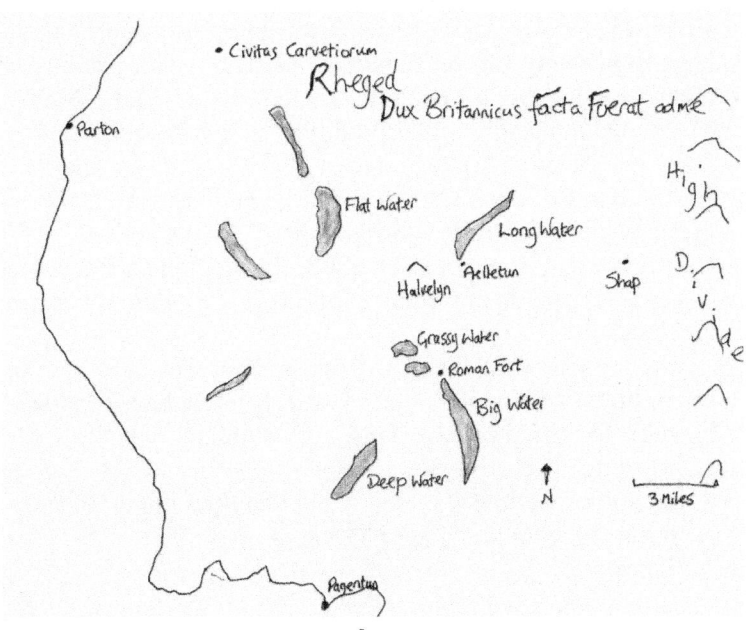

Prologue

Myrddyn was dead. The wizard who had helped my father save our land from the Angles and the Saxons was now buried beneath the sacred mountain of Wyddfa. He lay in the same tomb as my father. My brother Gawan had buried him. That news was not common knowledge. Only a few knew that he was dead. Most of our people just believed that he was somewhere else. The travels of Myrddyn the wizard were legendary. For the last few years, he had been rarely seen. Most of my people worshipped the old gods and Myrddyn the wizard was seen as someone who was greater than an earth-bound body. So long as the land of Rheged survived then there was a belief that Myrddyn and the spirits were responsible.

My equites, my lords and my brother all told me we had much to be happy about. King Oswald had been defeated. Northumbria, which had been joined was now two Kingdoms, Bernicia and Deira. The closer of those people, the Angles of Bernicia, stayed in the east. Our ally, King Penda of Mercia, kept the south safe for us. Our world should have been more secure than at any time yet I could not rouse myself from the stupor and sadness at the death of the wizard who had made me what I was. I was Hogan Lann, the Warlord. I was Dux Britannica. I should have been happy and yet I was not. Not only had my family been taken from me, but we had also lost the island of Ynys Môn, Mona, and the lands around Wyddfa. There had been a time when my father had ruled the west of this island. We had been the last outpost of the Roman Empire. I had lost that. It was gone. We now controlled an island of land with Civitas Carvetiorum at its centre. The old Roman legionary fort was a bastion. Around us flowed a sea of Saxons, Angles, Hibernians and Picts.

It was my brother, the wizard and warrior Gawan, who roused me from the self-indulgent pit of despair into which I had fallen.
"Brother you need to speak with Myrddyn."
"Myrddyn is dead."
He nodded, seriously, "I know but that does not mean that you cannot speak with him. Go to his cave."
"His tomb?"

"No, brother, do you not remember? He used to visit a cave a few miles south of Halvelyn. You went there with him. Copper drank from the magic pool! It was a special place for him. His spirit will be there."

My brother knew a world which I could not enter. It was the spirit world and he knew things I did not. If he told me to go there then I would but I knew not what I would find. "I just go to the cave?"

"Go there, light a fire and drink this." He handed me a small jug. "It will help you to enter the dream world." He saw my worried look. "Brother, fear not there is no poison here. You can trust in me."

"I know that Gawan but I am the warrior and you are the mystic. I am uncomfortable with this."

He shrugged, "Then do not go. This is the only way you can settle that which disturbs you."

He was right and I took the jug. I had neither wife nor child. I needed no farewells. However, my equites would not let me travel alone. Llenlleog insisted upon accompanying me with two of my scouts. Geraint and Tadgh. As we headed south through the steep-sided valleys of the land of Rheged I was glad of their company. My warrior, Pelas, had been killed by a poisoned blade and he would have been with me otherwise.

They all understood my mood. We did not need to fill the silence with empty words. They were alert to danger and that allowed me to enjoy the land we had protected from the Saxons. The journey south took us through high sided valleys with the brooding mountain, Halvelyn to the east. We had had to compromise with King Penda of Mercia. His people had been our enemies. When he had allied with King Cadwallon, then that had made us allies. Cadwallon was now dead but the alliance remained; for the moment. I did not think that there would come a time when we would be free from Saxons but I hoped for a time when we would not be swamped by them. Myrddyn had prophesied that the descendants of my brother would one day defeat the Saxons. Our blood would rule this land. I had to believe that would happen. If it did not then my whole life would have been wasted.

Saxon Sword

Unconsciously my hand went to my father's sword, Saxon Slayer. It was a link to the past. It was Roman and older than any other precious object that I possessed. It had come to my father from one of his ancestors. He had dug it up from a long-abandoned farm. I had to believe that there was some pre-ordered pattern to this. The sword had come to my father and that had begun the resurgence of Rheged. Myrddyn would return and he would tell me.

It took all day to reach the cave. It was summer and there was little risk of rain for the skies had been clear. The path wound up through the trees and the cave itself was surrounded by a tumble of rocks. When we reached its gaping maw, we made a camp outside with a large fire and my scouts cooked the meat we had brought.

"You go in alone, Warlord?"

"I do. No matter what you hear do not enter. I will be safe. Myrddyn will not harm me." Neither my scouts nor Llenlleog wished to accompany me.

I walked into the cave. On my left was the pool which Copper had drunk from. According to my brother, it was magical. I had yet to see evidence of that. I left Copper with my men and I entered the cave. I took a torch. The place was special. I felt it the moment I stepped under its foreboding ceiling. I saw kindling in the centre of the cave. The warrior in me wondered who had placed it there and then I realised this was a magical place. Logic had little to do with it. I made the fire and lit the kindling. The flames licked around the dried kindling and then flamed onto the logs. Suddenly the cave seemed like a warrior hall. There were four large logs around the kindling and I sat on one. What would happen? I was a warrior and the realm of the spirit world was not mine. It was the world of Gawan and Myrddyn. I was about to leave when the fire flickered. It was as though I was being spoken to from the Otherworld. This cave was a portal and I disobeyed the spirits at my peril. I had to obey. Taking the potion, I drank it down. I knew not what was coming but my brother had given me the draught and I would take whatever the Otherworld threw at me.

All went black. It was as dark as I could remember. If I had not trusted my brother I would have been convinced that I was in the Otherworld already. Then I saw Halvelyn. It was below me and I was a hawk high in the sky. I knew I was a hawk for I could see my shadow on the earth as I soared high above the mountain. I spied the Reed Tarn. Then I saw another shadow. It was bigger than mine. It was an eagle. Was I being hunted? I had been hunted before but never as a bird. I swooped down, looking for shelter. As I flew I found myself over Wyddfa. I recognised the place we had found the blue stone and I dived towards it. As I raced earthwards I saw a black hole. It looked too small for me but as I drew closer, it grew larger and, folding my wings behind me I entered the blackness of the hole.

I stopped and waited for the eagle to plunge after me and tear me apart. The hole had been larger than I had thought. Nothing happened. I put my wing to my face and it was not covered in feathers, it was my hand. I began to walk. In the distance, I saw a light. It was a blue light. I walked towards it and as I came closer to the light I saw it was a pool of blue water. Sitting on a rock in the middle was Myrddyn.

"You took your time getting here. Did the bird frighten you, Warlord?"

I nodded, "You were the bird."

"Of course. Gawan sent you, did he not?"

"Wizard, you left too soon!"

"I stayed too long! Your father's time was my time and I stayed too long to protect you. The spirits are unhappy. This is wyrd."

"But my work is not done!"

"Mine is! You and Gawan, not to mention Arturus, will have to make do without me."

I saw that his reflection in the pool was not a true reflection. It showed a young man. Was this the Myrddyn my father had first met? I looked into the water and I could not see my reflection.

"What will become of me? Will I defeat the Saxons?"

He shook his head, "Do not expect me to give you hope where there is none. The Saxons are spreading too quickly. Saxon Slayer cannot kill them all. You will lose."

"Then I should just accept their presence. I might as well give up."

He laughed and his laughter was so loud that ripples appeared on the surface of the pool. "You cannot do that. It is not in your blood. You will fight and you will die. Those that you love and care for will also die. The island that we live upon, all save this one will become Saxon. Only Rheged will remain. Save Rheged all will forget the old gods and all will be forgotten."

My head sank. All the deaths, all the pain, all the compromises we had made were in vain. My father had sacrificed himself and it was without a point. I put my hand down to draw the sword, Saxon Slayer. It was not there. It was gone.

"The sword is but a tool. When you die then Arturus will not have it. Your people will no longer have the sword which holds such power. Arturus does not need it. His sword is his blood. It is his seed. He will die and the people will mourn but they will remember him. Many generations from now there will be another Warlord, and another and another. Each one will have someone like me. There will be a guide from the spirit world to help them. This land you love will change. Men will bleed and, in that blood, which seeps into this land, will be a strength and steel which will conquer the world. Remember this pool. It is the home of the sword. This is where it must lie."

"And me?"

"You will be forgotten. You will be a memory, briefly, and then a legend. You will be a story told around campfires by warriors. The story will change and Hogan Lann will not even be mentioned. You will become a mailed warrior on a golden horse who saved folk from the Saxons. Your father, you, and even Arturus will become one man. People will believe that you lived forever."

"I cannot, simply, give up."

"No, you cannot. You have to fight. You will face foes who are more terrible and fierce than any you have encountered thus far. One will kill you but that is not the end. That will be the beginning. Make Arturus your heir. Make him the last

Warlord. Your father and I have a place of honour waiting for you. Fear not."

"But who is this enemy?"

There was no answer for he had gone. I rose and found that my legs felt like lead. I waded into the water. It was icy. I slipped on a stone and plunged into the water. When my head broke the surface, I was back in the cave and I was in the magic pool of Myrddyn. I had had counsel but it was not the counsel I wanted to hear. It was the counsel of death!

Part 1

King Oswald

Chapter 1

My men had heard shouts from within the cave. They had heard splashing but they had been told to stay outside and they had obeyed orders. They were curious about what I had dreamed but they seemed afraid to ask. To be truthful I was uncertain what to tell them. Did I tell them that no matter what we did we would lose to the Saxons? You could not send a warrior into battle with those thoughts in his heart. I was unsure how I would manage it. I had been convinced that Saxon Slayer would if wielded by a true warrior, defeat the Saxons. Now I had learned that the sword was just a tool and that Arturus who was still in the east with his mother, was the weapon which would, in time, see our people rise again. This was not the message I had hoped for when I had left my home.

I smiled at them, "All is well. I have dreamed and I have spoken to Myrddyn."

Llenlleog asked, "And?"

"And if Myrddyn wished you to know then he would send the dream to you. Come, it is time we rode home."

My answer did not satisfy Llenlleog. He was my first equite. I was aware that I was shutting him out. It did not sit well with me. It was getting on for dark when I saw the white walls of Civitas Carvetiorum in the distance. "I am sorry, my friends. I know that you wish to know what happened in the cave. All that I will say until I have spoken with Gawan, is that I spoke with Myrddyn. He is in the spirit world but he did not give me the counsel I sought."

Llenlleog nodded, "That was ever his way, Warlord. When it comes down to it then swords will be needed and not magic. Magic can help us enter Din Guardi. Magic can make weapons of war which terrify the enemy but it will be a piece of steel which wins a battle and a warrior with a true heart who knows how to wield it."

I would not end Llenlleog's dream but I knew he was wrong. No matter how brave the warriors we led we would, inevitably, lose.

Gawan was waiting for me at the gate. His face showed that he knew what I had dreamed. I did not know how. He might have saved me a two-day journey and a night on a stone floor. I was being unreasonable. No matter what Gawan knew I had to speak with Myrddyn.

"Take Copper to the stable. Thank you, my friends. I would not have done that alone."

Gawan put his arm around my shoulder. "It must have been hard to hear what Myrddyn's spirit told you."

"What little hope I had before I entered the cave has now gone. There is no point."

He shook his head, "You are wrong. There is always hope. Arturus and his mother are on their way home."

"Then your family will be reunited. For that I am happy but it does not change things. We still lose!"

"And yet the wizard we both trusted for our whole lives told us that Arturus' seed would save our people."

"And that is so far in the future that… I cannot even see beyond the new grass! Arturus is barely become a man and has no wife let alone a child."

"You are not becoming a follower of the White Christ, are you brother? That is the way they think. We are at one with the land. The land endures no matter what people do. Our folk were here before the Romans and they will still be here when the Saxons are but a memory. Your task, and mine, is to ensure that our world survives even though a Saxon darkness descends."

Perhaps he was right. I threw myself into making our equites, squires and archers as strong as they could be. We had lost warriors like Pelas and new men needed to be trained. Agramaine had proved himself and he would be an equite. We had precious few of those. Our mounted horsemen were the greatest advantage we held over the Saxons. When our foes made a shield wall then the horsemen could fix them and our archers destroy them. Mailed and with lances, our horsemen were feared throughout the land. The land had been visited by a plague. It had taken many of the warriors who could have fought our foes. It had made us weaker.

    King Oswald was still a threat. Along with his brother Oswiu, they sought to make this whole island Christian and Northumbrian. I wondered if Arturus, who had left a youth, would come back a man. Would he be ready to take on his warrior duties? I hoped that he might have learned, as I had learned, of secrets from the east which would give us an advantage over our foes. While Gawan sought a mystical solution to the problem of Oswald I worked with Llenlleog and Kay to find a military solution. We sent Geraint and Tadgh to scout the land of Bernicia. When we had entered their castle and killed the witches we had hurt the King. He purported to be a Christian and yet he had used witches to defeat Myrddyn. Gawan had just said the Saxon was being practical and using whatever method he could.

    While my scouts were away we began training our squires and archers. We no longer had a huge army. Our battles had bled away the best and we could now muster barely two hundred men all told. I had just forty equites. All were worth twenty Saxons but when we fought it would be against twice that number. The Saxons bred well. They rutted like feral deer! We made some of our older squires who were now ready into equites. Youths who had shown promise became their squires. Our archers were not chosen they were bred. They had broad shoulders and powerful arms. They were harder to rear than even equites.

    Another of our strengths was our commerce. We had two ports: one in the north, Civitas Carvetiorum, and one in the south, Pasgentün. We used large ships to trade with the rest of the world. It cost us for we had to crew them with men who could fight as well as sail. They would all have made good equites. That trade, however, brought us riches denied the Angles, Jutes and the Saxons. It meant we would buy good iron and make good mail. We lived well and that was another reason Oswald sought to defeat us. He wanted that which we had. His White Christ did not help to drag them from their huts. They still lived like barbarians. We clung to the old ways and we lived well. We had stone buildings, walls and baths. We had retained the best of Rome. The barbarians had destroyed what the Romans had left.

As well as having equites, squires and archers, we also had farmers, ironworkers, miners and artisans who could fight. We did not take them as an army to fight beyond our frontiers. We used them to man our walls and defend our home. There had been a time, long ago, when we had protected our people and they had not needed to fight. That had ended with the loss of our lands and the death of the King. We had no King. The last members of the royal family had died. I had no doubt that there were some with the blood of King Urien in their veins but the throne was empty.

Cadafael ap Cadwallon was now King of Gwynedd. Cadwallon had died without issue and Cadafael was a shadow of the man he replaced. However so long as King Penda rule Mercia and continued to war against Bernicia then we might survive. The dream and Myrddyn's words had been depressingly dark. I wondered what fate awaited me. King Oswald had sworn vengeance upon me for I had slain their king, Edwin. The Christians had made him a saint.

Our scouts returned and they reported that the Angles kept to their lands. There were no warbands and they had not mustered an army. The thegns would have their heart weru and that would be all. Their news did not make me feel any less apprehensive.

Arturus and his mother arrived some months after my dream. Their arrival lifted all of our spirits for Arturus had been a golden child. He had Gawan and Gwyneth's good looks. With long flowing hair which was gold coloured hanging down his back, he looked like some sort of Greek god. He had his hair from his father and his looks from his stunningly beautiful mother. He had adopted the Greek style of shaving his beard and so was clean-shaven. He had their intelligence and he had his father's martial skills. He had shown some skills in magic but he had been away at the court of the Emperor for a long time and no one knew if he would have lost those skills. Gawan and Myrddyn respected the knowledge held there in the east but both knew the power of the land of Rheged had a more powerful influence.

Arturus had grown. He was no longer a boy. He had come back a young man. He stepped from the ship with bronzed skin and flowing locks. He did not look like the boy who had left. He had been transformed. His mother still looked the same. I spoke with Arturus as she and Gawan embraced. My brother had missed his beautiful wife.

"Are you pleased to be home, nephew?"

"Now that I am here and see the rugged hills climbing to the sky I am. I will be truthful, Warlord, I was reluctant to come home. Constantinopolis is a wondrous place. It enchants and it intoxicates. Know you that the Emperor offered me a place amongst his own equites?" I nodded. Gawan had told me. "I would have accepted. In fact, I had decided that I would accept when I had a dream and Myrddyn came to me. He told me that I was needed here in Rheged. He said the spirits would forgive me for abandoning the old ways if I came home."

"When was this?"

"Four months since, why?"

"For that was when the wizard was dead."

"Ah. Now I understand why he is not here to greet us."

I had heard the name, Myrddyn, and that had been all that I had heard. Now as I looked at his face the rest of his words surfaced. "Abandoned the old ways? Did I hear you aright?"

He took, from beneath his tunic, a silver cross. "I became a Christian. My mother did the same."

It felt as though my nephew had slid a blade into my back. We had been betrayed. If the hope of our people lay in one who was not a Christian then what was our future? My silence and my face told my nephew what lay in my heart. My brother and his wife had gone to the side to speak alone. Others were fetching chests and bags from the boat but I stood in stunned silence.

Arturus reached up and put his hand on mine, "Warlord, I am still the same Arturus. I will still fight for this land."

His hand was soft. He was no longer a warrior. Already the priests of the White Christ had begun to turn him. "How can you fight those who are Christians? Your religion says that you turn the other cheek! They are your brothers now and it is we, the ones they call pagans, who are your enemies."

He smiled, "The Emperor and his men are more pragmatic than that, uncle. They do not side with someone because he shares their religion. They have a new enemy there. The followers of a man from the desert worship the same god but his followers, the men of Islam, make war upon Christians. The Emperor and his men do not turn the other cheek. They fight. I will fight."

I turned his hands over and put my hand next to his. My hands were calloused and hard. "Are your hands the hand of a warrior, Arturus?"

He shook his head, "Not yet but they will be. I confess that I have neglected my training. Now I am back then I can work with Pelas and…

"Pelas is dead. It was not just Myrddyn who died. Others fell. We have fewer men than when you left. We are an island within an island. The mountains are all that stands between us and destruction. Like you, I have dreamed and I have seen the end. Perhaps it would have been better had you stayed where life was easy and there was a place for a Christian warrior with soft hands."

I was angry and I had said that which I should not. I turned and walked back to the stronghold which might soon be besieged by our enemies.

"Warlord!"

I did not turn when Arturus called me. I had dreamed and Myrddyn had spoken with Arturus. I had been deceived by both. I went to the stable and, mounting Copper, rode south to the hills. I wanted to lose myself in them.

It was almost dark by the time I had calmed myself and felt ready to return to my home. The hills and valleys did that. This land was untouched by all, even the Romans. Only their handful of roads crossed it. I had realised that my brother would now need me for he had been betrayed too. His wife and his son had abandoned him and been seduced by the White Christ. King Cadwallon had shown us that the followers of the White Christ could be cruel men. He had butchered women and children. We had not done that. The men of Bernicia and Deira had also shown that they could be ruthless and kill those who could not defend themselves. My equites and squires would never do that.

Arturus' betrayal was more fundamental than that. If we abandoned the old ways then the land would abandon us. It was at that moment that I finally understood the dream. Myrddyn had known what Arturus would do. He had said, '***His sword is his blood. It is his seed. He will die and the people will mourn but they will remember him.***' This was meant to be. I might not be happy about it but I would have to learn to live with it. It would break my heart but I would have to watch as Rheged died so that it could be reborn sometime in the future.

As I entered my gates I saw Gawan waiting for me at the entrance to the hall. I dismounted and a sentry led Copper away. "Give Copper a good rub down and some oats. I rode hard."

"Aye Warlord."

Gawan just smiled, "Brother, this was meant to be. My wife and son are still the same people they were before they left. It was practical to become Christian in the court of the Emperor."

"Then they will abandon the cross?"

"No." My brother would not lie to me even if it meant causing me pain. "I am no Myrddyn. I cannot see into the ripples of time from this stone which has been thrown into our pond. We do what we must here and now. Let those who come after us make sense of what we do. You have hurt Arturus for he feels he has let you down. I beg you to make him your squire. Show him how to become an equite. Mend the fences which now lie broken."

"He is your son. Why do you not have him as your squire?"

"With Myrddyn gone it falls to me to be the wizard. I have fought too much and forgotten that which I was taught. I must relearn. The power Myrddyn had I can never have but I can become stronger than I am."

I saw apprehension on Arturus' face as I entered. His mother's countenance was like a mask and I could not see beneath it. Gawan was right. Arturus would be the next Warlord. Myrddyn had said he would be the last such Warlord. I owed it to my father and those who had died before to make him the best warrior I could. I smiled, "Arturus, you have enjoyed your time in the east. What say I make a warrior of you? Agramaine, Pol and Llewellyn are now equites. Will you be a squire so that I can make you an equite? If you are to be Dux Britannica then you will need skills."

Gwyneth asked, "Why does he need warrior skills? The Emperor does not fight!"

I turned to Gawan's wife. I was not fond of Gwyneth. "And this is not the Empire. This is a tiny outpost and all that remains of what was once Rome. Arturus would not wish men to die for him while he sat in comfort, would you?"

I was proud of my nephew and spied hope in him for he stood and said, "I will train, mother. I may not be able to wield Saxon Slayer but I will become an equite. It may be a losing battle but I will fight our foes for our freedom." And with that, he came under my wing.

The next day we went to the horse master and selected two horses for him. One was for war and would need to bear a mailed warrior one day. The other was for travelling the land and carrying weapons. I then resumed his training. Before he had gone away he had been in training. All young men were trained for war. Those of higher birth learned to use a sword and to ride a horse. Those of humbler stock used a bow and a spear. We held competitions for all on a regular basis. Like our swords, we were honed.

The soft life Arturus had enjoyed soon manifested itself. His hands blistered and then bled. His thighs and calves chafed. His buttocks ached. It said much for my nephew that he did not ask for time off to rest. He was there each morning with the other equites. As he wielded the wooden practice swords his muscles hardened. It would take time and that was in short supply.

Arturus and his mother had brought servants with them. They had been slaves but manumission brought with it, loyalty. Arturus' two were Atticus an older slave and Demetrius who was a similar age to Arturus. Atticus proved a godsend. He had been a warrior who had chosen the wrong side and he had been destined for the galleys until Gwyneth had bought him. She saw, in him, someone to protect her son. Grateful that he was alive Atticus worked hard. It was he who made the salve for Arturus which helped his hands. It was he who gave him advice. Demetrius was more of a body servant. Born into the life of a slave he was skilled in the art of massage and his hands eased Arturus' muscles. Six months after their return Arturus looked and acted differently. His mother did not approve but my brother and I did. The other squires knew he was the best of them and he could have easily become an equite without waiting any longer. It was Arturus himself who determined that he would wait.

"Warlord until I have fought in a war and bloodied my sword then I will not be blooded. I am content."

When war came it was swift and it was sudden. I had known that King Oswald sought revenge for our attack on his stronghold. The fact that we had breached his walls had terrified him. Rumours of Myrddyn's demise were spoken in the Angle villages but as he had not been seen within the walls of Din Guardi then they remained a rumour. The Angles were now Christian. How did they reconcile a wizard with their god?

The King did not come himself to wreak revenge on us. He wanted his revenge served cold. He had bided his time and then acted. He sent killers. He hired mercenaries. As my equites and I practised by the river a rider, galloping on a hardy little pony, reined in. "Warlord I bring dire news. I am Raibeart ap Ardel. Lord Lann Aelle and all the warriors of Aelletün have been slain. Raiders came in the night."

"Angles, from Bernicia?"

He shook his head. "My father, Ardel, lived long enough to tell me that they were Saxons. They had tattooed faces and were savages. Those that they did not kill they took as captives."

"And how did you escape?"

"I had been to the Big Water. My uncle has a farm close by the old Roman fort."

"Then ride back to Big Water and warn them there of the danger. Tell every village through which you pass. Until we have dealt with this danger then all are threatened."

Even as I turned Copper to ride back to Civitas Carvetiorum I was planning how to deal with this threat. My first priority was the recapture of the captives. As much as I wanted to bury my cousin he was dead and beyond my help. Once we had the captives back then I would deal with King Oswald. The mercenaries were the least of my worries. Once they were paid off then they would depart for pastures new. I would have my men keep watch for them. Saxons with tattooed faces were rare.

I waved over Geraint, "Ride ahead. I need our scouts and archers preparing for war."

"Aye lord."

As he rode off Arturus asked, "Where will they take the captives?"

"The road by Long Water heads northeast. If they were without captives they might try crossing the high ridge where the Roman Road, High Street, runs. I cannot see that. They will head up the water and cross the bridge close to the deep pool. From there they can make the old Roman Road and pass by Banna."

"Was that not fortified?"

"It was but the plague which took so many while you were in the east, took the men who lived there. We have not got around to manning it again." I shook my head, "I am not the Warlord my father was. I allowed self-pity to distract me. My cousin's people may have paid the price. It was, perhaps, aggravated by his lack of vigilance." He gave me a questioning look. "His land was the frontier. When we had the fort at Banna there was a buffer. We will catch them. Their nearest stronghold is on the other side of the Great Divide. They have made the old Roman fort to the west of Hagustaldes-ham their frontier. If we cannot catch them before they reach it then we should not call ourselves horsemen!"

"Do not be hard on yourself Warlord. You have not made a mistake."

"Llenlleog, in my position I have to anticipate what our enemies will do. I have looked within for too long. Now I need to look beyond our borders!"

One innovation that Arturus and Atticus had brought was the Roman cavalry saddle. It was a strange piece of horse furniture. It had four horns and held the rider in place. You could not mount a horse the normal way. You have to vault over the back. For that reason, we only used them for the equites but it meant that we could now use a spear or a lance from its back. The horns held us in place. They had worked in practice but we had yet to try them in war. This seemed the perfect opportunity.

Geraint's arrival and the summons to my scouts and archers had alerted the fortress. "Put the new saddles on the horses. Equites we ride."

Kay and Bors emerged. They were already mailed. I wore just a leather jerkin. "What is amiss Warlord?"

"Mercenaries have killed the men of Aelletün. We ride to recover the captives. We will take the road to the south of the Roman wall."

They nodded and raced to fetch their squires and horses. I saw Arturus trying to put my saddle on Copper. Despite the fact that it was one of his ideas he was struggling. I went over to help him. "Remember Arturus that you and the other squires are there to help us this day. If we look in danger then you come to our aid. Our archers and equites should be able to deal with any danger."

"Aye Warlord. Now that it is here I am a little fearful. Does that make me a coward?"

"No, it makes you a man. If you said you were not afraid I would not trust you."

Just at that moment, Daffydd ap Miach rode up. He had a horse farm to the south of the town. "I heard, lord. I only have forty archers ready to ride. The rest live too far away."

"This is a warband we hunt. The men we take will have to do." I waved to Geraint to lead the scouts. They would need no orders. Their task was to find the enemy and watch them, unobserved. It sounded easier than it was. There were eight of them and they would send a rider back to keep us informed of their position.

By the time we left our home, heading east, the mercenaries had more than half a day's lead over us. We rode steadily along the road. Always the wall to our left reminded us of the old boundaries of Rheged. Now they were more fluid. Had I been the mercenaries then I might have been tempted to cross the wall and disappear in the forests of Dál Riata. It would have been harder for us to follow and they would have been able to move as quickly as our horses in the thickly wooded land. I knew that they had not done so for my scouts had not returned. We could steer our course along the Stanegate.

There were few settlements along this part of Rheged. It was too close to the Angles and in the winter was exposed to the weather. There would be few places for the mercenaries to hide. The long ride along the desolately empty road gave me the time to think about this raid. King Oswald had used mercenaries for a reason. They would be more ruthless than his own warriors.

They were not his people and if they failed he would have lost a few coins. The normal arrangement was half the payment before the job was done. Another reason for the mercenaries was, perhaps, to lure me east where he could fight me on ground of his choosing. I thought that this was a real possibility. I had come east with a relatively small number of warriors. The miscalculation appeared to be where they would fight us. We would catch them well before they were in Bernicia proper. Once we neared their captured fortress beyond Hagustaldes-ham then there would be danger. For the next twenty miles, the road and indeed the wall was exposed. Once we passed the abandoned fort close by Steel Rigg then we might be able to see them. Our scouts certainly would.

We were close to the fort with the baths when Tadgh rode in. "Warlord, they are ten Roman miles ahead."

"They have made good time."

He shook his head. "I am sorry to say it is at a cost. Have you not noticed the bodies in the ditches, lord? They have been slitting the throats of those who could not keep up and have abandoned them in the drainage ditches to the side." He pointed to one such ditch. I saw the arm of an old lady. Our eyes and minds had been so focussed on the road ahead and we had trusted our scouts so much that we had not seen that which was before our eyes.

I mounted, "Enough! If we save our horses then our folk die! Ride like the wind!"

My helmet rattled against the new horns of the saddle as I urged Copper on. The new arrangement meant that I had, as well as Saxon Slayer, two spears. When we caught up with them then we could give a good account of ourselves. "Tadgh, how many are there in this warband?"

"We counted at least a hundred. There may be more. We spied scouts ahead of them."

"But not behind? They were not watching for pursuit?"

"No, Warlord. It is as though they expected us to follow and we did not pose a threat."

I now regretted not bringing Arturus' father with us. He would have been able to read what we could not see. I had thought this was a simple task. The further east we went the more I realised that this was anything but. With squires and archers, we had less than seventy men. We should have been superior to the Saxons we chased and yet they had killed every man in Lann Aelle's town. He had men who had fought with us against King Oswald before. Their leader knew we were coming. Was he playing with us like a cat with a mouse? I suddenly saw ambushes behind every bush.

When we reached the ridge, which overlooked the Tinea I spied them. They had halted on the far side of the Roman bridge. The Roman fort they used was not far away. Why had they halted? Even as we watched I saw a warrior with a long sword, half as long again as Saxon Slayer, walk to the centre of the bridge. Two men dragged a woman. Even at a mile distance, I recognised Freja. It was Lann Aelle's wife. Before I could race Copper to her aid I knew that I would be too late for I could see what the savage would do. He swung the sword and took her head. He shouted something and another woman was brought over. This was deliberate. He was taunting us and yet he risked us riding through him and his men. We would slay them all.

I was about to urge Copper and my men to wreak revenge on the huge Saxon with the long sword when Geraint and Aedh suddenly broke from the cover of some trees. "Warlord, it is a trap! It…"

Aedh said no more for two arrows were sent into his back and he tumbled from his horse. More of the Saxons suddenly rose from the drainage ditches. They were fifty paces from us. Had not Geraint and Aedh warned us then they would have been upon us before we could do anything. I pulled out a spear and threw it at the half-naked Saxon archer whose body was heavily tattooed. It had hidden him in the ditch. We had not expected the ambush but he had not expected me to throw a spear from horseback. With no mail to slow it the spear tore into his chest. Even so, he tried to wrest it from his body.

There were well over eighty Saxons and we were hard-pressed. Arturus was behind me and I could do nothing to aid or advise him. He was having a lesson in warfare. I hoped that he would survive. I used my second spear like a lance. I galloped down the road towards the bridge. I could see the Saxons there, led by the huge warrior with the long sword, as they drove the remaining captives up the hill towards the Roman fort. They would escape us! I plunged my spear so hard into the chest of the next Saxon that it came out from the middle of his back and when he fell he tore it from my grasp. Drawing Saxon Slayer, I was aware that I had not donned my helmet. The Saxons had archers. They were poor ones but even a poor archer might get lucky.

Luck was with me. As I leaned out and swung back an arrow flew through the air. It passed over my head. Myrddyn had been watching out for me. I swung my sword as I galloped. Timing was all and my sword hacked into the chest of the Saxon whose spear was rammed at my chest. My mail held. His chest did not. My blade broke his breastbone and tore open his chest.

Suddenly the Saxons were gone. Even as I looked I saw them fleeing towards the river. My archers had dismounted. Daffydd ap Miach and his archers would kill many but more than half would escape. They would risk the waters of the Tinea. Up ahead I saw that the road was empty. The leader with the long sword had escaped me. The battle here at the ambush was not over either. Most of the Saxons had fled but my men were searching for others while my squires chased the ones racing across the fields to the river. I saw Kay about to despatch a wounded warrior.

"Hold Kay. I wish to question one of them!"

"Aye lord, but you had best be quick. This one has not long for this world."

I dismounted and sheathed my sword. I had the opportunity to examine him. He wore leather breeches. What I had taken to be a leather belt was actually a ring of iron. His body was tattooed as was his face. It was hard to see flesh that was not blue and it explained why they were so hard to spot. Kay had speared his knee and his lifeblood was seeping from the wound.

We had fought enough Saxons to know their language. I saw from his amulets that he was not a Christian. Perhaps that was why Oswald had hired them. If he was not Christian then there was hope. I had something to bargain with.

"Where are you from and who is your leader?"

He spat at me. It was bloody phlegm. Kay made to strike him but I held up my hand. "Horseman, kill me for I will not tell you!"

"Suppose after you told me what I need to know we give you a sword and a warrior's death? Then you can go to the Otherworld and meet your dead brothers."

His eyes agreed. "I will tell you for it will do you no good! We are the Clan of the Snake. We are cunning and we are killers. Lang Seax is our leader and he eats the hearts of those that he kills. He will kill you." His eyes were filled with joy.

I nodded and moved closer to the wounded Saxon, "Give him a weapon Kay."

Even as Kay gave him the sword I saw the movement in his eyes. He was going to kill me. I had been expecting it and the seax I held in my left hand ripped across his throat.

I stood.

"Lang Seax?"

"It means long sword in Saxon. It is the warrior I saw on the bridge. We have a name and now we ride to the stronghold. I fear that it will be in vain for we are too few to take it by storm."

We had not lost any equites and for that I was grateful. But for our squires, it was different some of those had been killed. Our mail only covered the tops of our legs and these Saxons had long swords. I respected the Saxon swordsmiths, they made good weapons. Luckily the Saxon warriors were not as skilled in their use as we were. I saw that Arturus had survived and that he had blood on his spear.

He looked at the spearhead as he approached me. "A man is harder to kill than I thought. I have hunted animals but even though my spear struck the Saxon's arm he almost managed to stab me with his sword." He pointed to Daffydd ap Miach who, along with his men was collecting undamaged arrows. "Daffydd slew him with an arrow. I owe him a life."

"You survived your first encounter. The others will not be any easier but at least you will have a better idea of what to expect."

The other new equites, Agramaine, Pol and Llewellyn had emerged successfully. These were the small victories I would take. When we crossed the Roman bridge, I saw that our archers had reaped a harvest from the fleeing Saxons. Some of their bodies lay against the piers of the bridge. Others were floating downstream. I hoped the Saxon leader, Lang Seax had been paid well for he had lost many men. Even as the thought came into my head I dismissed it. Mercenary leaders could always find men to fight for gold. They could be replaced.

We stopped two hundred paces from the walls of the old Roman fort. The Saxons had repaired it. They had not done a good job but it would stop us. I would need to muster every man in my land to take it and that was not worth the price. I would have to try negotiation. It did not sit well with me but I had little choice. The walls were lined with warriors. Some were Angles from Bernicia. Others had the tattooed faces, chests and arms of the mercenaries.

"I would speak with the one they call Lang Seax."

One of the Bernicians shouted, "I am Thegn Aethelfrith and I command here. You can speak with me, Warlord."

"Were you the one who abducted the women and children from Aelletün?"

He shook his head.

"Then you are not the man I need to speak with. I would have my captives back."

He laughed, "And how will you get them back? I count less than a hundred men here. You have not enough to scale the walls and defeat us. You are horsemen. Go hence. The captives are now our slaves."

I nodded, "Aye we are horsemen. Have you enough meat and food within these walls? My horsemen can make certain that nothing gets in or out of this Roman fort. My archers will rain death on your walls. They will stop you from reaching the river for water. There is grazing for our horses and we can hunt."

"King Oswald…"

"King Oswald will do nothing. If he could have his revenge then he would have come himself. The fact that he sent mercenaries tells me much." I paused, "We have magic. Perhaps I should return to Din Guardi. This time I might end the life of King Oswald. How about that?"

I could see that I had him worried. The Angels had been shocked that we had managed to gain entry into their most powerful fortress. They were Christians but they feared our magic. "You are a pagan! Go hence."

"Not without my captives."

He disappeared and I waved over Daffydd ap Miach. "Could your best archers hit the men on the walls?"

"Probably but once we send arrows then they will take shelter and use shields."

"I count twelve of those who ambushed us. Kill them. It will send a message."

"Aye, Warlord."

He dismounted and whistled over his archers. They dismounted and Daffydd ap Miach explained what he wanted. Once they nocked and drew then the men on the walls would know what they had planned. My Captain of archers was clever. He used the horses to disguise his intentions and his men nocked, drew and released without warning. Eleven of the tattooed men were hit. Not all the wounds would be mortal but we had shown what we could do. The rest took cover.

A short while later the voice of the thegn could be heard, "Warlord, I would speak with you. Do I have your word that I will not receive an arrow for my trouble?"

"You have my word!"

He stood and exposed his head and chest. I might be an enemy but my word was trusted. "If we give you the captives then do we have your word that you will leave?"

"You do but I do not say that I will forgive this attack. I will leave but one day I will return and this Lang Seax will see how a sword should be used. I do not use mine to butcher women!"

The warrior called Lang Seax appeared. He was a good head taller than the thegn. "I will fight you anywhere and any place, old man! You were a warrior with a good reputation but that is long gone. I have heard that you have lost your wizard! I do not forgive either. This excuse for a warrior might return your captives, it matters not to me for I will be paid anyway, but there is blood between us now. Your archers slew my brother. I will have weregeld for him."

Just then the gates opened and fifteen women and children ran out towards us. I shouted, "Lang Seax, thank the thegn for he has just saved your life. I gave my word." Without turning my head, I said, "Daffydd ap Miach, as close to him as you can manage."

In one movement my master archer sent an arrow to smack into the parapet just below the Saxon leader. A chip of stone flew up and scored a wound along his cheek. He put his hand to the wound and wiped away the blood. He grinned as he tasted it. I could see that he had filed his teeth. I had heard of barbarians who did this.

I pointed Saxon Slayer at him, "Saxon Slayer cares not if it kills kings, princes or bandit chiefs. It drinks the blood of Saxons and it shall drink yours."

"We will meet again, horseman."

The captives had reached me. One, I vaguely recognised as the wife of one of Lann Aelle's oathsworn, grabbed my hand and kissed it. "Warlord, you have saved us! They were terrible men."

I patted her hand, "You are safe now. Is this all?"

"It is all that is left. Those who were slow on the journey back they slew. Long Water has many bodies within it. Lady Freja defied them to the end. She said that you would come for us and she was right."

I waved over the squires. "Each of you, take a captive and have them ride double." As they did so I shouted, "Daffydd ap Miach watch our rear. I trust not these blue-skinned savages."

On the long journey back to Civitas Carvetiorum we learned more about the attack on Aelletün. The sentries who watched the walls had had their throats cut and the barbarians had been within the settlement before Lann Aelle and his men knew. His stronghold had little stone. It was mainly made of wood. That was ever our weakness. When we went to war, our equites had mail and could withstand the blows of any enemy. Even though Lann Aelle had less than twenty such equites had they been mailed then the Saxons would have been defeated. They were attacked individually. Lann Aelle had fought bravely but without armour, he could not survive. Before he fell he ordered all to flee. Some escaped. That alone gave me hope. When we returned to Aelletün we might find some survivors hiding in the hills.

The captives were exhausted and we were forced to stop and make camp for the night at Banna. I sent half of my archers back to Civitas Carvetiorum to tell Gawan and his family that we were safe. I ordered Gawan to take the equites who remained to search for survivors. We kept a good watch on the walls of the old Roman fort.

I sat with my equites and Arturus. If he was to succeed me then he needed to know how his uncle spoke to the equites who were close to him. Llenlleog said, "Warlord do not berate yourself. You could have done no more. I confess I thought we had lost the captives. Your words saved them."

I shrugged, "It was a bluff but the thegn did not know that. Lang Seax did. Had he been in command we would have been given the bodies of the captives. He is a ruthless enemy."

Kay was a thoughtful man, "Warlord, these men of Bernicia say they are Christian and yet they conspire with witches and hire those who are savages and do not believe in their White Christ."

"Oswald is a king for whom his religion is but a veneer." I turned to Arturus. "You wear the cross, Arturus, how do you explain this Christian king?"

"They are practical. My mother was closely protected in Constantinopolis. I was privy to much that went on at court for the Emperor was fond of me. They are pragmatic men. If they can use what they call a barbarian then they will do so. The Emperor has many mercenaries who serve him. Often, they are the most barbaric of men and when they serve the Emperor then they are ruthless. This Oswald seems to be the same."

There was hope for Arturus. Perhaps the baptism had not changed him too much. "I can see that we will have to revert to our system of long patrols."

Agramaine, Pol and Llewellyn were among the equites who, like Arturus, had been too young to have experienced the equites' quests, as we had called them. I saw the question in their eyes. They would not ask amongst the equites such as Bors, Kay and Llenlleog. They would not wish to appear foolish.

"In my father's day and when we had Ynys Môn each equite and his squire, along with a couple of archers would ride abroad for half a moon. They would seek signs of enemies and strangers in the land. Then we had wars and the plague. We ceased our patrols. We lost land and retreated behind our walls. We stopped building in stone and we have paid the price. Even if we rebuilt

Aelletün in stone it would take too long to offer protection and the other settlements are the same. It is just those like the one in which we sleep tonight, Pen Rhudd and the like which are solid enough to be protected. For the rest, we ride abroad. We have thirty-six equites who remain, me included. Six will ride a quest each moon. That will allow us to still retain thirty should war come."

Arturus looked at me and shook his head, "That is not enough men. The Emperor has two thousand mailed men to watch his palace! There is a Bandon of five thousand men camped just outside the walls of his city."

Llenlleog smiled, "And that is the Empire. We are but a shadow of the Empire. Until the sons of the equites become old enough to train I fear that this small band will have to do it alone."

Arturus was like a dog with a bone. He would not let it go. "But how can four men stop a warband like the one we saw?"

I answered for Llenlleog, "Put simply they cannot but they can watch. They can hunt enemy scouts. They can warn settlements. Our folk have one thing in their favour. All are trained as warriors. They might farm or fish. They might work in wood or metal but if a foe comes and they are ready then they can fight. That is all that the equites' quest can do, it can give warning. If Lang Seax and his men had been seen when they were on the Roman Road then we might have met them at Pen Rhudd or here at Banna." I smiled at Arturus, "Perhaps you should have taken up the Emperor's offer. Your life would have been more comfortable."

He shook his head, "I would have had little sleep for I am sure that Myrddyn would have haunted my dreams until I did as I was bid!"

Chapter 2

For four moons we sent out our equites to watch our eastern borders. Gawan was the one equite we did not ask to ride abroad. He was angry with himself as he had not seen the danger to our cousin. He and I were now the last of our line. The three brothers who had forged our people had had sons. Gawan and I were the last two. He was the wizard and he strove to be as powerful as he could be even though that would only be a shadow of the power that had been Myrddyn. Myrddyn had used his mind to seek out foes as they approached our land. Gawan could not see as far.

I rode on the fifth such quest. Arturus and I had Judicael and Dai with us as our archers. Both were young. Llenlleog was not happy about the arrangement. He was now my first equite. Along with Gawan, he would command in my absence. "Warlord, both Judicael and Dai are young. Arturus has the least experience of any. Why do you take the risk? Have Daffydd ap Miach with you."

I shook my head, "I will be fine. The young have to learn and these white hairs in my beard tell me that I might have something to teach."

"Warlord this land cannot afford to lose another Warlord."

"And we will not."

I had told Gawan of Myrddyn's words but neither of us thought that there would be any benefit in telling the others that I was doomed to die. Myrddyn had been as enigmatic as always. As Gawan had said there was no time given for my death and Gawan had not yet dreamed it. However, in light of what he perceived as his failure to detect the Saxons, he was lacking all confidence in his skill. He told me we needed a real mage and not a half one.

We had more to carry and so I took Star. Star was a bigger horse and Copper was getting old. Dai led a pony with our supplies. We had to survive for fourteen nights. At least two of those would be in one of our settlements but most would be in the wild land of our borders. Each of the six equites would ride to our borders and back. So far, the equites we had sent out had seen little evidence of Saxons. Agramaine had caught and killed a couple of bandits but that was all. They had been travelling abroad in the snow. Now the new grass was here and that was another reason for Llenlleog's unease. The new grass was when we might find signs of an enemy.

We were in the centre of my line of six patrols. We would be together for the first few miles and then we would diverge. Bors would head south to the sea. He would pass the Deep Water. Pol would head north to the land of Dál Riata. We would head to the stone they called Shap. It was a natural boundary for us now. At one time we had had a fort called Brocauum. It was further east and had been close to the lands of Northumbria. That had long been destroyed. A deep trough-like valley descended from the rock called Shap and headed north to Carvetitas. It was the headwaters of the Eden. We would ride there and look for signs of Saxons and Bernicians. The time of the new grass was the time of rain and it was easier to track. This would be a lesson in tracking for Arturus.

We had to pass Aelletün on the way and it was sad to see the place where my cousin had fallen. The dead had been buried and the survivors discovered. There had been more than we had thought. The survivors were hardy folk and they still lived by the river but there were fewer of them. We stayed the night and then headed up through the steep-sided valley to the rock of Shap. We made a camp in the lee of the craggy rock. We would not light a fire. We did not wish to be seen by enemy scouts. These quests were not pleasurable. We slept on the ground and ate cold rations. After we had emptied our ale skins we would drink brown, iron filled, mountain water. The horses were happy for it was lush new grass which they ate. The spare horse carried our shields and spears. Once we made the camp I took off my mail hauberk.

We watched the sun set in the west. It held the promise of a dry night. At this time of year and at this altitude it would be cold but we would endure that. We had furs in which to wrap ourselves. Mine was that of a wolf I had killed. Arturus was surprised that he would have to stand a watch. I shook my head, "I will stand one too. Is it right that Judicael and Dai should have to share the whole night watch? This will do you good. When you watch you learn how to hunt in the night. Often that is a skill we need. We do not always fight our foes in daylight."

I had the second watch and I gave the last watch to Arturus. It was too much to expect him to be able to wake and then get back to sleep. For Judicael and myself this would not be a problem. When Dai woke me, I was alert in an instant. It was something I had taught myself. I made water and checked on the horses. They were fine. After a mouthful of ale, we had to husband it, I went to the rock which overlooked the valley and the camp. I wrapped my cloak about me and hunkered down. The secret was to move as little as possible. I quite enjoyed these solitary watches. It was when I felt the closest to my father. I had been at his side when he had been killed and that meant my last memory of him was as he looked up at me, dying. It was that memory which had steeled me to continue. He had made a sacrifice for his people. I had managed to lose most of what we had had and if I lost this last little island how could I face him in the Otherworld?

As I watched, looking for shadows which moved I sought a solution to the problem of Oswald. I did not have enough men to fight him. I could hurt him so that another might defeat him but King Penda was the only one with an army big enough and he was safely behind the borders of Mercia. King Cadwallon's death had ended our dream of defeating Oswald and his brother Oswiu. We could stop him from invading my land. We had to hope that our land would help us to stop him before he could ravage it. There were many passes where we could hold him. There were places where he could be ambushed. I knew he would not come, at least not until he had built up his armies again. He had sent mercenaries to punish us but he feared the wrath of the Warlord. My fear was another mercenary raid. Lang Seax had lost too many men to be an immediate threat but he would have had gold from the Bernicians and gold is a great lure for those with no honour.

I saw false dawn and knew that it was time to wake Arturus. I shook him awake. He rose with a start. "Peace, it is your watch. You will not have the dark for long. Check the horses and then sit on the rock and look down the valley. Keep still for you are looking for shadows which move. When the sun has risen then wake me."

Arturus' first watch passed successfully in that nothing happened. We ate and then saddled our horses. We would leave the packhorse with our shields and spare weapons at the campsite. We headed north. Llewellyn, who had borne the standard once, was now an equite and he would be north of us. We had not planned a meeting but if one happened then we could share information.

We dropped down into the valley and followed the twisting trail which rose up to the high ground to the east. It had been the trail I had watched. It was wide enough for two men on horses, no more. It zig-zagged up the side. We were looking north and when we turned, it was south. We were heading to the deserted village of Chonoc-salchild. None had lived here in my lifetime. When the Angles had first come and fought King Urien the villagers had been wiped out. It was a difficult enough place in which to live at the best of times but the Angles ended the life of the village. My father and I had hoped that, if we were successful, then people might return. They had not. I had failed my father. Now four of us rode through the once-thriving village.

This would be our halfway point. It was noon and so we rested, watered our horses and ate dried venison. Judicael was on watch and he whistled. Dai and I had our weapons out and we had stood before Arturus even realised what was happening. When Judicael stood and waved we knew that there was no danger.

Llewellyn and his men rode in. "You have made better time than us, Warlord."

"Did you see any sign?"

He nodded and pointed north, "Radgh discovered where the mercenaries must have crossed when they attacked. We found an old fire."

"Aye, Llenlleog and his men found it two moons since. There are no fresher signs?"

"Apart from the fire, there is no evidence that the Saxons were ever here."

"I would not expect them over the long nights. Now we can expect them. Keep a good watch."

The next day was equally uneventful. We rode south and met Pol. He, too, had seen nothing. He turned south and we headed back north. Arturus seemed almost disappointed. I explained to him that this was the life of the equites. There was more boredom than fighting. We had reached our camp early. The next day we would head due east for our deepest penetration into the land of the enemy. After I had taken off my hauberk and while Judicael and Dai saw to the horses we sat with our backs to the rock of Shap. The sun was getting lower in the sky behind us making the shadows sharper.

"This is hardly glorious, Warlord."

"No, but it is necessary. Was hunting the mercenaries glorious? Was there pleasure to be derived from seeing our people slaughtered?"

"No, but I thought an equite would do battle with our foes."

I laughed, "Being a warrior means being watchful for the longest time and then fighting for your life for the shortest. The hardest lesson to learn is patience."

Just then something caught my eye. The slowly setting sun helped. I shaded my eyes and stared at the opposite side of the valley. There were four men and they were descending the track on the eastern side of the valley.

"Be still." I gave the low whistle of alarm. The other side of the valley was more than six miles away. They would not hear us. It was movement which would give us away. Judicael and Dai would make their way around to join us. "You have younger eyes. Tell me what you see."

"I see nothing… wait. There is movement. It is four men. They have leather caps on their heads and they carry swords. On their backs are their shields. They are Angles. They are not the Clan of the Snake."

The two archers slid next to us. "Angles on the other side of the valley. They are heading south."

Judicael said, "They will camp soon. Further south there is a small river with a stand of trees. It will give them shelter." My archers knew the land well.

"We wait here until the sun has set and then we hunt them. They are warriors." I had a dilemma. To ensure that we captured them it would have been better to warn Pol and Llewellyn. To do that I would have to send my two archers and that would leave me with Arturus. He did not have the skills I needed. We would have to risk taking them with the four of us together.

The four of us watched them as they twisted and turned. Occasionally we saw the flash of white as they peered up at the western skyline where we sat. I know that Arturus was convinced we had been seen but the bright sun would have blinded them. We would be invisible. If they were good then they might detect movement. They reached the bottom and then briefly disappeared behind some scrubby elder, hawthorn and blackthorn bushes. They reappeared and their backs were to us.

"We move." The sun had dropped behind the skyline. It would still be shining at Civitas Carvetiorum but here Halvelyn and the other mountains hid its rays. We saddled our horses. Arturus went to fetch his helmet and shield. "No, we do not need them. I will not wear mail. It might make a noise. Now we shall see if the night watches have given you the skills we need." As we mounted I said, "We need one prisoner!" My archers nodded.

By the time we were saddled night had fallen completely. We headed down the track to the valley bottom. It took some time. If the Angles were not camping then we would lose them. They must have travelled a long way for they camped and they lit a fire. We saw it three miles or so down the valley. It was a pinprick of light which appeared and disappeared as men stood before it. Then it vanished altogether. I knew that Arturus was desperate to speak to me but I had impressed upon him that we needed silence. He would be alarmed that we had lost the Bernicians. It was not so. They had been moving around and now they had settled down for the night. Their recumbent forms hid the fire from us. Like Judicael and Dai, I had the position of the fire fixed in my mind. It was above the track and the water. These men had experience. They would not risk a rainstorm and a flooded camp.

It was a clear night and the track was relatively flat. The Angles had hurried down the valley sides to avoid travelling over it in the dark. Then it would have been dangerous. That they were scouts was obvious but scouts normally returned to an army when they camped. These did not and I wondered why.

When we could smell the wood from their fire we stopped. Slipping silently from our horses we tethered them. Our horses were all trained to be silent. I knew not how the horse master managed it but he did. They would eat the grass and graze on leaves but they would neither whinny nor neigh. I drew Saxon Slayer. Arturus had the sword he had brought from Constantinopolis. I would have preferred he had wither a Saxon sword or one made by our smiths. I knew their mettle! Judicael and Dai had their bows. At their waists hung short swords and seaxes but they would feel more comfortable with a bow in their hand. I led. Judicael and Dai might be better scouts but I was the leader and it was my responsibility to face danger first. The wind was coming up the valley and as well as the smell of wood fire it brought the smell of greasy unwashed bodies. The Bernicians might worship the White Christ but they did not bathe. It was the smell which identified their sentry. He was to the west of their camp on the other side of the stream. He was watching the west. He was seeking the men of Rheged,

I tapped Judicael on the shoulder and pointed. I wanted him to take the westernmost sentry. He nodded. He slipped his bow over his back and drew his seax. If he used a bow to slay the sentry then there was a risk that the falling body might alert the others. Now that we knew where the sentry was I waved for Dai to go to my right and Arturus to my left. I slipped my seax into my left hand. If this was to become knife work I would simply drop my sword. We moved more slowly the closer we got to the Angles. My eyes were completely adjusted to the dark and I saw the twig on the path. It had been placed there deliberately. The Angles had laid traps around to alert them of danger. I hoped that Arturus was using his youthful eyes well.

I stopped when I saw their fire. They had built it within a ring of bushes. There had to be a way in but it was not immediately obvious. Dai did not need telling. He would find the way in. I moved to my left and hand brushed Arturus. His eyes widened as he saw me. I nodded my head and he moved to his left. We had to climb up. There was a small shelf. Once there I gestured for Arturus to get behind me. It was as he did so that he made his mistake. It was a small one but it was expensive. His foot sent stones skittering down the slope. The Angles were up and ready in an instant.

I heard a cry as Dai killed one. A second ran at me with a sword in his hand. I acted instinctively. I deflected the sword and then stabbed into his guts. He fell at my feet. The last man swung his sword. It was a lucky blow for it struck Arturus on the side of the head but as it was the flat of the blade it just rendered him unconscious. Then the Angle was off. he disappeared into the darkness. Dai and Judicael appeared. "Get after him!"

I turned Arturus over. He was breathing. I heard a moan from behind me. The man I had gutted lived. I saw by the light from the fire that his guts were spilling out. I knelt next to him. "You are dying." He nodded. "Would you like me to end your pain? Let you hold the cross of the White Christ?" He nodded eagerly. "Where is your King and where were you headed?"

Like the Saxon prisoner, he thought to answer me with an insult but a sudden spasm of pain made him arc his back. "He is at Iedeu. We were sent to find a safe way south. I swear."

I believed him, "Go to your God." I slit his throat and he died with a soft sigh.

The Bernicians had put water to boil. When I went to the sentry Judicael had killed I saw that he had a couple of doves he had trapped. He had been plucking them when my archer had slit his throat. They would have been meant for the pot. I took some of the boiling water and after letting it cool slightly used it to bathe Arturus' head wound. The skin was broken and he would have a bad bruise but as first wounds went it was nothing to worry about. His mother would, that I knew. We had another five days before she would see it. By then it would be just a bluish brown. As the archers returned Arturus came to.

His first reaction was one of guilt, "I am sorry that I made a noise." He looked at Dai and Judicael who were grinning at him. They were finishing plucking the birds. "None of us were hurt?"

"Just you, nephew and it is not a bad wound."

Judicael said, "Sorry, lord, we lost the last one. He could have gone anywhere. Come daylight we can track him if you like."

I nodded, "We will all track him. We will cook the birds and get some rest. In the morning we will pick up his trail. I am guessing that he will head home."

Dai asked as he jointed the bird, "Is their army not close by?"

"The one I questioned said they were finding a safe way south. The King is at Iedeu. We will discover the truth of that tomorrow."

It was a wet morning. The rain started during my watch. It made tracking the Angle difficult. We rode back up the trail they had descended. We went beyond Chonoc-salchild until we could see the other Roman road which crossed over the highest part of the High Divide. I did not expect to see the escaped scout but when we did not see an army or even a warband we turned and went back to our encampment at Shap.

The horse we had left had drunk all its water but the rain must have given it enough to slake its thirst. "Tomorrow we ride a short patrol south. Pol might be wondering where we were. The horses have ridden harder in the last two days than I intended." I gestured for Arturus to join me as the two archers saw to the horses. The rain had stopped hours earlier but the grey skies promised more. We would have to make a shelter. I waved Arturus to sit by me in the lee of the rock, "Come let me see your wound."

We had cloth to bind it at the camp and applied honey and some of Gawan's salve. Gawan swore that it would stop a wound from becoming poisoned. I applied it. After wrapping a bandage around the wound, I gave him the small axe we had with the horses, "Go and cut down some of those elder branches. We will make a shelter for the night." We did not need to light a fire, we had eaten one hot meal but I decided that we would. Shap and the shelter would hide us from prying eyes and the night promised to be misty. It would be low cloud which would make everything damp and dank. It did not take long to make a shelter. The fire meant we could cook a second hot meal and as we ate the wild greens, herbs and dried venison we spoke of what the presence of the scouts meant.

"If there is no army close by then this is a scouting expedition for later in the year."

Arturus nodded, "And it also means that we are not the intended target." We all looked at him. He shrugged, "They were looking for a safe way south. Their home is north. What lies to the south?"

"Mercia."

He nodded, "They have books on strategy in the Emperor's palace. I read some and had slaves read to me the ones I could not. I think I understand King Oswald. The Mercians and the Welsh almost defeated him. When he destroyed King Cadwallon that left just one major enemy, King Penda."

I gave a wry smile, "We are not a major enemy?"

"We are, Warlord, but one he is afraid of. Why else would he hire barbarian mercenaries to destroy us?"

Judicael said, "Perhaps I should have Dai hit me with the flat of the sword. Your squire makes sense Warlord. He sent the mercenaries to kill you."

Dai shook his head, "No, Judicael for he killed Lann Aelle. He did not come for the Warlord."

"I think he did." Arturus had finished eating. He wiped his hands on the wet turf. "This Lang Seax is clever. He brought the Warlord to him. He thought to ambush us and it nearly worked. I think that if the ambush had succeeded then the garrison would have joined in and we would all be dead."

Arturus' words made sense. It would affect what we did from now on. We would keep watch for the Bernicians heading south. We would follow them and we would warn the Mercians. I now saw a chance to defeat the Bernicians.

When we returned to Civitas Carvetiorum the other equites had also found and caught two other groups of scouts. Ours had been the only one where a scout had escaped. King Oswald would have to find another route. There was, in my mind, a safer one south of Eoforwic. The west posed too much of a threat.

Arturus had almost healed when we returned and I just received scowls for my pains from Gawan's wife. We had a table which was large enough for thirty equites. As six were on patrol it worked out well and we shared our news around the table. Gawan was there too. He had been an equite. He sat in the chair that Myrddyn had once occupied. The old wizard had had it carved from the lighting struck oak. He thought it had magical powers and none of us was willing to argue.

My equites were all equal. The table was round to reflect that. I sat next to Gawan because he was my brother and Llenlleog because we were of an age. Agramaine was one of the youngest equites and he occupied the seat next to Gawan while Pol was next to Llenlleog. Six of us had been on a quest and we enjoyed the wine and the food more than the others. Half a moon was a long time to endure dried venison. We had been lucky that the Angles knew how to hunt!

After we had shared our news Gawan said, "Oswald will not risk riding down the valley of the Eden. We have not enough men to defeat his whole army but we could hurt him before he was able to fight Penda."

I nodded. "I agree. The road which passes Eoforwic is too far from us and there are few places to ambush."

"You must ride to meet with King Penda. The road south of here is clear. He must be warned of the danger."

"But this land needs protection too."

"You need not take a large number, brother. I was thinking four equites and squires with twenty archers. Daffydd has been training up new ones. You could take those with you."

Kay nodded, "The squires who are in training are almost ready to be equites. The blacksmiths are making their hauberks now. The attack on Lann Aelle focused their minds. We lost good equites and those who live in the west, where it is safe are keen to replace them. There is no lack of courage in Rheged."

I sipped the heavy red wine which Gwyneth had brought from Constantinopolis. Perhaps I needed to leave the land, briefly. It would show me if it could survive without me. Myrddyn had foretold my death. I had already seen fifty summers. My father had not seen many more before he was killed. The question was should I take Arturus or leave him to learn more about the land of Rheged?

Gawan said, quietly, "Take Arturus with you. He needs to learn from you and not his father. He will not be a wizard." My face must have shown the surprise. He laughed, "Did you think that Din Guardi was an accident? I can read your thoughts brother. I do not travel far these days and I use the land. While you were on your quest I was in the cave of Myrddyn and I spoke with him. When you travel south to Mercia take my son to see Myrddyn and his grandfather. It is meant to be."

And so it was decided. I went south with Llenlleog, Agramaine and Llewellyn. Daffydd ap Miach and nineteen young archers came with us. Left Kay in command of my equites and Gawan as ruler in my stead. He did not see death in my journey but the spirits had played tricks before now. We would put plans in place.

Chapter 3

It was just after high summer when we left. There was a temptation to travel by ship but storms could come from nowhere and there were Hibernian pirates. It was safer and easier to ride. Geraint and Tadgh came with us. That was their choice and their decision. Although both had families and farms their wives and sons who lived by the Grassy Water did all the hard work. Geraint and Tadgh hunted. This was not the time to hunt and so they came. I was grateful for them. They were like Gawan. They sensed things which others, me included, could not even see. It took a day to reach the small port where Prince Pasgen had lived. We still called it Pasgentün. His sons had died but his daughters had survived and they lived there. Their husbands were warriors. Two of their sons, Coen and Coel were squires. We stayed one night for when we left we would be in the land between Rheged and Mercia. Until we had allied with the Mercians we had fought over this bloody ground. Now our people and Mercians farmed the fertile plain and harvested the shellfish rich waters. We headed for the old Roman fortress that had been called Deva. Nearby was Tatenhale. Eorledman Ethelbert had a home there. We had fought alongside him before now. We would visit with him. It had been more than a year since we had seen King Penda. Saxon politics were complicated. Eorledman Ethelbert also knew how the Kings of Gwynedd ruled. Cadwallon I had known. He had been a shield brother. He had changed from the young squire who had ridden behind my father. I did not know his successor. I would take a Saxon's advice on the new king. That was a change from my father's time. The only thing he took from a Saxon was his life.

The old fortress of Deva had been used both by us and by the Mercians. The walls were now too damaged to be defensible and no one had the time or the ability to rebuild. I knew that we were lucky at Civitas Carvetiorum. We just had minor repairs for the structure of our walls was sound.

We neared Tatenhale close to dusk. The Mercians did not ride their land for they did not use horses for war. When we neared

Tatenhale we caused a stir. Geraint and Tadgh had told us that there was no danger from enemies but the Mercians of Eorledman Ethelbert just heard our hooves and ran for the shelter of their walls. We must have been recognised for the sentries did not slam the wooden gates shut. The Eorledman was in his hall and he came out to greet me. He had been a thegn and, as a reward for his service the King had made him Eorledman of the lands around Deva. I thought it a poisoned chalice for if their allies, the men of Gwynedd changed their mind about allying with the Saxons then it would be Tatenhale which would have to fight off an attacker and the walls would not stop a determined army. He was a big man and almost my age. He had battle scars on his arms and his face. He fought in an open helmet and his armour was leather. Since fighting against Edwin and Oswald he had had metal plates sewn on.

"Warlord, I would say this is an unexpected pleasure but you do not make visits to chat about the hunting."

I nodded, "Nor do I speak out in the open when what I have to say is for your ears alone."

He frowned, "I trust my men."

"That is good for I trust mine and yet I would not speak of important matters where the slaves and common ceorls could hear."

His frown turned to a smile. "You are wise. I am unused to men like you. Come, your men are all welcome. It will be a little crowded and a little more pungent than you are used to but we are all men who have fought together."

Saxons ate the same food as we did but they prepared it and served it differently. I had to smile at Arturus. It was as far from Constantinopolis as it was possible to get. Everyone ate in the hall. There was a cacophony of noise. There were no platters neither pot nor wood. Knives were used to spear cuts of meat. The vegetables had just been cooked. There was neither dressing nor sauce on them. The rest of my men had eaten like this on campaign but Arturus had had just half a moon with his uncle. Perhaps this was why Gawan had wanted his son to come with me. He needed to forget about the Emperor. This was now his world.

One advantage of the noise was the fact that Ethelbert and I could talk. We put our heads together and I told him what I had learned. He drank his ale and wiped the froth from his beard. "I have heard of this Clan of the Snake. They came over from the land of the Saxons beyond the sea. One rumour is that they were banished by their own people. They are wild and cruel."

"Then as we killed almost half of their band they will not be such a threat."

"Would that it was true. The wild and the evil leave other clans and tribes. The outcasts of every Saxon, Jute and Angle village on this island head towards them."

"And, where are they?"

"You would seek to end this blood feud?"

"I would."

"Now they are at Hamwic in the south. They are raiding the island of Wihtwara. It has managed to survive until now. I think that Lang Seax sees it as his kingdom. The King of the West Saxons is happy to have him off his island."

That was too far away from my home for me to do anything about it but I now had a better idea of how the clan gained new members.

"And I have news of danger for Mercia. Oswald is sending scouts to find an easy way south. We have deterred him from a passage down the west coast. Tatenhale may be safe."

"They will head for Lincylene. King Penda will need your news."

"And his allies, the men of Gwynedd?"

"The men are good allies but the King? Cadafael ap Cynfeddw has no spine. He is no Cadwallon. The King of Powys, Cynddylan ap Cyndrwyn is a warrior alongside whom I would fight." He gestured to my horn which was almost empty. "More ale?"

I shook my head, "I am of an age where I would be up and down all night making water."

He laughed, "I am getting like that. I will have some men come with you. Some Mercians just remember your father. They have forgotten our alliance. I would not have harm come to you."

"Where will he be?"

"Tomworðig." He smiled. "If Oswald comes south to Lincylene then he is in for a shock for the King is close to there already."

I felt a little better about my visit after speaking with the thegn. Our business done, he and his men took to that activity which the Saxons seemed to enjoy more than any other; they began to get drunk. My men did not and I saw the amused looks on their faces when men with whom they had been talking sensibly gradually became so drunk as to be incoherent. Even Ethelbert joined them. The only exception appeared to be a young Saxon from his hearth weru. Thingfrith was a young warrior. He had the battle bracelets of a Saxon who has fought for his lord but he still looked young to me. Perhaps that was my age. He must have been a good warrior for the thegn to have chosen him for his hearth weru.

He smiled at me as Thegn Ethelbert fell face down in the remains of the wild boar he had been eating. "Warlord, if you would help me take the thegn to bed I would appreciate it. He is not getting any lighter."

I nodded, "Arturus." My nephew rose and joined us. He had said little all evening for he had been too busy watching the Saxons. The Thegn was a big man and it took the three of us to carry him to his sleeping mattress. His wife was there already and she was asleep. Like many Saxon women she might have been pretty once but now she was almost the size of her husband. We laid him down and left them; both were snoring.

Few of the Saxons had managed to leave the table. Some still drank. Thingfrith saw Arturus' shocked look as a Saxon who had just vomited began to drink again. "It is a game for some of these men, young lord. Tomorrow they will boast about how much they have consumed. We do not do this every night but the visit of the Warlord is a time to celebrate."

Arturus was astute, "Yet you do not join them."

"I am the youngest of the hearth weru. One day I will do that which Angeltheow does, I will lead the hearth weru. I will be captain of the thegn's men."

Arturus nodded. He could understand that. They both had much in common. They came from different people and cultures but they had similar ambitions. The difference was that Arturus would get his by right when I died. Thingfrith would have to earn the right.

"I will go and see to the horses, Arturus. I will join you later."

"I will come, uncle."

We left Thingfrith who went to the semi-conscious Angeltheow to help him to his bed too.

When we were outside Arturus said, "These Saxons are not to be feared for they have no discipline."

"Yet they are wild fighters. These men are not Christian. The ones who are Christian have had some of their barbarian edge taken away. It is why Penda was able to defeat Oswald."

"And he had the Welsh and the men of Rheged."

I laughed, "That is true but I believe he would have won anyway. Perhaps Penda would have lost more men but victory would have been his." We checked on the horses. Saxons did not understand war horses. Sometimes a thegn would ride a horse. He might even take one to war but he would not ride to war. They saw horses as a tool to carry goods or pull a plough. They would not harm our animals but I knew I would sleep easier having seen that they were not distressed.

Despite the heavy drinking the hearth weru and Ethelbert were ready to march first thing in the morning. I sighed with disappointment when I saw that only Ethelbert rode. The rest would be marching on foot. It was seventy miles. Where we could have made it in a quick two days it would take three or even four days to reach Penda's stronghold. Surprisingly, however, and despite the drinking, the Saxons kept up a good pace. We only needed two rests along the way. We stayed one night in Nantwich at the home of Ethelbert's nephew, Aethelfrith, and a second in the hall of a warrior called Eccles. Both were wary of my men and I could see why Ethelbert had accompanied us. We might have been offered violence. Ethelbert was a wise warrior and he knew the value of our alliance.

Tomworðig was the biggest Mercian settlement I had seen. It was bigger than any of Oswald's towns save Eoforwic. Din Guardi was a fortress but it could hold few people. Tomworðig had a wooden wall and just a single gate. Not as formidable as Din Guardi it still had ditches, wooden towers and a fighting platform. Even more impressive were the one hundred men

Saxon Sword

Penda had in his personal guard. It was too many to be called hearth weru. Angles and Saxons did not keep a large number of men in a standing army. They used ordinary farmers and townsfolk to do their fighting for them. Penda's oathsworn were the most impressive Saxons I had seen. Each had a helmet and a leather byrnie studded with metal. Their swords were the finest I had seen and they had large round shields. They looked to be heavy but I knew that they could take a great deal of punishment. Each of them had an identical spear. That was unusual. Most Saxons made their own and used whatever wood came to hand. This way their shield wall would be hard to break. Finally, they all had a cloak. It might have been red once but the sun had faded it to a rusty brown.

When King Penda saw me looking at his men and assessing them he smiled, "When you were our enemy, Warlord, we learned from you. These are not your horsemen in mail but they will suffice for me."

I nodded, "I am impressed, King Penda."

He waved a hand, "This is my son, Peada and my brother Eowa whom you have met before and that is his son, Alweo. Come inside for you would not journey here unless it was important."

King Penda might have copied some of our warrior ways but his hall was the same as all Saxons. Our men stayed outside and I took just Arturus with me. With his brother, son, nephew and Ethelbert the only other present was the captain of his personal guard, Pybba.

Slaves came with ale. On the ride over from Tatenhale, I had suggested that Arturus pretend to like the Saxon beer. The Mercians seemed to think that any who did not like their golden ale was to be viewed with suspicion. He smacked his lips convincingly when he drank.

"So, Warlord, what brings you from your mountain lair?"

"Oswald. He has sent scouts to find a way through my land. We have killed them but I think it means that he is heading south. The only reason for that is to make war on you."

I saw Penda considering that. Eowa said, "But surely that helps you, Warlord. If Bernician fights Mercian then you win."

Penda looked up, his eyes angry. "Brother, the Warlord is our guest. If it were not for him and his horsemen then we would not have had the victory we did."

Eowa nodded but I could see that he bore me no love.

"Thank you for that information. We have spies in Eoforwic and I had heard that he was gathering his forces." He looked at me. "If he comes will you bring your men to our side again? Will the alliance still hold?"

"I will ask you, King Penda, can you rely on the men of Gwynedd?"

He smiled, "Since Cadwallon fell they are less than reliable but the men of Powys are doughty." I nodded. "You have not answered my question. Will you bring your horsemen and archers to our side?"

"I will bring men to aid you, aye King Penda."

Eowa said, "But not all."

"Not all, Eowa. If I bring all then I leave my land and my home in danger." I fixed him with my eye and then turned to King Penda. "I will bring enough to make a difference for that is what you want, is it not? You have men for the shield wall but you need the quick strike of mailed and mounted men who can strike anywhere on the battlefield. You need the accuracy of my archers who can punch a hole in a shield wall."

"That is precisely what I want."

"Then when we are summoned we will come. It will take two days for a message to reach us and two days for us to march here."

The King nodded but Ethelbert said, "If it is here." We all looked at him. "I know that the Warlord thinks that they will not come through the Eden valley. That does not mean that they will strike from Lincylene. There is another way!"

The King frowned, "Where?"

"There is a pass over the High Divide. It is south of Rheged and close to the old kingdom of Elmet. It comes out close to the old Roman settlement of Mamucium." He smiled, "I know for it is close to my hall. What if he comes that way?"

King Penda nodded, "Then you will have to watch for him." He stroked his beard. "I had forgotten that route. He would be able to divide us from Powys and Gwynedd. It is good that we have you, Eorledman Ethelbert, to watch the west."

Alweo was the one who looked the least happy. I could not discern the reason and I put it from my mind. The King asked, "What will be the quickest way to reach you? Your home is far to the north."

I nodded, "We live in parlous times, King Penda. I would need some sign that the message was from you. King Oswald has shown that he can be cunning. The attack by the mercenaries was evidence of that. I will have an equite at Pasgentün. That way you could send a ship or a messenger but how will I know that it is from you?"

King Penda looked around and smiled, "I can see that you have lived this long because you are wise and wary. Before you go I will speak with you privately."

His brother, Eowa, said, "Do you not trust us, brother? We are family."

King Penda smiled, "Let us just say that I have not yet thought of a safe and secure way. Besides, I have yet to contact my Welsh allies. I will let you know brother. After all, if anything happened to me then you would be the Regent who would ensure that my son attained the throne." I saw the look exchanged between Eowa and Alweo. There was a conspiracy here. I feared for our coalition. I had hoped for unity between the Mercians and the Welsh. It seemed we did not even have unity amongst the Mercians!

"Of course, brother."

The King smiled, "We will hold a feast in honour of the Warlord. If you would come with me now, Warlord, there is a pleasant walk through my orchard. The apples are just beginning to ripen. I can tell you of the methods we might use to stay in contact."

When we left Pybba pointedly walked behind us to discourage any from following us. "It is strange, Warlord, that you, a former enemy and the son of the bane of the Saxons should be the only one I can truly trust even in my own court."

"A bold statement, King Penda. How do you know that you can trust me?"

"In all of our dealings, you have never once broken your word. Why, even with mercenaries who do not deserve the courtesy, you kept your word. That is rare. I have no doubt that should we fall out you would be a fearsome enemy but I will not allow that to happen."

I stopped and looked at him, "How can you be so sure?"

"You care for Rheged and Rheged alone. The days of Lord Lann, Dux Britannicus, are long gone. You have more modest ambitions. I can tell you now, Warlord, that I have no desire for the smallest part of Rheged. The land is rock-strewn. With steep valleys and high mountains, it holds no attraction for me. You may keep it and I will keep in return your friendship and, more importantly, the swords of your horsemen."

I nodded, "That is refreshingly frank of you."

"More, as part of our friendship and to show how much I value you I will send you a herd of one hundred horses. I have had them bred in the south. If I thought for one brief moment that my men could learn to ride I would keep them but my men prefer the shield wall. I will have men drive them north for you."

"And in return…?"

"Just remain friends, come when I call and watch my family for treachery."

"Your family?"

"Eowa and Alweo think that I am blind, deaf or stupid; perhaps all three. I am not. They plot and they conspire. Pybba has men who watch them. I know their every move. Someone once told me to keep your family where you can watch them. Wise words."

"And Ethelbert of Tatenhale?"

"I trust him. I show him no favouritism for fear of incurring the ire of my enemies. He knows that I trust him. However, Warlord, I pray that you do not mention what I have told you to him. I trust him but there are some of his men whom I do not trust."

"I will keep a good watch. And the signals?"

"Simple." He took out a metal disk on a leather thong from his purse. He handed it to me and I examined it. There was a wild boar upon one side and on the other a Roman numeral III. "This is yours." He took out a second from his purse. On it was the

Roman numeral I. "This is mine. There is a third which has the Roman numeral II. If a messenger comes with the numeral I then you are to believe the messenger and come to my aid. If, on the other hand, he has the one with II upon it or does not have one then he is a traitor and you should hold him."

"Then you knew I was coming?"

He shook his head, "I hoped you would come but if you had not then I would have journeyed north. I planned to come at Samhain for the Christians fear to travel at that time of year."

"And why do I need one?"

"Should you wish to send a message to me."

I liked King Penda. He was determined and knew what his kingdom needed. A king needed to be ruthless and he was. We spoke of the men I might bring and he gave me his assessment of our enemies. From him, I learned that Oswiu was more dangerous than his brother. We returned to the hall just before dusk. I saw questions on everyone's faces. Now I had heard the King's words I looked at them differently. Who was a traitor and who was not?

Arturus was the one who pestered me for information. My equites and captain of archers did not. They knew that I would tell them what they needed to know when it was the right time. "Wait until we are in our hall, nephew. There will be time. For now, watch all that is around you. The Mercians are our friends but most Saxons are not. Learn all that you can so that should you need to fight them then you will have that most powerful of all weapons, knowledge!"

At the feast, we watched Saxons once more engage in drinking contests. The exceptions were Eowa, Alweo, Pybba and Ethelbert. The thegn's bodyguards, our squires and my archers dined in a second hall. This time Arturus was less shocked and I could see that he was being more observant. Halfway through the evening King Penda said, "I nearly forgot, Warlord. When I need you, I will use a rider on a white horse to bring you the message that I need you. If the rider has any other shade of mount he is not from me. That way Oswald and his allies cannot lure you into a trap."

Eowa and his son looked smugly at each other and I saw my equites and Ethelbert frown. They wondered why King Penda had made such a public announcement. Any could now send a rider on a white horse. They did not know of the seal. I confess that it was an act of genius. Eowa and his son had taken the bait.

The King retired earlier than the rest of his thegns. Pybba watched him to bed and then returned. He stood where he could watch me. I do not think it was a threat, rather the opposite, King Penda was ensuring that his ally did not die in his hall. Worryingly when Eowa and his son saw Pybba return they both left. I saw a smile crease Pybba's face. It was further confirmation of their treacherous intent. The King was playing a dangerous game. How and when would he trap his brother and his nephew?

I stood and my equites stood with me. I turned to Ethelbert, "I will see you in the morning. We have a long ride west ahead of us."

He raised his head. "You could head north from Congleton and save forty miles."

I shook my head, "I have another task after we reach your hall. All is planned."

Arturus asked, "Planned?"

"Your father asked me to take you somewhere. It will not take us long and might do you good."

I found it hard to sleep. I knew that I needed to speak with my men but King Penda had warned me of traitors and spies. I would wait until we were at Myrddyn's cave beneath Wyddfa. I rose early and found the King and closest hearth weru eating. He had a priest close by him and King Penda was dictating something to the man who scribbled on a wax tablet. My face must have shown my surprise for he said, "You find it strange that a pagan such as me employs a priest?" I nodded, "Yet I have heard that you did the same. I do not persecute Christians. I allow priests in my land. If they can convert any then so be it but few choose the soft way."

I took some food and placed it on a platter. King Penda used metal platters. I poured a horn of ale and sat at the table. Other men arrived and King Penda gave me a knowing look. Whatever was said would not be private. The words would not help an enemy. My equites joined me and then Ethelbert. He sat with the King and, with Pybba watching, they spoke briefly. When Eowa joined us, he was alone. Perhaps his son had too much ale the night before.

I finished and Ethelbert said, "If we are to make good time, Warlord, then we should leave now."

"We are ready." I turned to King Penda. "When you call then the men of Rheged will return."

The King nodded, "I am counting on it."

Eowa looked at us from beneath a furrowed brow.

We headed along the road the Romans had built to destroy the power of the druids. It was remarkably straight and King Penda ensured that it was well maintained. The border with old Northumbria lay just beyond it. I saw a piece of high rough ground to the south of us when we were about ten miles from the King's home. At the bottom were trees but I spied, at the top what looked like earthworks.

"What are those Eorledman?"

"That is called Castle Ring. I have lived here for twenty years and I have never seen anyone there. When we first came it was empty. Men say the spirits of the ancient ones haunt it."

To the north was a village on the ridge. We would pass by within a hundred paces of it. "And that?"

"Ridgeley."

Riding a horse afforded me the opportunity to view this land. I did not know if one day I would have to fight here. The old hill fort would be a good place to stand off enemies. The trees which had grown were nearer to the road. The castle ring still had a good view.

We were almost at the village when Thingfrith suddenly threw himself to the ground and held his stomach, "Lord, I have the gut ache. I have been poisoned!"

The two groups of warriors reacted in different ways. My men reached for weapons and used their elevated position on the backs of their horses to scan the land to the north and south. Geraint and Tadgh peered ahead while Llenlleog's squire looked behind us. I had Saxon Slayer in my hand instantly.

The Mercians, Ethelbert apart, all ran to the aid of the stricken hearth weru. He was a popular warrior. The spear, when it was thrown would have struck the Eorledman had not Arturus whipped up his shield hand, almost instinctively and the spear thudded into it.

Daffydd ap Miach loosed an arrow into the woods to the south and shouted, "Ambush!"

Spears, arrows, stones and throwing axes rained down from the sky. Some were thrown from Ridgeley while others came from the woods. The hearth weru were not mailed and men died. My men needed no commands. I spurred Copper and we took off towards the woods. It was Mercians who had ambushed us. Even as I leaned from the saddle a spear whistled over my head. The thrower was a warrior I recognised. He was one of Alweo's oathsworn. He tried to turn to run but a warrior could not outrun Copper. I brought the sword across his spine, laying it open to the backbone.

The trees were thin and spindly. Their foliage had hidden the attackers but they did not stop our horses. A Saxon turned with his shield and spear to try to strike at Copper. A charging horseman always has an advantage. He is moving so quickly that, with a good horse he can change direction in a heartbeat. I did that. The Saxon's spear was over his shield and I jinked Copper to my left. The warrior's right side was exposed and I swung Saxon Slayer sideways. It hacked through his upper arm. The blood which arced told me that it was a fatal wound. Copper's hooves crushed a warrior who was trying to avoid Llenlleog. He did not see us and he died instantly. The ground was rising and the trees thinning. It had been a large ambush. There were still twenty men fleeing us. I could not see what was happening on the other side of the road. I had Llenlleog, his squire and Arturus with me. I knew that Daffydd and some of his archers would be close by but they could not use their bows from the backs of horses; at least not riding through rough scrubland. Had the Saxon fleeing us turned and made a shield wall they might have survived. As it was they hurtled up the hill for the safety of the old hill fort. We slew half of them before they even made the first of the earthworks.

Behind me, I heard the voice of my captain of archers. "Warlord, just stop them from moving and we will have them!"

Daffydd knew his business. There were no walls on the hill fort. There were ditches and ramparts. Two of them stood on the ramparts with their shields before them. My archers' arrows hit their unprotected legs. No one else tried that tactic. The Saxons hid in the ditches. When arrows fell vertically men were hit. The four of us moved closer to the ditches. Six men broke cover and ran south. We caught them. Arturus made two kills. He was well on the way to becoming an equite. I watched as he swung his arm back and used its momentum and the speed of his horse to hack into the neck of the Saxon.

When all were dead we headed back. We were a good mile and a half from the ambush. The Saxon ambushers had been on their last legs when we finally slew the last of them. Arturus asked, "You did not keep a prisoner, Warlord, why?"

"I knew what they would tell me. Alweo and his father were behind this. Alweo was not in the hall this morning and I saw at least two of his oathsworn. We will not find him and we have no proof but we do not need any. Eorledman Ethelbert will speak with their King."

When we reached the ambush, I saw that half of the hearth weru were dead. They had killed their ambushers but there was one body which had been hacked so much that it could not be identified.

I looked at Ethelbert. "It was Thingfrith. He was a traitor. You warned me to beware spies and I did not. I will not be remiss again. And you, Master Arturus, I owe you a life. I would have been dead but for you."

I dismounted and said, quietly, "Alweo was behind this and probably his father too."

I gave him my reasons and Ethelbert nodded. "The King suspected as much when he spoke this morning. I had been expecting an ambush but Thingfrith's deception fooled us. He had shown no sign of treachery and I truly thought that he had been poisoned. I was a fool."

"And your men have paid the price." There was little point in being sympathetic. This was a cruel world which did not forgive mistakes. "Now you need to search the hearts of the rest of your men and discover their true loyalties."

Chapter 4

We stayed a day longer at Tatenhale than I had intended. Ethelbert needed my help to make his home stronger. The ambush and the traitor in his midst had shaken his confidence. He had also decided to invest the old Roman fort at Deva, with men. It might not be as strong as it once had been but it would be somewhere his men could defend. It would be a sanctuary for the people. He had an old warrior, Egbert, whom he would put in command. The Eorledman would have to make the difficult journey back to Tomworðig so that he could tell, in private, King Penda of the ambush. As we headed south-west towards Wyddfa I wondered if we would be needed in a war against Bernicia. It seemed to me that there was too much dissension in the Mercian camp. I could not see how they could make a united front against Northumbria.

Arturus had been little more than a babe in arms when we had lived under Wyddfa's shadow. The men of Gwynedd were our distant kin and allies. We would be in no danger but, as we rode over familiar roads I was saddened and depressed by the ruin I saw. The roads we had maintained were now tracks. The stone towers and walls we had built were now robbed out and used for houses. It had only been a few years and yet there was already little trace of my father's hand. He and his brothers had forged a line of defences against the Saxons. They were now gone. Gawan had warned me what I might see and I think, for that reason, he had wanted Arturus to see it before it went.

When we passed the island, we had known as Mona, it felt as though my heart was being wrenched from my body. It had been the jewel of our land. With Wyddfa so close we thought we were protected by its power. That was until Morcar killed my father. Like Thingfrith he had been above suspicion and he had cut down the Warlord from behind. I wondered about the motives of the two warriors. As I looked west I saw that the two strongholds on either side of the Narrows were gone. What saddened me most of all was that we saw few people. The monks at the monastery of St. Asaph shut their doors when we rode by and the farmers fled at the sound of our hooves. We had been their protectors and their saviours and yet now we were shunned.

We headed up the narrow path which led to the cave. It had been many years since we had been called the Wolf Brethren. Those of us who still bore the wolf amulets as clasps for our cloaks were fewer in number. The plague and the wars had had an effect but as we wound up through the trees towards the entrance to the cave I felt the wolf's blood rising through my body. Myrddyn had made the tomb. It was fashioned to look like a wolf. He had begun many years before my father had died. He had dreamed his own death. He had prepared his own part of the tomb too for he had seen that death also. It was an extraordinary construction all the more remarkable in that it was carved from stone. It was part of the mountain. When he had been building it, he had had lights burning within and the locals spoke of the giant wolf sleeping below Wyddfa's snowy peak. When Myrddyn ran short of magic he used his considerably powerful mind.

Llenlleog had been here before. He turned to me as we reached the clearing where the stream bubbled over a waterfall. It was a lovely place. "We will not be able to descend until morning, Warlord. We will have to camp close by."

I knew what he was saying and I was prepared. I only needed Arturus and myself to enter. "I know. I am not afraid but if there are those who fear the dead then they can stay here and make camp." I turned and said, "Arturus and I will be camping by the tomb. If you do not wish to then you can stay here. The water is sweet and the air refreshing."

All chose to come with us and we wound our way up. I could tell that Arturus was nervous. He clutched at the cross around his neck. His fear was understandable. He would be entering a truly pagan world. Myrddyn had come to him in a dream but I knew that both his spirit and that of my father resided here in this cave we would soon enter.

"The spirits who are in this cave cannot hurt us. Our enemies should fear them but Lord Lann was your grandfather. Myrddyn watched over you as you grew."

"I know but does this make me less of a warrior to fear that which will not harm me? I am afraid simply because it is the unknown."

"All men fear the unknown but this is not unknown. Let the spirits enter you."

"Will we sleep inside the tomb?"

"I know not. Myrddyn has not spoken to me. Your father wished you to see it. He did not specify when."

The squires and archers who had never seen the cave were awed when they saw it. Perhaps they had been expecting a hole in the ground. The carved mouth, muzzle and ears of the wolf were incredibly lifelike. The closer you came to it then the features were more indistinct but from a hundred paces below it and against a sky already turning pink it was a huge open-mouthed wolf. What Myrddyn had built could have been seen in the east where kings and emperors lay buried.

"Our people made this?"

"Under the guiding hand of our wizard aye." I turned, "Make camp. I will take Arturus in before dark. We will light the fire. Arturus, fetch kindling. I will go into the tomb first." I had, in my saddlebags, a candle which Gawan had made himself. It would burn all night. Using my flint, I lit the candle. A sudden breeze seemed to sigh and made the flame flicker. Myrddyn was here.

I stepped into the tomb, "I am here, father, wise one. I have brought Arturus as Gawan told me." As soon as I entered I could feel that my father was here. He was not in the mummified body I saw on the shelf. His spirit filled the cave. It was as though I was inside his spirit. Gawan had told me the same except that he felt the spirit was that of Myrddyn. Each man felt something different.

The light from the candle threw long shadows in the cave. Its flickering flame made the rocks look like the pillars in a Greek church. The stone flecked ceiling seemed to shimmer with the candlelight. I saw the mummified body of my father on one side and on the other the newly buried body of Myrddyn. I turned as I heard something drop. Arturus was not in the tomb he was still outside. He had seen the wolf's eyes light up when I had lit the candle. When Gawan had come to bury Myrddyn he had brought a metal candle holder. It had been fashioned so that a wolf head had a shield upon which the candle would sit. I placed the candle upon it.

I turned to go to the blackened hearth in the centre. There was no chimney but the cave had been cunningly formed so that the smoke rose and was drawn out of the wolf's nose. I took the kindling from Arturus and made a fire. It should have been his task but I knew that he was taking in all that he saw around us. When the fire was going the whole tomb was bathed in a soft red and blue light. The blue was reflected in the blue stone in the rocks.

I stood and went over to my nephew. Putting my arm around his shoulders I said, "Your father wished you to see this. I know that you are a Christian and what was done here is what the priests who baptised you in Constantinopolis, would have called pagan." I pointed to the shelf in the rock where the Warlord lay. Men called me the Warlord but I knew that I was a pale imitation of the real one. "There lies Lord Lann. I believe he is sleeping. Come."

I walked over to the shelf and saw the patina of dust which now covered the body. We had not put face masks upon them but he wore his armour and his helmet. We stood and looked. Arturus said, in little more than a whisper, "Why does he not hold Saxon Slayer?"

"My father found the sword. It had been left for him by an ancestor. It was buried. When he died it was taken. I recovered it." I turned and looked at Arturus. The thought had been placed in his head. Perhaps, as the son of a half wizard, he was more attuned to the spirits than I was. Had they told him something? I took out the sword. "You think I should lay it upon his body?"

He shouted so loud that it made me start, "No!" The word echoed around the tomb.

I heard feet at the entrance. Our men were startled. Without looking I waved a hand to dismiss them. "Why not? What did you hear?"

He looked at me and there was a mixture of fear and awe in his voice and on his face. "I heard Myrddyn in my head. He said the sword was needed yet." He looked at me and his eyes pleaded. "I do not understand this. How can Myrddyn speak to me? I dreamed him but that was a dream. I often have fantastical dreams. But now I am awake and I heard his voice inside my head. It was as though he was here."

"Dreams, Arturus, are the way that the spirits talk to us. Some men never dream. You dream often?"

"Aye I do and since Myrddyn came to me in Constantinopolis I have dreamed more and more. I see beautiful visions and terrible ends I…" he shook his head, "I cannot speak of it here. Can we go now? I will see it again in daylight but the night is falling. I am not afraid but…"

I put my arm around him and led him from the tomb. "There is no compunction for you to stay. We will go. Daffydd and his men will have hunted. There will be hot food."

Every face turned as we left the cave. Llenlleog said, "Warlord some of the men have asked if they can visit the tomb."

I nodded, "My father and his wizard would like that. We need to feed the fire."

Llenlleog nodded, "Of course. We will go in but in small numbers. This is a holy place." He turned to Arturus. "When I came here the first time I dreamed. I dreamed my death and I have taken comfort in that."

Arturus started when Llenlleog said that and he looked at me.

"You have dreamed your death?" Llenlleog clutched at the wolf amulet he wore. I smiled, "Do not be afraid. All men die. I know that it will be in battle and I need to know no more. Unlike Llenlleog I do not need to see my own death. I have seen more than fifty summers. Its day is coming. Let us see to the horses and then we can eat."

After we had seen to the horses and headed back to the camp I smiled as I saw the stone wolf with flaming eyes and smoke coming from its mouth. The men who lived in these mountains would see it. Their battle sign was a dragon. Few if any dared to come to this pagan place and to some they would see it as a dragon wrapped around Wyddfa and protecting the mountain. Then their belief in the new White Christ would weaken. They would think of the old ways when this land was ruled by druids. They would not ascribe the sudden appearance of the light in the night to us. It would be as though some spirit had woken beneath the mountain. It was *wyrd*.

Normally my men were like chattering magpies when we camped. Here there was silence. The fire crackled and the stew bubbled. Men's feet sounded on the stones as, in ones and twos, they entered the tomb and paid their respects. I saw Arturus watching some as they emerged. They had light upon their faces. I knew, for it had happened to me, that they would be better warriors. They would have felt, as I had, the presence of my father. That gave a warrior hope. If he died in battle then this was his fate. He would be in the spirit world.

Arturus picked at his food. He was distracted. "How can there be a Christ and the spirits of the dead?"

I shrugged, "I know not. My beliefs have not changed since I was a child. Yours have and I do not envy you the battle which will rage within you. I see now why your father wished you to come here. He and I will soon pass into the Otherworld and it will be for you to rule what remains of Rheged. It may well be a fusion of the old ways and the new." I shook my head. "I honestly do not know. What I do know is that I have dreamed and seen a dark world ruled by Saxons but I have also seen," I pointed to the wolf's eyes and the red light which burned there, "a warrior in the future who wields a sword and sees Rheged reborn."

He stared into the campfire and laid down his bowl of food. "I too have dreamed. I know that we lose. I have not seen my death but I have seen rampaging Saxons and other wild men. I saw naked Hibernians and fierce Picts. I saw Civitas Carvetiorum burning."

Llenlleog had been listening, "Arturus, I have seen the same. Do not despair. What we do will become the stuff of legend. So long as that dream exists then there will be hope for the future. I have not seen this seed grow but I believe it is there. When we are dead we will watch from the spirit world and, many years from now, we will see a wolf warrior. He may look different from us but we will see Arturus in his eyes and in his sword. All of us here are sworn to see you become an equite and ready to take on the Warlord's mantle. It is meant to be."

Arturus saw that the men around the fire, equites, squires and archers were all silent and looking at him. It was as though scales had fallen from his eyes, "That is why all of you are so hard to defeat. You are not afraid to die in battle."

I nodded, "Our death will not mean defeat. For those of us who die it will be another journey and, in our death, we will take enemies of Rheged with us."

Although it was not cold I lay wrapped in my wolf cloak. I was one of the wolf brethren. There were few of us left now and I knew that when I returned home then we would need to resurrect that which I had pushed to the back of my mind.

I dreamed.

I saw that I was being chased but I could not run as fast as I wished. I was wounded and I had many enemies. I climbed a steep path. Every few steps I turned to slay another foe but they were like grains of sand on a beach. No matter how many I slew there were more following. When the last one plunged his sword into me I fell into a black hole.

I woke with a start. Daffydd was picking at the remains of the stew. There was a thin grey light to the east and Arturus was gone. My captain of archers nodded towards the mouth of the tomb. "He went in some hours ago, Warlord. He is sleeping there."

I nodded and rose. I walked over to the cave. I was glad I had my wolf cloak for it was colder now. I saw that my men had kept the fire burning and Arturus was lying parallel with his grandfather. He was dreaming. Gawan had known this would happen.

I turned and went to make water down the path. By the time I returned dawn was beginning to break.

Daffydd said, as he offered me some of the leftover food, "I am pleased we came here, Warlord. My father was born not far from here and he died close by too. I am sad that this is no longer our land but Rheged is a fair copy, is it not? Halvelyn is no Wyddfa but it is a special mountain. My family will be safe there when I am gone."

We were all ready to ride when Arturus finally rose. He looked different. He turned and looked back at the cave and knelt briefly. He turned and came over to me. "I prayed for their souls." He smiled at my face. "It is a Christian word but it means the same as spirit, uncle. I dreamed and I think that I understand now. It is time for us to return to Rheged. We have much to do if I am to be ready to take over from you."

His father had shown his wisdom or perhaps he had been directed by Myrddyn. Arturus changed after that night. He began to learn to be a leader.

It took us ten days to return home. I knew that his mother was worried but his father was not. As we headed up along the Deep Water and saw the crags all around us the next Warlord was looking around to take it all in. He had thought the east was that which he desired. He had been seduced by the life in Constantinopolis. Whatever he had dreamed had driven it from him.

For myself, I felt energised. I had my blacksmith make a copper-covered wolf amulet for each of the new equites and Llenlleog and I worked with the squires so that they could become equites. The gift of King Penda's horses proved timely. They were bigger than our horses and our horse master began to breed bigger horses to carry equites. I asked Arturus if he wished to be made an equite. His performance against those who wished us harm had shown me that he had the skills but he told me he was not yet ready. That was a clear sign of leadership.

Over the winter we saw no signs of the Bernicians and I received no news from Mercia. Neither was welcome. I knew that both the Bernicians and King Penda's enemies were up to something but we were blind. Gawan offered to go in disguise to Eoforwic to spy upon the enemy. As he told me Myrddyn had often done that.

"While we had Myrddyn we also had you, brother. We cannot risk losing our only wizard."

"But I am a shadow of my mentor."

"Even so there is no need. Let us take no news as good news. Our quests still watch the Eden valley. King Penda and Ethelbert watch the road to the west and we know that the Bernicians will not come in winter. When the new grass comes we will have more equites, archers and squires. With King Penda's horses, we can move quickly."

He smiled, "Brother you have changed."

"It began with the dream in Myrddyn's cave but I have seen your son change too and he is the hope for the future."

His eyes saddened, "And I have seen the curse of the wizard. It is bad enough to dream your own death but I have seen my son's death too. I know that it is not the end but it feels that way." His countenance changed to a smile. "That is some way off for to die he needs a son who is grown and he has yet to take a bride."

Our eyes began to turn south as the weather improved. We had more equites now and we kept one equite, a squire and two archers at Pasgentün. Like the ones to the east, they spent half a moon there. It was too early for the changeover when we saw Bors with his quest heading north. They had with them a rider on a white horse. It was a messenger from King Penda. I sent for Gawan. He was working with two young men who had shown an aptitude for magic. He was not certain that they would even attain that status but he hoped that they could become healers. Llenlleog and the other equites joined me.

"Is it war do you think, Warlord?"

My equites knew of the boar's head seal and of the white horse. I shrugged, "It could be but speculation will gain us nothing. He will soon be upon us."

Bors dismounted, "This is Ecgfrith. He has come from King Penda." I looked at the warrior as he slid from the back of his white horse. He had no battle scars. I would have put his age at, perhaps, twenty summers. From the chafing on his legs, he had ridden hard. He was no rider. He had a short sword and seax as well as a leather satchel across his body.

He bowed, "I bring word, from my king. War is upon us."

I nodded, "What is the message?"

"King Oswald has left Eoforwic and he is heading for Lincylene. My king would have you meet him at Tomworðig."

I kept my voice calm, "When?"

"He would have you leave immediately, Warlord. It will take you three days to reach him and the enemy is closing with us. He says not to worry about your full muster. You and your best equites are what we need. I was sent because I know of a road which will take us through the quiet part of the land and we can reach my king without being observed."

I nodded, "Llenlleog, have my equites and captain of archers gather in my hall. I will speak with them."

Ecgfrith looked relieved, "Thank you, Warlord. King Oswald brings a mighty army."

Saxon Sword

"How many are there?"

"He has twenty warbands, lord."

That was a large number of men. That was more than we had fought when we had killed Edwin. "Come we will have some refreshment before we ride." I put my arm around his shoulder. "Was it a hard journey?"

He nodded, "Aye lord the high passes still had some snow."

"You came that way?"

For the first time, he looked nervous. "It was the quickest way, lord."

I smiled, "That explains why your legs are so red. That is a hard way to come."

"Aye, it was."

"And did King Penda give you aught else for me?" He looked puzzled, "A letter, a ring, a seal perhaps?"

He smiled, "No lord for he did not wish a message to be intercepted. That is why he sent me on the white horse so that you would know that I was a true messenger."

We had reached my hall and Agramaine had been listening intently. As we reached my hall I said, smiling, "And how did King Oswald learn of the white horse?"

He turned, fear and guilt all over his face, "I told you, Warlord, that I came from King Penda."

"Agramaine, bring him into the hall. We have questions we need to ask. Arturus search his horse."

Arturus left and we led the struggling warrior into the hall. "Lord I swear." Gawan was watching and he gave the slightest shake of his head. He had read the young man's mind.

I reached under his tunic and pulled out the cross. "You swear by your lord, do you? You are no Mercian. You are Bernician. You can prove your innocence by laying out, on the table, the contents of your satchel. That will prove it one way or another."

He began to lift out what was within. There was a second cross, wood this time, which proved him a Christian. There was a small stoppered jug and there was dried venison. "I am a Christian, lord but King Penda suffers Christians."

"That I know but you are not from him. That I also know."

His shoulders sagged and, in one movement, had taken the jug, pulled the stopper and downed the draught. Gawan ran to him. "That is poison!"

We were too late. His back arched and he fell writhing to the floor. It was a painful death but swift. "That is the final proof if proof were needed."

Arturus entered, "There is nothing of note on his horse."

"And that leaves us with a dilemma. He has come from King Oswald. When he said the High Divide, I knew that. Where does he wait to ambush us?" I was asking the question of myself.

Gawan said, "I just detected his falsehood and not where the threat lies."

"Arturus fetch our scouts. When Llenlleog returns we will hold a council of war." He left. "Have this body removed. He was brave; foolish but brave."

Left alone with Gawan I asked, "What do you think?"

"I think that a mixture of King Penda's suspicions and the spirits have given us a chance to hurt King Oswald. He may be waiting to ambush us in which case we can ambush him. On the other hand, he may be trying to lure you east to give him a safer passage down the Eden Valley."

"Then he will have spies watching my land. We will appear to take the bait and rely upon the skill of my scouts. I will let my equites discuss the matter."

"But you have made up your mind."

"Let us see if they have a better solution."

When I explained what we had learned to my equites they offered many solutions. The younger ones thought we ought to ride north and ravage the land of Bernicia. Pol said, "Warlord if they are waiting to ambush us then their land will be unguarded."

The older ones, like Bors, were more practical, "We ride south towards Eoforwic. If we know they are waiting then that gives us an advantage."

Agramaine said, "Why do we need to do anything? We know that this is not a message from King Penda. We just wait for the right message."

Llenlleog said nothing until a silence descended, "Let us ask Gawan. What is the point of having a wizard if you do not use him"

Saxon Sword

Gawan smiled. He and Llenlleog had been squires together. You learned much about a man when you shared the experience of mucking out horses. "We use our skills and our warriors' strengths. We know their plan from their spy. He was to lead the Warlord to a specific place where he could be attacked. He told the Warlord that King Penda wanted the Warlord. He did not need his full army. It is my brother that they seek. King Oswald thinks that if he takes the head then the dragon will die. If we do nothing then they will know that their plan has failed and they will plan another. Let us spring this trap. We lost the vital knowledge of which road they wish us to take when the spy died. We need to find it. Our scouts are better than any Saxon. They will find the enemy. We need bait for this trap and what better bait than my brother? We use the Warlord and six equites. It would seem to me that we use archers on one flank and the equites on the other. When the Bernicians spring their trap then we spring ours."

They all looked at me and Daffydd ap Miach said, "I am not happy about risking the Warlord. Surely there must be another?"

I stood, "My brother's plan is a good one. I trust both Llenlleog and Daffydd ap Miach to keep me alive. Who else would draw the Bernicians? Myrddyn is dead. I am the one they want. The problem I see is which equites would accompany me for it would be a quest filled with danger."

In answer, all of my equites stood and shouted to be the ones to come with me. I saw Llenlleog and Gawan smile.

While our scouts rode forth we prepared. I chose Kay, Llewellyn, Pol and Agramaine to ride with me. We would also have twenty of the garrison with us. They would wear helmets and mail so that the Saxons would think we were a larger force of equites than we really were. With King Penda's new horses, we might fool the enemy. We gathered supplies for the short campaign. We had good maps and knew, roughly where they would ambush us. To the northwest of Loidis, the ground rose and was perfect for an ambush. We would have to travel close to there if we were heading for the old Roman fort at Lincylene.

It took two days for our scouts to return. "We have found them, lord. They have eight warbands and they are camped close by the old Roman fort of Virosidum along the Ray Valley. There is a large fort there and they are using it to disguise their numbers." Geraint smiled, "They have scouts out for there are a number of roads you could take south. They have chosen this one because they think their scouts will give them a good warning."

I nodded, "And they will for they will see us head toward them. The road passes by the forest?"

"It is not the main road. It is a minor one but it has a good surface. If you were trying to move across the land undetected then you would choose it."

"They think they know me. If we travel down the road then we will do what they expect us to. Our archers could use the woods?"

Easily for it is not a thick wood."

"And the land on the other side of the road?"

There is a hill and farms."

Llenlleog asked, "Could we hide our equites behind it and then come to the Warlord's aid?"

"You could."

Gawan said, "Then we have the plan."

As the squires who would be travelling with me would be in the greatest danger we gave them short mail hauberks. Geraint looked a little like the spy and he would ride with me riding the white horse. Gawan deduced that it would help us for two reasons. Firstly, it would allay any suspicions they had and secondly, they would not press home the attack on me quite so vigorously. We left the next day. Gawan had wanted to come with us but there was much risk involved in this and I needed a good hand on the tiller.

Aware that there might be spies watching the roads the archers, squires and equites led by Llenlleog and Daffydd took the longer northern road to get into position without being seen. They rode hard and we did not. Even if there were no spies close to our land Geraint and Tadgh had seen a ring of them five miles from the place they had chosen. As we rode I asked Geraint for the detail of the place.

"The Roman fort is a small one, Warlord. It is like the one at Glanibanta. From the looks of the walls, it has been abandoned for a long time. The warbands have camps which are spread amongst the wood. As I said it is an open wood. There are many deer there. The village is a small one and they have the leader of the Bernicians there. He has four warbands with him."

"It is not the King?" He shook his head. "Nor the Clan of the Snake?"

"They were Bernicians, lord. I saw their standards. They were not tattooed and they wore helmets. They were not the savages."

"Good," I turned to Kay, "When they attack us we fall back to the village. That will allow Daffydd and his archers to attack those in the woods while their attention is on us. We will be charging towards their leader with half of the Bernicians. They will be confident and that will be their undoing. Llenlleog and our equites will tear through their ranks from the rear."

We camped close to the place we had killed the Saxon scouts. I did not envy the rest of our men. We had the steep-sided valley to travel. They had to follow the upper Dunum. They had the waterfall to negotiate. They would be hidden from enemies but the land itself would be a foe to be conquered. As we sat around the camp I saw that Arturus now sat with the other squires. Since the tomb, he had realised that he was the future of our people. The squires would be the equites he would lead. He had to get to know them. I saw him describing our night attack. He would be telling them of his error. A good leader had to show his men that they could make mistakes so long as they learned from them.

I was silent for I knew that where we would fight was not far from the village my father and his brothers had been born. It had been the place the Angles had come and destroyed their way of life. Had not King Urien found them then who knows what might have happened? They might have ended as bandits fighting against the Bernicians. It would not have ended well. King Urien had been sent to give the brothers purpose. He and his horsemen had ridden these lands much as we had done. The difference was that we were better mounted, armed and mailed than they had ever been.

We made one more camp before we reached the small Roman Road. We could have done the journey in just two days but I had to be certain that my men were in position. They would have ridden hard. Daffydd and his archers would have tethered their horses and be filtering through the trees. Llenlleog and the equites would be with Tadgh. They would be lined up and hiding below the village. We would be arriving at noon. I had planned that before we left. In lieu of a horn which would alert the Bernicians, we would use the sun as our signal.

We rode in a tight formation. Ahead we could see the high point of the moor but the Romans had built the road south of it. The road ran along the valley bottom. The River Ure was little more than a bubbling stream. It would be no obstacle. Even as we had turned east we had seen the forest. It stretched north to the high ground. My archers would have made their destination easily. To the south, I saw the valley sides rise. My equites and squires would have had a harder task. If they had not reached the unguarded side of the ambush then the men I led would be hard-pressed to charge uphill and defeat four warbands.

Garth led the men who were posing as equites. Their cloaks hid the fact that they wore no mail but they all had a helmet. With their round shields and the spears in their hands, they would look, from a distance like equites. He and his men followed the four real equites and their squires. When we charged we would have eight men at the fore with Garth and his men as two lines behind. I had spoken with Garth and impressed upon him that if our trick failed that he and his men were to ride to the forest. Daffydd ap Miach would be their way home. If they did that then they would be reporting our deaths.

Geraint looked up at the sky. "Warlord, we need to ride faster if we are to reach the ambush at noon."

I nodded, "And you need to get slightly ahead of us. If you were the spy then you would not wish to be caught by your comrades. Ride, Geraint, and take cover when the attack begins. You are a scout and not a warrior."

"I serve you Warlord and I am a man of Rheged. I will fight and if this is my day to die then I will die happy knowing that I have served you." He dug his heels into the flanks of the white horse and galloped off down the road.

We were mailed and we rode with helmets. It was what the Bernicians would expect. We rode in a column of twos. Arturus was next to me and he carried my banner. I dug my heels into the flanks of Star and said, "Remember Arturus, when we charge, drop the banner." He nodded. He had a spear held next to it.

"And think back to how we hunt animals. Thrust down and twist else the spearhead can become stuck. These Angles wear no mail. You do not need to strike deeply. A horseman with a spear can hurt an enemy on foot; even one in a shield wall."

"Aye, Warlord." I saw him lick his lips. He was nervous. That was good. It would not do to be overconfident on this day.

Our gait was an easier one for riding and the road, while not a perfect surface, allowed us to get up a good speed. I saw Geraint ahead of me. He would drop his arm to his side when he spied the enemy. They would not hide from him. They thought he was the goat leading the flock to its doom. I glanced to the hills to the south of me. The shadows told me that it was almost noon.

Geraint dropped his arm. "Prepare for the ambush!" The village was less than half a Roman mile from us and the last burst of speed had brought us close to where the Bernicians waited. We were four hundred paces below the cluster of huts when the warriors charged down from the forest to the north of us.

"Wheel right." This was where our training would show. As we dragged our reins around to head up the tilled fields by the river we pulled up our shields and prepared our spears. Arturus dropped the standard by the road. It fell into the ditch. We would recover it when the battle was over or, if not, then in the future some farmer would pick it out and wonder what had happened here in this lonely valley.

The Bernicians, streaming from the forest were running downhill. They had little order for they did not need it. They would be attacking the rear of the thirty-two horsemen. I did not look back. That could be fatal. We kept our line straight. It was asking much of the four squires to fight a single warband let alone four of them but if Llenlleog was in place then all would be well.

The four warbands emerged from the village and made a double shield wall. Sixty men backed by sixty others faced us. They had a cross behind them and two standards. I saw priests. They were confident. We were two hundred paces from them and the slope meant we were not yet travelling quickly. I chose the spot we would hit. It was in the centre of their line. Not all of the men we faced had helmets but they each had a shield. I saw that some did not have an iron tipped spear but a fire-hardened one. They would hurt our horses but not us. When we were just a hundred paces from them I heard the wail of the dragon banner. Llenlleog had unfurled it. The hooves of more than a hundred horses thundered as Llenlleog and my equites charged the shield wall from behind. The village buildings meant it would not be a continuous line but it did not matter for the second ranks of Angles turned to see their new enemy as the eight of us struck the centre of their line.

There was indecision on the faces of the men who faced us. A spear came towards my chest but it was struck without conviction and the Bernician was hit in the throat by my spear. Star's hooves clattered into the back of the Bernician behind and I was through. I urged Star towards the Bernician warlord and his standard. Llenlleog and his men were already ploughing into the Angles.

The priests dropped to their knees and clung to their crosses. I would ignore those. Their incantations prayers and pleas would not harm me. The Bernician warlord was a different matter. He had, with him, two of his hearth weru and a standard-bearer. They locked their shields. I had hoped that I would have Kay and Llewelyn by me but the slope and the Angles through which we had charged broke up our line. I had Arturus and Pol's squire, Gareth, with me. It was not what I wished for but it would have to do. Star was ahead of the other two and I used my horse's forelegs as a weapon. As the spears of the Bernicians were pulled back I reined in and pulled back Star's head. Leaning forward the horns on the new saddle held me in place. Spears were thrust blindly at my horse. One scored a wound along Star's foreleg. It made my horse angry and it clattered down hard with two mighty hooves. One smashed a shield and a forearm while the other crushed the skull of the standard-bearer.

When Star's hooves landed I was inside the ring of defenders. As Arturus ended the life of the warrior with the broken arm Gareth thrust his spear at the remaining hearth weru. I rammed my spear at the warlord. His shield had a boss made of metal and my spear merely forced him backwards. I could see that he was torn between killing my horse or killing me. His arms were covered in the marks of combat. He was experienced but perhaps he had never faced a horse before. I wheeled Star to my left which allowed me to strike down. The Angle's spear came at me at the same time as mine went towards his chest. His spear rasped along my mail. Mine was deflected into his left shoulder. The head came away bloody.

I completed my wheel. As I briefly saw the forest to the north I saw that Daffydd had defeated the Bernician warbands. They were fleeing down the valley. Coming around I saw that the priests had taken shelter behind the warlord. Gareth and Arturus were busy protecting my flanks from other members of the Bernician chief's oathsworn. The sounds of battle filled the village but I saw more equites than Angles. It would end when the chief fell. I did something which I would not condone in one of my men. I hurled my spear. The chief was not expecting it. His wounded left arm made him slow to raise his shield and a spear is no weapon to use to stop a missile. It struck him square in the centre of his chest. Thrown from less than three paces it entered his chest and emerged from his back. He stood, briefly, and then tumbled backwards, falling on the frightened priests.

It was over. I drew Saxon Slayer and looked around but we had won. Some of the enemy surrendered. The wounded were being despatched. I took in that Arturus lived as did most of my equites. Geraint rode up on his white horse. He said, "We have broken them, lord. They flee home."

We gathered the prisoners. The priests we did not touch but we took three fingers from the right hands of the warriors. They would live and they could work but they would never hold a spear or a sword. They would not be able to use a bow. The relics we had taken from the priests we burned, along with their crosses. I could see that Arturus was uncomfortable when we did that.

"Go back to King Oswald. Your wounds are a punishment for the treachery of King Oswald and his spies."

Chapter 5

We had lost men but fewer than might have been expected. The warlord and his men's attention had been on the road and the valley. The ambushers were ambushed. The villagers had fled and we spent the night in their homes. The Bernicians had left food and we ate well. We took three days to reach Civitas Carvetiorum. There was no rush to get home and we wanted to conserve our horses. It made it an easier journey for the wounded too. Gawan had dreamed and knew of our success. We sat in the bathhouse. I had had it repaired. It was luxury and it made us feel civilised. Arturus also enjoyed it and he would normally have been with us but he had stayed with the other squires. They too would be celebrating but in a different way.

"My son did well?"

I laughed, "Do not fish for compliments brother. You dreamed. I saw a hawk above the battlefield and know that you know that he did. You lost not a moment's sleep."

He nodded, "I know but the dream world is not as clear as the battlefield."

"Then you have forgotten what it is like to fight in a battle. You know that which is within the length of your spear. For the rest, you trust to your men. It is why we win more than we lose for we have men who know what they are doing and can follow orders."

"Yet, brother, there will come a time when even with men following orders explicitly you will lose because there will be a sea of enemies. Are you ready for such a day?"

"You mean ready to die?" He nodded. "I am for your son has shown me that he can be a leader. He is not ready yet but he will be. Have I time to mould the clay of the warrior into the shape of a Warlord?"

"You have. I have not dreamed the time of your death merely the manner."

I shook my head, "That is a comforting thought."

"Besides he needs a bride. Our family's seed must be planted. You and I are the last of the line. Arturus is the only male who lives."

"I will worry about that when Oswald is gone. I must send a messenger to King Penda. He needs to know of this failed ambush."

"Send Agramaine. He has something of the wizard in him."

"As has your son."

"We need to protect Arturus as much as we can until he is ready. A butterfly is beautiful but while a caterpillar and a pupa it is in danger. Let us cosset my son."

I laughed again as the servant brought in more hot water, "Then I ought to keep him from battle."

"Brother, while you fight by his side then he is safe for your death is a lonely one. Arturus is not there."

With that sobering thought, I turned my attention to preparing my army for the war that would come.

I sent Agramaine and six archers to King Penda. I gave my equite the wolf boar token. I wrote nothing down but made him commit to memory what had happened. He would take the route we had taken earlier. He would go first to Tatenhale and then Tomworðig.

He returned half a moon later. That was faster than I had expected and it was with the news that he had met the King at Tatenhale. The news I received was that he was building a better alliance with his two neighbours in Wales. He would be ready for war when it came. Agramaine brought back the token. The system had worked and I was relieved.

I decided to build up my own alliances. We had allies to the north. Some had fallen in battle and others had drifted away. I needed to buy time for Arturus to grow into the leader I hoped he would become. I would head north and speak with the King there. Eugein ap Beli was the King of Alt Clut. His enemies were the warriors from the islands and the Picts to the north of him. Myrddyn had once escaped from the stronghold that was Alt Clut. It was even stronger than Din Guardi but we rarely had to make war on the people there. In the days of Ridderch Hael, we had been close. That had been in my father's time and now, whilst not estranged, we had little traffic between the two kingdoms. I took just six equites and squires. I left my archers preparing for the war against Oswald. Agramaine had said that King Penda expected it to be the following year. My pre-emptive attack had weakened him. The thegn I had killed was one of his most powerful warriors.

The land north of the river was similar to my land. It was easy to see why the invaders had found it so hard to wrest it from us. Each town was well defended. I was known and given a guarded welcome at each town through which we passed. It took two days to reach Alt Clut and we discovered that the King was in residence.

Eugein ap Beli was unknown to me. I had met his father once. He was a tall man with brooding, not to say glowering features. In battle, he would appear fearsome. When he greeted me, however, his face broke into a smile. "The cub of the wolf warrior! I am pleased to finally meet you."

I could not help but like him. There appeared to be no deception in his face. His arm clasp was firm and he looked me in the eyes.

"And I am pleased to meet you. Our fathers knew each other but thus far we are strangers."

"And we can end that this night. We will hold a feast to celebrate your arrival." He lowered his voice, "And then you can tell me what brings you here for this is unexpected. Is there danger?"

I shook my head, "No more than there is normally. King Oswald, however, is planning to go to war with Mercia. If he wins… we do not know how the land will look."

He nodded, "We will talk when you are cleaned and refreshed. The Romans did not build many roads in my land and I know that the ones we have built are not as clean as we might hope."

We had commented on the roads as we had ridden here. The recent rains had caused mud and soil to wash onto the already poorly maintained roads. Our horses, cloaks and mail were all besmirched and grubby. Our quarters were clean and we had our own chambers. There were four of them allocated to us. This was different from the Mercians. I did not like the communal halls. The water was warm and the towels were clean. I felt much refreshed when I joined the King in his hall. In this part of the world, they drank oat beer but I had brought a flagon of wine which had come from Constantinopolis.

I held it up, "King Eugein, please accept this gift of wine from the Empire."

He nodded, "only if you will share it with me." I nodded as he waved over a servant, "I confess that I like the taste but it is so hard to get. My father told me of a time when Imperial ships would trade here and now there are few."

"We still get a few. If you like this then I will get some for you. We have ships which trade that far east. They make two journeys a year. The Empire likes our copper and our iron. We like their wine, their fruits and their spices. It is an equitable trade."

As he gulped down the wine Eugein nodded, "This is a fine drink. But now tell me, why did you come here Warlord? You did not come here to bring me a flagon of wine and to flatter me."

"You are right. We are both of the old people and we are both assailed by enemies. I think that one or both of us will be attacked. I would rather put in place an agreement to help each other now before we need it. That is all."

"I am agreeable but I confess that we have more to gain from this than you do."

"Not so, King Eugein, we had a vast land which we held and now we have a tiny enclave of beleaguered land. I have fine warriors and the best of horsemen but we are few in number. War will come again and we will need help. Who knows, King Oswald or his brother Oswiu may cast covetous glances at Alt Clut. This stronghold would never be taken but you would not wish the Angles to run rampant across your land."

"You are right." He tossed off the wine and poured another, "You have my agreement, of course, but my men march on foot and if you sent for aid then it would take some time for us to reach you."

"That is not the problem. We have strong walls. We can laugh away a short siege. Just so long as you reached us might make the difference."

"Then you have my agreement." He nodded to my equites and squires, "As a king, I can only dream of having men like that to serve me. They are invincible. How could any warrior defeat a man encased in mail?"

"It happens but most of our success comes through training and discipline," I told him of the ambush we had thwarted.

"Your horses make the difference. We are not riders. We can stand toe to toe with a foe and we can best him but sometimes our enemies are as thick as the sand on a beach."

"We just do what we can, King Eugein."

When we left, the next day, I felt happier. If we were summoned by King Penda I would be leaving my land with someone to aid us. Each of my strongholds could hold out for a moon. The King of Alt Clut could reach us in seven days.

On the way home, I spoke with Arturus. I had hoped that King Eugein had a daughter but he had only sons. Part of my reason for going there was to see if there was a bride for my nephew. It was not the best plan but having an alliance backed by a marriage was often a safe and secure way of ensuring that promises were kept.

"Arturus, your father and I have decided that you need to be wed." He looked at me open-mouthed. We had not discussed this at all. I smiled, "This sounds like something we have conjured from nowhere but we have both thought this was your next step to becoming Warlord."

"You are still Warlord! We need not another."

"That spear which tore my mail could easily have broken the links. Then I would be dead. You need a bride. You need to father sons. I failed. You are the last of the Warlord's line."

"Your daughter…"

"Has no sons and she is my daughter. Like it or not Arturus, you will lead our people. I know that you have embraced the life of a warrior but you have more to do. When we visit the Mercians I will be looking for a bride of noble birth."

"But if I do not like her?"

"It matters not. As Warlord, you have few choices over your own life. Your choices are about more important matters such as the survival of our land and our way of life." I saw his crestfallen face. "This is not imminent but it will come."

As Gawan had suggested I had sown the seed. Now we would have to see if it took root.

Winter came and went. Our warriors became fathers and that was hope for the future. The new horses we had from Mercia were in foal. When spring came we would see how fruitful our land would be. A good year would show that the gods were with us. If they were not then we would fight on. To do other was inconceivable.

The message which came from King Penda arrived a month after the new grass. King Oswald was heading south. Our vigilance meant he could not use the Eden valley. He was, instead, forced to use the High Divide. His warriors would not have a pleasant journey. There would be little in the way of food and they would have a harder time. When the battle came that might make all the difference.

The messenger, who came on a brown and plain mount with a boar token told me that the King of Mercia did not have enough men to face the foe at Tomworðig. His plan was to draw Oswald towards Powys. His Welsh allies, his messenger, a thegn told me, were reluctant to move into the land of Mercia. We were asked to ride to Tatenhale and join Eorledman Ethelbert who would travel across the land of Gwynedd.

As we prepared to leave Arturus asked me, "Why do we ride over the hard mountains of Gwynedd, Warlord?"

"We are the bane of Oswald. King Penda is cunning and he hides us from view. There will be scouts and they will watch for more than two hundred horsemen. A horse is easy to track. Even without hooves, a horse leaves a mark on the land. Oswald will think that we wait here in Rheged. We will be the surprise which might turn the battle."

We took Gawan with us. He needed to be there. He gave an argument that as we were fighting closer to Wyddfa and the tomb then Myrddyn might be able to help us. I think he wished to be with us for he wanted to watch his son. We left perilously few men watching our homes. We had many horses and I took three of mine. I sent a message to King Eugein asking him to watch my land. This would be a test of his commitment. We took servants and horses laden with spears and arrows. This was a war. This was not a raid. We would be fighting the might of

Saxon Sword

Bernicia and Deira. If Penda lost then Oswald could turn his attention to us. I was under no illusions. The men who fought and died in Powys would be fighting for Rheged. If Arturus did well then I would make him an equite. He still needed more experience but I needed him as a leader. Others could fight but Arturus was as important as Saxon Slayer.

We reached Tatenhale without incident and Eorledman Ethelbert had many men waiting to follow him. He had ten small warbands. There were three hundred warriors. Only his hearth weru, all fifteen of them, wore mail but they were a formidable formation. He had culled his hearth weru and rid himself of any whom he thought shared the beliefs of Thingfrith. My men camped with the men of Mercia.

As we ate with the Eorledman I asked, "Is all well done, Eorledman? Will the alliance hold?"

"There will be three armies, four if we count yours. To hold together such a disparate group of men will not be easy but I believe that King Penda will succeed.

"And Eowa?"

He nodded, "His son, Alweo, has disappeared. Some say he fell in the ambush but I do not believe that. I am convinced that he is with Oswald. Eowa pretends that he supports his brother but the King has him watched constantly. If there is treachery then we will know of it."

We headed due south the next day. These were little more than tracks over which we marched. In many places, we had to use single file. We were, however, free from observation. A hawk or an eagle might have seen us. Gawan seemed to grow in confidence as we headed close to Wyddfa. Its power reached out to my brother. In his head, he saw the armies of Bernicia and Deira as they headed south. He knew their numbers. We had rested at a col. We overlooked a long piece of water and the hills all around were reflected in it. I thought that this would be a good place to hold off the forces of Oswald. We could not use our horsemen here but they would break themselves against Mercian shields and our archers could slay them. When we had more even numbers our equites would swing the scales in our favour.

"They will outnumber us but this is not Oswald's land. Powys is close to the holy mountain and its power will add strength to our warrior's blows. We will prevail." I looked at him and saw him shake his head, "You will not fall here. That web has yet to be spun."

I stared at him, trying to see into his mind, "Web brother?"

"We both have many steps to take before your death. When a spider spins its web, things happen to break strands and make weaknesses. It changes the web as it goes. What we see at the end is not the web which was started. The end remains the same but the journey there is not yet written."

I laughed, "You are becoming Myrddyn. He said many things that I did not understand. The way you read my mind is most disconcerting."

Llenlleog had been listening to our words he said, "Warlord it does not need a wizard to know that you were thinking of this as a place to do battle. Each time we have stopped I have watched you assessing the ground and wondering if this might be the best place to fight the Bernicians."

"It will have to be upon Mercian soil that we fight. King Penda can only move back so far and then the retreat becomes a rout and Oswald will have that which he wants, Mercia's heartland."

We began to descend down little more than hunting trails to the east. We saw the camp of King Penda. He had gathered not at the ancient hill fort to the north but on a flat piece of ground. The warlord in me disapproved of his choice of ground immediately. If there was high ground then you used it if only to deny the enemy. I saw that the hillfort was slightly overgrown. Some of the stakes of the old palisade had been green and now sprouted into trees. They could be easily cleared. I saw nothing of value on the ground he had chosen. There were only a few strands of scrubby trees. There was no river to use as a defence. I saw one solitary hut and a single huge tree. The ancient people had worshipped such trees. People had not chosen this as a place to build a home. They had come, in the past to worship at the tree and take refuge in the hill fort. Why fight here? Perhaps this was not the ultimate site for his battle.

Gawan chuckled, "Brother we are but a few miles from King Penda. Let us wait and then he can tell us why he has chosen this place to do war."

As we neared the camp I saw that there were fewer Welsh warriors than I had expected. Had his alliance not been honoured? If King Oswald was coming then he would bring the full might of old Northumbria as well as the men of Lindsey and those of the East Angles. This would be a battle for Britannia. Whoever won would control the island for some time.

Most of the camp had gathered in clan and family groups but there were five tents in the centre. I saw Penda's boar standard and the red lion of Powys. The dragon of Gwynedd was absent.

Our arrival prompted men to stand and stare. We were the only horsemen. My men's mail shone and sparkled in the afternoon sun behind us. We looked like a shimmering dragon. With our fluttering standards and red plumed helmets, we must have looked like an imperial army. A fluke of wind made the dragon begin to wail. It was not the howl of a charge but it was eerie enough to make the Christians amongst the Welsh clutch their crosses. It drew King Penda from his tent. Next to him was another warrior wearing mail. I took him to be the Welsh King.

Gawan said quietly, "We have made quite the entrance brother!"

"I would that we had the same effect on Oswald but I fear that he knows us too well. He will have plans to defeat the equites of Rheged."

I climbed down from Copper and King Penda stepped forward to clasp my arm, "Welcome, Warlord, to Maes Cogwy. This is King Cynddylan ap Cyndrwyn, King of Powys and King of Dogfeiling."

I had been right. The king looked to be of an age with me. There were flecks of grey in his beard. I had never met him but knew that he was a strong king. His grip, as he clasped my arm, confirmed it. "Warlord, I have waited many years to meet with you. You and your father are legends. Our bards sing songs of your mighty sword and your shimmering soldiers. I would not have thought that any who looked so beautiful could be so terrible and yet the stories we have heard cannot lie. Llenlleog,

Gawan, Bors, Kay, those names are known in our mountain valleys. With you at our side then Oswald will be defeated."

I nodded, "I do not see King Cadafael ap Cynfeddw. Gwynedd has mighty warriors too."

The two kings looked at each other and King Penda said, "Come, the flies will soon congregate, let us go inside my tent and talk." He saw Gawan, "Your brother's advice would be welcome."

I nodded and handed my reins to Arturus. "Llenlleog see to the camp."

"Aye Warlord."

As I stepped into the tent I saw the mighty Pybba waiting to ensure our security and privacy. The interior of the tent was dark but I could see that there would be just the four of us. Where was Eowa? Pybba stepped in with a lighted candle and its glow threw strange shadows around the tent. It allowed us to see each other's faces and that was important.

"You wonder why we have chosen this strange site for the battle, Warlord?" King Penda seemed to be a mind reader too for he launched straight into that which was on my mind.

"Aye and I wonder at the absence of Eowa and King Cadafael ap Cynfeddw."

"There are all connected with our choice of battlefield. We had planned on meeting north of here at King Cynddylan ap Cyndrwyn's kingdom of Dogfeiling. There we could have used the hills and mountains to hold off our enemies. King Cadafael agreed to bring his army thence. My brother betrayed us. Suddenly King Cadafael said that he could not make war on a fellow Christian and that he would remain in his palace of Aberffraw."

The King of Powys said, "Oswald must have bribed him. Cadafael is not the king his father was." He smiled sadly at me, "Perhaps had he trained as an equite like his father then events might be different."

"Perhaps, and Eowa?"

"Fled to join his son and King Oswald. He has been promised the throne of Mercia when Oswald wins. Some of the men of Gwynedd joined us in defiance of their King. They are archers who live close to Wyddfa. They are good men."

Gawan asked, "But why choose here? My brother is the strategos but I agree with him, this site has little to commend it."

"We draw Oswald further away from his home. His men will have had to march almost half the length of this island. This place is called Maes Cogwy. It is marshy. Our camp is on solid ground. The Bernicians and their allies will have to march over the marsh and they will be slowed down. Our archers and the men led by Daffydd ap Miach will be able to slaughter them as they approach."

"Then you did not need my equites for we cannot charge over marshy ground."

King Penda smiled, "You saw the old hill fort as you approached?"

"Aye, it is a mile or so to the north of here. That would have made a good place to defend."

"And also to wait. We would have your standard with ours here by the camp. You, your equites and your squires will secrete yourselves at the hill fort. Oswald and Eowa will think you and your men are here with us and fighting on foot. When they are engaged then you charge. There is a solid area between the hill fort and the place the Bernicians will use. That is why we chose this site. It is a trap. They will cross the harder ground which you will use and not know of the marshy ground ahead. We had to find somewhere that Eowa did not know. This is Powys. King Cynddylan chose it."

The Welsh King smiled, "I may not have fought with you or your father but I have spoken with those who have and know the best way to use your horses. The sight of your men charging and the sound of the dragon standard will terrify the Angles."

I smiled. We had a chance. "I will ride there now and see it close up. Where are the Bernicians?"

"They are at least a day away."

"We will need to discourage their scouts. I know they do not use them well but your brother and his son know me."

Gawan said, "I will come with you and Arturus."

It was not far to ride. I noticed that the ground sloped gently up towards the hill. As I neared it I saw that it was man-made. Some tribe, in the dim and distant past, had used a slight bump in the ground to make a refuge. There were four ditches while the

Saxon Sword

entrance was from the west. This had been built by the Welsh. We rode up the entrance ramp. It was no longer smooth; stones and soil had fallen in and bushes lined the sides. I took in that the ramparts had begun to fall down into the ditches but for us, that did not matter. We could wait in the topmost ditch which was not as steep-sided as the others. There the rain and time had eaten into the ramparts. A screen of spindly trees and bushes hid us from the east. We dismounted and walked through them There were more on the far side. When we reached them, we had a fine view to the east and, more importantly, to the south.

Gawan nodded, "This will work but the plan needs adjustment."

"Adjustment?"

Oswald, Eowa and Alweo, not to mention Oswiu know you, brother. They will be looking for you. We need them to see you."

"I will not have another lead my equites!"

"And I am not asking you to. My mail and my helmet are the same as yours. Our beards are the same. It is only the colour of our hair which is different. Wearing a helmet will hide it. If I ride Copper, which is your most distinctive horse, and if my son has the standard near to me then it will allay the enemy's fears and draw them to us."

"But you will be in great danger."

"I am a warrior, brother. You cannot protect me forever and besides, I have not yet dreamed my death."

"I would rather ride behind the Warlord."

I turned, "Arturus, if they see just your father wearing my mail they may think that it is another taking my place. Your golden hair, lack of beard and distinctive features mark you as Arturus, my squire. If you do not sit astride your horse next to Gawan then the ruse might fail. If we have surprise then it could bring victory. If they know where we are then it invites disaster. I do not ask this of you, Arturus, you are my squire and I command it."

"And who will be your squire?"

"I need no squire."

We did not return the way we had entered. I wanted to see if we could ride down the southern side of the hill fort. We discovered we could not. The ramparts were unstable there. I pointed to the entrance of the hillfort. "We will have to wait there. I will have a couple of Daffydd's archers in the top. They can use an arrow to signal when we attack. Come let us ride from the entrance. I would like to see how long it takes to reach the camp."

I estimated it to be less than a mile to the camp. I had to try to visualize the Bernicians as they attacked. As we trotted I turned Copper to my left. We would need to attack the right flank of the enemy. They would not have shields facing us. If they turned to face us then they would be exposing their backs to our arrows. I dug my heels in and Copper sped up. The ground was still in our favour and sloped down slightly. It was barely noticeable but Copper was moving easily and that told me that the gradient was helping us. When we were parallel to the camp I reined in. "I am happy now." I smiled, "I will upset Llenlleog. Tomorrow we make a new camp by the entrance to the hill fort."

The two kings were happy about the new plan. They saw it as a way of refining what had already been a strategically sound one.

More men arrived during the evening. Some were from Gwynedd. King Cadafael was not as popular as his father had been. Warriors came in defiance of him and to honour the old alliance with Rheged. I knew that the King had indulged his son too much. Cadwallon had thought that when we defeated Oswald we had the whole of Britannia under our control. He was wrong. When he had fallen by the wall at the Battle of Heofenfeld, it had been a disaster not least because it left Gwynedd in the hands of a poorly prepared king. Other warriors came from the lands around Tatenhale. Once the Bernicians had moved south towards us then the threat to the homes there dissipated. In all, we gained two hundred men. Their quality did not matter it was numbers which counted.

Daffydd chose two of his archers, Dai and Garth ap Geraint to come with us. I sat up long into the night speaking with my brother and the two kings. When dawn broke we would break our camp and move to the hill fort. We needed signals and commands establishing for the whole plan relied upon timing and surprise.

We rose early and headed to the hill fort before dawn had broken. According to the Powys' scouts, the enemy warriors were still a day away but I did not want to risk the surprise element. We would not have tents and we would not be able to use fires but they were minor considerations. The two archers came with us. They would camp at the top of the hill fort.

"When you spy them in the distance then one of you come and tell us. You know when to send the arrow?"

"Aye, Warlord, when they are committed to their attack. And can we then join in, Warlord?"

That was typical of my men. They were warriors one and all. Llenlleog said, laughing, "Of course so long as you stay from under our horses' hooves."

The other squires ensured that Star was cared for and they asked if I needed my sword sharpening. I think that many of them wished to touch the magical weapon. "Arturus sharpened it before I left the camp." I took the equites and squires up the hill so that they could see the battlefield. Having an aerial view like this would help them when they charged. None of us exposed ourselves. We were all too experienced for that. We spied the road down which the Bernicians would come. King Oswald was not coming to talk. He was coming for war. He wanted King Penda dead. Now that he had a Mercian who would do as he was ordered then he could add Mercia to his conquests. Cadwallon had been the last High King. Oswald, despite his conversion to Christianity, wanted to be the next! When we were all familiar with the landscape and before we were seen we headed down to the camp. The squires hurried off to prepare us food.

My most experienced equites sat with me. We had some logs on which to sit. "It will be strange not to be riding beneath your banner, Warlord."

"It may add to their confusion, Llenlleog. If they see the equites follow your banner it may make them think that you have left me."

He laughed, "We are all oathsworn, lord, that will not happen."

They were in good spirits and I was honoured to lead them but they needed the truth. "You know that we are all doomed to failure?" They looked at me. "Our numbers dwindle and those of the Angles and Saxons grow. Our old allies are weaker. Cadafael is not the leader his father was. We slew many when we killed King Edwin. How many more were there to defeat and kill King Cadwallon? We slew six warbands and more in the Ray Valley and yet, according to the scouts he has come south with an army which is greater than the ones we destroyed."

Llenlleog nodded but did not seem at all discomfited or put out, "True we have fewer warriors now than we did but that means there is greater glory for us. My sons have not seen seven summers but in another seven they will become squires and then train to be equites. Our numbers will grow. We know that one equite is worth ten Saxons!"

The other equites cheered. Only Bors and Kay had served longer than Llenlleog and he was the leader of the equites. None was braver and none a better warrior. I felt reassured. If I fell and Arturus was not yet ready to be the leader then Llenlleog could lead the equites.

I felt happier and I smiled, "You are right! Myrddyn's death still weighs heavily on me. I am seeing this chalice as half empty. When we destroy Oswald, he will have to build up his army again and you all have sons who will become equites!"

During the night we were woken as Oswald's scouts clashed with the Welsh warriors who were our outpost. Our wisdom in making our camp early was rewarded. I knew that when dawn broke we would see the armies of Bernicia and Deira, of Oswald and Oswiu, lining up to fight us. Despite my best efforts, I could not return to sleep. Defeat was not something we could countenance. If we were to lose then Mercia would be lost and any of my men who survived would have to fight their way north through hostile lands. It would be the end of my equites and archers and that would mean, ultimately, the end of Rheged.

Chapter 6

As I could not sleep I rose and made water. The squire on duty was walking amongst the horses and did not see me as I climbed up the hill. I was pleased that I could still move quietly. Dai was on watch. He was an experienced archer and scout, he had heard my approach. "Best keep your head down, Warlord, they have their camp less than a mile away. I can see their fires."

I wriggled next to him and lay on the damp turf. Their fires spread out in an untidy sprawl into the distance. I could see that they had followed the line of King Penda's fires. It meant their line was at a right angle to the hill fort. Having seen no fires there they had assumed that it was unoccupied and ignored the hill fort. They probably thought it was a mistake on the Mercian's part. Peering east I saw a grey line on the horizon. Dawn was on its way. It had been many years since I had done this. I had been a squire when last I had scouted out a foe. This was the easiest position from which to do so. As dawn broke I saw the Angle army take shape. They had just four tents and there were standards leaning against them. They would be the kings, the leaders and the priests. It soon became obvious, as the light improved, that this was an enormous army. The scouts had said that elements of the East Angles had joined them but I also saw flaxen-haired Jutes from Cent moving around. More than half of the camp was too far away for me to estimate the warriors.

I said quietly, "Keep a good watch. I will go and rouse the camp."

I slithered back through the bushes. I did not stand until I was fifty paces from the spindly trees. The camp was awake when I descended. Kay looked red-faced with anger, "We thought you had been taken!"

I laughed, "Without a struggle? If they could have done that then I would deserve to die. There are many of them and their battle lines are at right angles to the hill fort. We will not now need to ride towards our lines first. We can form up in our lines here and ride directly at them. Dai will tell us when they form their lines."

As we went to our horses Llenlleog said, "Kay was angry and berated the squire. It was Pol's squire, Gandálfr. Pol was not happy."

"Llenlleog, when I am not here you need to exert your authority. Kay means well but we both know that he is not subtle. He charges at everything. That is a worthy virtue in battle but less so amongst his warriors."

Llenlleog nodded, "You are right. My problem is that I assume all the other equites are the same as we. They are not. Each one is unique. Your boots are hard to fill Warlord. You make it look easy."

We had reached the horse lines and the squires were busy saddling the horses. "Remember that I followed my father for many years and watched him. I was there when he formed the equites. You and I see them the way they are and not the way they were. It is why I have much to do with Arturus."

"I will watch over him when you are unable to."

"When I am dead."

He nodded, "You seem a little preoccupied with your mortality at the moment."

"The Warlord did not reach my age. I have no uncles left alive and there is just Gawan and Arturus left of my family. Is it any wonder?" I paused, "And Gawan has dreamed my death. I must prepare. My father knew he was to die and I had no warning. You have."

He looked at me with new eyes. I saw realisation set in.

One of the squires had saddled Star and he gave the reins to me. Llenlleog turned to look north-west, "I wonder if Wyddfa and Myrddyn's spirit has something to do with your mood?"

"Probably although I would have thought the presence of those spirits would have lifted mine."

As we led our horses away he said, "I think the fact that the King of Gwynedd is not here has something to do with that too. We fought for that land. We helped Cadwallon become the king he was and his son has deserted us. We lost equites and archers. It is understandable."

Dai suddenly appeared above us and began to run down the entrance of the hillfort.

"Mount!"

There was a flurry of activity as we all mounted. By the time he reached us the equites had mounted and the squires had handed us our spears. "Warlord they are forming their ranks. It is as we thought last night. They have formed an arc. They mean to surround King Penda and his men."

I nodded. "We await your arrows!"

We formed up in four lines. We had two lines of equites and two lines of squires. My intention was to drive through the enemy and reach their leaders. We did not have enough equites to kill huge numbers of warriors but we could hurt their leaders. If we took the head of the beast then King Penda could destroy the body.

It was strange, as we sat there, to hear the sounds of the two armies. We could not see them but we could hear them. The Bernicians were chanting some paean to their White Christ while King Penda and his Mercians were banging their shields and chanting threats and curses; the sounds blending into one another. The horses were snorting impatiently as we awaited the arrows which would tell us that it was time. A cheer went up from beyond the hill fort and then I saw the two arrows fly and land a hundred paces from us.

I raised my spear, "Forward!"

Having ridden this once it was easier to pace Star. We trotted until we were beyond the hill and the battle unfolded below us. The army of Oswald and Oswiu was just clashing with the Mercians when we saw them. Dai's arrows had been perfectly timed. They were six hundred paces from us and we saw only their backs and their side. The standards were in the distance more than eight hundred paces from us. The kings had chosen the large sycamore tree we had seen the night before around which to place their tents. I think it was said that Christ's cross was made of such wood. I thought it ironic that the tree had probably been worshipped by pagans and yet the priests and Christian kings gathered around it!

All eyes were on the standards of the two kings and Gawan and Arturus. Those four were the only ones who were mounted.

It was deliberate. It was the lure to draw the enemy on. I kept the pace steady for as soon as we began to gallop the vibration and the sound would carry to the enemy. I wanted them engaged by the Mercians and unable to disengage before we alerted them. I watched as waves of arrows from the Welsh archers and Daffydd's sailed over the heads of the front ranks. Those at the rear who had shields used them but many more had not and they died. It made them press even closer together desperate to take advantage of the shelter of their comrades.

At two hundred paces I shouted, "Charge!" Our horses were unleashed and they opened their legs. The ground thundered and shook. I saw Bernicians looking to the skies for signs of a storm!

A shield wall is a powerful weapon save that it relies on the shields being locked and facing its enemy. The moment the wall is broken it is like a thread from a woven kyrtle. It unravels and vanishes. The Bernicians who were on the extreme right flank were before us and facing the Mercians. Three rows deep they had shields above their heads and before them. Then the ones at the rear and on the right heard us and turned. As they did so some of our archers' arrows found flesh and they fell. The Mercians facing them began to push forward and hurt those in the front rank. As more men heard us they also turned and it was like a wave surging down the serried ranks of Angles and Jutes. We had not even drawn blood and the enemy began to flee. Our line of horses must have filled their world. Had they been with others and holding locked shields, supported by those behind then they might have stood and faced the shining wall of armour which hurtled towards them. Perhaps it was the dragons and wolves on our shields, the red plumes fluttering behind us or the sound of the wailing dragon standard which made them flee but the ones before us did not risk our horses' hooves. I pulled back my arm for a fleeing man cannot outrun a horse. The men we chased had no armour. I reined in Star a little to make a more accurate strike. I punched, twisted and pulled. I did not need to penetrate deeply. The first Angle fell dead and his body was trampled by the horses following me. Even with Star just cantering I was still catching those who had fled. More were now joining them for the Mercians on our left flank had managed to turn the shield wall. They were hacking and attacking at the side of the Bernicians without shields. The arrows which still flew killed and wounded more. The behemoth which had been the Bernician horde was now writhing in pain.

I spied the two kings and their allies. They were surrounded by their hearth weru and priests. I turned to Llenlleog. He was on my right and his squire held the banner which would command our equites. "Wheel to take the kings! Let us end this!"

He turned and shouted. The standard pointed north and we began to wheel. Those on my right had to urge their horses faster while those on the left slowed down. Only well-trained equites and squires could manage this manoeuvre. I believe it won us the battle that day for it caught the Bernicians, Deirans and Jutes by surprise. They had expected us to plough on through their shield wall. For us, that battle was over. King Penda and King Cynddylan would finish that fight.

The hearth weru formed a shield wall. This would be a substantial one. These were the best of warriors. They had all sworn to die for their kings and thegns. The only horses they had with them belonged to the two kings and their two standard-bearers. Even as we closed with them, trampling over the bodies of men slain by arrows, I saw King Oswald and his standard-bearer dismount. They gave their horses to two priests. The four horses galloped away. King Oswiu was leaving. King Oswald showed his courage that day. The flight of the Deiran King and their standard prompted the Deirans to flee. The Jutes had no king to lead them. When the Angles left to flee north they joined them. I heard a roar from the Mercians as a third of the men they faced fled. Swords now rattled on shields for the spears were shattered. Men cried out as arrows plunged into flesh no longer protected by willow shields.

The battle, however, was not over. It would not be until the two hundred or so warriors who remained were dead. We were in a looser formation, my foot no longer touched that of Llenlleog and Bors. There was, however not enough space for a warrior to pass between us. We had used all the slope that there had been and now our horses were tiring. Some had been cut by the spears of dying men. The shield wall would hold us. As we neared it I changed my grip to hold the spear overhand. I threw it down and over the shields. The Angle had leather mail studded with metal but I was close enough for my spearhead to find his bare neck and he fell. As he fell he created a slight gap. I drew my sword and pulled back on Star. His mighty forelegs and hooves clattered into the shield of the Angle behind. His spear scored a line through my leather leggings and drew blood. It was nothing. It was his last act for he fell as Star dropped and the warrior's skull was crushed.

"Equites, fall back! Squires throw your spears!" It was a risky manoeuvre but with well-trained men it was possible to hurt the enemy more. The hearth weru did not understand my words. They thought they had won and they cheered and banged their shields as we withdrew by turning left and riding in a circle. Arturus had read, as had I, that it was called a Cantabrian circle in Roman times. I saw four empty saddles. Equites had fallen and that was a tragedy. You did not replace an equite easily.

The hearth weru had no bows and their slingers lay slain near their shield wall. They were impotent to hurt us. Ordinary warriors might have raced after us but not these veterans. When the squires formed up they reformed their ranks and the gaps were filled. We had killed a third of them already but they were confident for our spears were now gone. The squires, led by Bors squire, Torin, rode as though they were going to charge and then turned left to head north and hurl their spears over the shields of the hearth weru. Each squire had three spears for they carried our spares. As they galloped to form up behind us I saw that more than half of the hearth weru had been killed or badly wounded. Even as I contemplated a second such attack I saw warriors pulling spears from their limbs and stepping back to try to form a line. It would be a single line. Their second line was Eowa, Alweo, King Oswald and their standard-bearers. The priests had fled and were running after the King of Deira.

"Reform!"

The charge of the squires had allowed our horses to catch their breath. As my equites lined up alongside me I saw that the Mercians were driving the enemy backwards. The Bernicians were dying for their King. He had not fled and so long as his standard fluttered they would fight on. They were however being pushed back. It would be hard and brutal. King Penda would give no quarter. If we lost he would lose his kingdom. The King of Bernicia had ensured that his kingdom would survive by sending his brother back. I had no doubt that he thought they could still win. They thought they had God on their side.

Once we had reformed I dug my heels in Star and shouted, "Charge!" I aimed my horse at Alweo's oathsworn. I recognised the design on their shields. We had beaten them once at the ambush. They had originally been in the second rank and it was only as a result of Bernicians dying that they were in the front rank. I leaned forward and to the right. Star compensated by leaning to the left. I had trained him well. The Mercian spear was thrust at my head. I had to trust in my helmet. At the last moment, I bowed my head and swung my sword blindly. The spear rasped and scratched along my helmet. The leather thong beneath my neck held and my sword connected. As I lifted my head I saw that my sword had driven across the neck of one of Alweo's oathsworn. He fell and I saw the fear on the face of Alweo son of Eowa. He did not have a spear. He had a sword. Holding his shield before him to protect himself from Star's snapping jaws he swung his sword at my left. I wheeled Star to the right and the sword smashed across my shield. Llenlleog had slain Alweo's father. A single blow decapitated him.

As his father's head flew Alweo's face showed his fear. He could not ask for quarter. He had betrayed King Penda and he could only expect death. He had to fight on but he was facing Saxon Slayer. I pulled Star to the left and the move took Alweo by surprise. I swung Saxon Slayer from on high and my blade hit his helmet hard from above. The Saxons made good swords. I had seen Alweo's and knew it to be a good one. His helmet was not as well made. His protector beneath did not do what it was supposed to. I saw his eyes glaze over and he stood stock-still. Then a tendril of blood dripped down his nose and he fell to the ground. He was dead.

King Oswald and his standard-bearer remained. My equites were finishing off the last of the oathsworn and I dismounted. I strode towards the King. Pointing Saxon Slayer at him I said, "You have shown courage today King Oswald, for you have stayed with your men but you sent mercenaries to attack my people. You killed my kin and for that, you will pay!"

"You are all pagans and you will rot in hell! I will go to heaven for the priests have heard my confession. Nothing that you do can hurt me."

He stepped forward and lunged at me. At the same time, the standard-bearer struck at me too. It was a dishonourable blow and might have succeeded had not Llenlleog had lightning reactions. His sword was used two handed, ripped deep into the standard-bearer to his spine. I saw King Oswald flinch as he heard the backbone break. I took King Oswald's blow on my shield and let the sword slide down the side. His sword was shorter than mine. I could have stood off and traded blows but while he stood then men were dying for the Bernicians would not stop fighting while their king lived. I swung my shield at his right side and he reeled. As he did so I stepped in and slid my sword upwards. His left hand was slow to fetch his shield around for he was unbalanced. And I found a gap. Saxon Slayer had a tip and the sword drove between the metal scales. It ripped through the leather holding them together. It entered the padded garment he wore beneath and up through his rib cage. I kept driving and saw the horror on his face as he realised that he was dying. One last push entered his heart and, with a soft sigh he died. He fell and lay beneath the huge sycamore tree. I pulled out Saxon Slayer and held it aloft. My equites and squires began banging their shields and shouting, "Warlord!" We had won.

Gawan and Arturus were the first to reach me. They jumped down, "We have won brother and it is down to you and your equites."

I nodded. "And there are four who have died. Was the victory worth it? Oswiu fled. There will still be a king of Northumbria. He will hide in Eoforwic or Din Guardi and build up his army. Is that a victory?"

"It is a kind of victory. It buys us time to build up our army and King Penda to extend his power. So long as he remains a true ally then all will be well." He lowered his voice, "I have not seen treachery in his mind."

Arturus said, "And this is the last time I watch you fight alone, Warlord. Had not Llenlleog had quick reactions then the standard bearer's treachery would have done for you."

"But it did not. We are all brothers in arms and protect each other."

King Penda rode up. He jumped from his horse and embraced me. King Cynddylan followed him. "I owe you much, Warlord. If we had twice the number of equites then we could conquer this whole island!"

"But we have not and can never have. We have a victory but not a complete one. Oswiu fled."

"Aye." He took his sword and went to the body of Oswald. "He wanted to be like his Christ. Let us help him!" He took his sword and hacked the body of King Oswald into pieces. He turned to Pybba. "Put Oswald on this tree and let his body feed the birds and warn all of the folly of attacking Mercia!"

The rest of his oathsworn did the same to the bodies of Eora, Alweo and the rest of the oathsworn. It looked like a charnel house. We left the bodies by Oswald's Tree. The Christians saw it as something holy. I heard that they made him a saint. Even as we walked back to the Mercian camp the crows, magpies, choughs and rooks were feasting on the dead.

Part 2

Gwenhwyfar

Chapter 7

King Cynddylan took me to one side as King Penda and his oathsworn spread the dismembered body over the limbs of the tree. "Is this well done?"

I shook my head, "But now that it is done it cannot be undone. You are a Christian. Will the church not think that he was martyred?"

"Perhaps." After studying the grisly tree, he turned to me, "I would travel back with you, Warlord. Ethelbert will march with his King to Tomworðig. I have fulfilled my commitment and I intend to visit King Cadafael at Aberffraw. I have a home at Rhuthun. I would deem it an honour if you would visit with me. I have a proposal to make."

I was intrigued but wary, "I have to get back to Rheged as soon as I can. I left scant resources should trouble visit us."

"One night should do it and it is but a few miles out of your way."

That evening we celebrated. We had taken treasure from the enemy. The religious artefacts went to King Cynddylan and the rest was shared equitably. There were many good swords and amulets. The clasps for their cloaks were also both well made and decorative. Some of the helmets the thegns, chiefs and kings had worn were also worth taking. The sword of Oswald I took. I had plans for it. It had a fine scabbard and the blade was engraved.

We buried our dead on the top of the hill fort. It had been built by the ancient peoples who did not follow the White Christ. They would sleep easily there. By the time we had buried them the Saxons were already half-drunk. We had captured vast quantities of ale brought from Bernicia and they had consumed most of that already. King Penda and I sat with King Cynddylan, Gawan and Llenlleog watching the victorious warriors become progressively drunker. I could see that the Mercian King was not happy about it but we had won a great victory and eliminated one of his enemies.

After he had seen two of his thegns suddenly jump up from the ground and begin fighting he shook his head and said, "It is a pity that Oswiu escaped."

I was not certain if he was criticising me but I chose to ignore it if he had. "It will take him time to build up his forces again."

"And us also, Warlord. Their initial attack cost us many men. I had hoped to take the war into their lands but that cannot be; at least not for a while."

Llenlleog was in a thoughtful mood, "He will hire mercenaries. The church will pay him to do so. The last thing they want is a pagan army attacking the Christian Kingdoms."

King Penda nodded. His face was not the face of a victorious general, "But our alliance still stands?"

We all nodded. King Cynddylan said, "And I will visit with Cadafael and discover why he failed to honour the alliance."

King Penda shrugged, "We did well enough without him."

"But think how much more complete would have been the victory with his archers and his light horsemen. Our father helped to train his men and while they are not equites they would have been more than capable of catching King Oswiu."

I thought back to my father's days when Cadwallon had fought at our side. My brother was right but we could not change what had already happened. "Gawan, battles are always easy to win after they have been fought!"

"Perhaps."

"We will use the same arrangements for sending a message, Warlord but next time you will not have as far to travel for I intend to attack him in his own land. After this setback, it will not be for at least a year. We need to harvest crops and have my men make more warriors as well as train men for war."

"We will come when you call." King Penda was a good general. His men had fought well and his plan had been a sound one.

We rode north and west the next morning. We went at the speed of the King's guards and they walked. King Cynddylan asked that Gawan and myself ride ahead of the rest. He wished to have words with us. Arturus did not mind for he rode with Llenlleog and the equites. "Warlord, we have an alliance of arms but I would have a closer alliance."

I was wary. "I am no king."

"I know I was thinking of an alliance of family. I have two daughters, Heledd and Gwenhwyfar. Gwenhwyfar is the younger and some say the fairer. Heledd will make a good wife. I would have one of them marry Arturus. Heledd would be the better choice. She could be a queen."

Gawan nodded, "And yet you would be happy for her to marry a warrior who will never be a king."

"If I am to be brutally honest I would have her marry a prince but Cadafael's son is too young and Peada, Penda's son has seen them and had no desire to marry either of them. I think his father wishes for a Saxon bride. Oswiu's daughter Alchflaed would seem to be King Penda's choice if warfare fails. I have no son and my wife has ceased bearing me children. I could take another but that would create dissension for my wife's family is powerful."

I took it all in and we rode in silence for a while. He had obviously married to secure his position as King of two lands. Admittedly one was a client of Gwynedd but he had power. "Arturus is not my son. His father is here. What say you Gawan?"

"It depends upon Arturus. He lived in the east for a while. That might influence him. Neither of us has any objection to Arturus marrying whomsoever he chooses but we will not force him to marry any. He is not a prince and that is not our way."

The King seemed a little put out by Gawan's comments and he too rode in silence. "I had thought that marrying a princess would be attractive enough for you to agree to this while we rode."

I shook my head, "Then you do not know the men of Rheged. Kings come and go but we stay to guard the land. My father helped King Cadwallon become a powerful leader and then we were abandoned. Now his son does nothing. An alliance with you is a good thing but if it depends upon Arturus marrying one of your daughters then I fear the alliance may end. We have fought on alone before now. Besides Arturus has some of his

Saxon Sword

father's powers. He will sense what is in our heads. He will have to be told before we reach your home. He is a strong-minded man."

"It seems I have little choice in the matter."

The rest of the journey to the King's stronghold was uncomfortable. I would not make Arturus do anything he did not want to do. Gawan rode to the rear to speak with his son and Llenlleog joined me at the head of the column. He knew nothing of our conversation with the King and his mind was already on replacing the equites.

"We have eight squires who could be equites."

"Eight, that seems a high number."

"Warlord, one problem with you leading all our attacks from the front is that you do not see the men behind you. I do. Seven you have not seen in action but the eighth you have."

"And who is that?"

"Arturus."

"Arturus? He has been training less than any of the others."

"He had more skill before he began his training. When he was in Constantinopolis he trained with the Emperor's guards. He studied with the strategoi and their learned men. He knows more of the ancient battles than any man I know and that includes you, Warlord. You and I are getting no younger. Bors and Kay should be at home boring their grandsons with stories of wars long forgotten. We need new blood. We need young blood."

"But I would not have Arturus' spilt."

"And you will not."

We rode in silence for a while. We were climbing to the pass which led to the Clwyd Valley. Soon we would be at Rhuthun. Things were moving quickly; too quickly. I glanced to the south and saw Wyddfa. In my head, I suddenly heard a laugh. I had not heard the laugh for such a long time. It was Myrddyn. His voice in my head was so clear that I had to look around to see if he was on Star's back with me.

'Have I taught you nothing? We each play a part in this game of kings and crowns. You and I did not wear a crown, nor did we wish to. Your time is coming to an end, Hogan Lann. You have done all that your father and I could have hoped. Make the new world one which is ruled by those who

follow on from Arturus. This is all meant to be. He will choose well. It may not be your choice, or his father's but it will be the right choice.' There was a silence and then Myrddyn's voice faded as he said, 'There is a place ready for you, Warlord!"

Gawan's horse nudged next to mine. He looked at me and said, "He spoke to me too." Shrugging his shoulders, he said, "We must follow the path even though we may not like it."

"And Arturus?"

He laughed, "He does not wish to marry a Welsh harpy whom he has never seen! It went well!"

We stopped to water the horses at one of the many streams which flowed from Wyddfa. As I dismounted and allowed Copper's head to drop I saw the sword of King Oswald. I took it from its scabbard. A shaft of sunlight suddenly caught the blade and I read the inscription it said **CALIBURNUS OSWALD MEC HEHT GEWYRCAN**. It meant 'my name is Caliburnus, Oswald ordered me made.

Llenlleog read it too. A fine sword. You are going to replace Saxon Slayer?"

I laughed, "I could never replace my father's sword. I was thinking of Arturus." I did not say that if I was to die alone then my sword would die with me. "When he becomes an equite I thought to give it to him. It is as long as Saxon Slayer."

"Perhaps Oswald had it made as a copy of Saxon Slayer. The jewels on the hilt look similar."

"Perhaps and this might have been sent to me for that purpose. Say nothing. I need to think on this." I sheathed the sword and wrapped it in sheepskin. Looking towards Wyddfa I knew that I would give it to him. It was a question of when.

We remounted and continued on our way. The King still kept alone. I was not certain if we had offended him with our apparent rejection of his offer or if he was thinking of something else. He was a hard man to understand. I saw Rhuthun in the distance. It was a well-made stronghold on a carefully chosen piece of ground. It had a good gatehouse, a ditch and a palisade around a large pair of halls. It was, however, made of wood. I had not seen any defences which could match Civitas Carvetiorum. We were lucky. King Urien and my father had not allowed the walls to fall into disrepair. We even had a functioning bathhouse. This was, for the area, a strong fort. There were few sentries on the wall for the King had brought most of his men with him. I wondered why he had left his wife and family here. Perhaps this was the land where her family held power.

We reined in just before the gates, "Warlord, my home is not large. I only have rooms for You, Gawan and Arturus. Your men will have to camp outside."

Was this a snub because of our words? If he thought to offend my men he was wrong. Llenlleog was close by. He nodded and smiled, "So long as there is food then we will be happy. Or we could hunt."

The King shook his head, "There will be food sent, Llenlleog."

The King had stable boys to care for our horses but Arturus went with them to make sure that our mounts were cared for. Our horses were everything to us. He would see to it that the saddles were taken off carefully and that the horses were rubbed down, fed and watered. We entered the hall. The King must have sent a rider ahead to warn his family for the Queen and her daughters were waiting in their finery. There were four thrones in the hall. The Queen sat on the one next to the King's and they were flanked by the two princesses.

The King had said Heledd was the elder and even before we were introduced I recognised her. She bore the same name as her mother and I confess that she looked not only like her mother, but she was also regal. I would have put her age at eighteen or so summers. With flowing auburn hair and a fair complexion, she was, indeed, beautiful. Gwenhwyfar, in contrast, had chestnut hair which was almost red and she was younger but she had striking features. She had blue eyes which were like deep pools and she had an impish smile which danced upon her face. If Heledd was regal then Gwenhwyfar was an adhene. The old peoples believed in them. They were a spirit of mischief. Gwenhwyfar looked like such a creature. It was well that the King wished Arturus to marry Heledd. She would be a good consort for Arturus. Gwenhwyfar looked like the wild young horse you admired but would never dream of riding to war.

"My Queen, this is the Warlord, Hogan Lann and his brother Gawan, the wizard."

They were Christians. Queen Heledd and her eldest daughter clutched at their crosses. Gwenhwyfar smiled. She was not afraid of magic. Had she been of our people I might have thought her a witch. The Christians saw such women as, somehow, frightening, a force of evil. It was not so. There were witches who were evil but far more were the healers in the villages and the source of great and ancient wisdom. They were the ones who ensured that babies were born safely. Some were said to have powers which rivalled the wizards like Gawan. I suppose that the blood of witches still flowed beneath the Christian bodies.

The Queen regained her composure. "You are welcome to my home. The messenger brought word of the great victory. You are doubly welcome Lord Hogan Lann. My father often spoke of you and your father, the Warlord. You kept this land safe. King Cadwallon kept this land safe. It is sad that his son is a shadow of the man in whom we put our trust and faith."

Just then Arturus entered. Our bodies hid him from the three women. The King said, "And this is Arturus ap Gawan."

We stepped aside and revealed him. Heledd smiled at him for he was, indeed, most handsome but Arturus did not even see her. He only saw Gwenhwyfar for their eyes were locked on one another. It was as though the rest of us did not exist. I saw a frown fall over Princess Heledd's face. She must have been told of the probable arrangement. The Queen also looked unhappy. King Cynddylan tried to make the best of it. "Arturus this is my wife, Queen Heledd and my daughters, Heledd and Gwenhwyfar."

Arturus dragged his eyes from Gwenhwyfar and bowed, "It is an honour to meet three such beautiful ladies. This land is supposed to have gold beneath its stones. I see a greater treasure here before me."

The flattery was given to all three but we knew it was intended for Gwenhwyfar. She giggled coquettishly. There was an uncomfortable silence as the two stared at each other. The looks were ones which should have been given in private, on a wedding night and the entire room shifted uncomfortably in the awkward silence of the hall.

Gawan acted first and he said, "We are dirty, King Cynddylan. Could we clean up somewhere and make ourselves presentable?"

The Queen seemed relieved that Gawan had broken the silence, "Of course. I have a chamber ready for the three of you." She clapped her hands and a servant came. He gestured with his arm for us to follow him.

The chamber had three beds within and jugs of water. The servant offered to stay and attend to us but I dismissed him. Gawan needed to speak with his son.

When they had gone Gawan put his hands on his son's shoulders. "Arturus I read your thoughts and those of Gwenhwyfar. She is fey. You have used your powers."

Arturus looked up guiltily. I said, "Powers?"

"He has not been trained brother but he has skills in magic. They are basic ones but he is able to detect a person's thoughts. Today he and the adhene shared thoughts."

"She has power too?"

"She does. She has greater powers than any woman I have ever met. Did you not notice that she did not touch her cross when we were announced? She may tell her parents that she is Christian but beneath that veneer is someone who follows the old ways."

"But father I thought that you wished me to marry one of them?"

"And I thought that what were the words you used, *'I will never marry a shrill-voiced, Welsh harpy,'* you would not countenance such a union?"

"That was before I saw Gwenhwyfar."

I spoke, "You were supposed to marry Heledd."

"I am happy to marry Gwenhwyfar but not the other. She spoke to me in my head and…" he suddenly blushed and I knew the thoughts which had been planted there.

This was the first time that Arturus had come into conflict with his father and me. I was in a difficult position. Gawan was his father but I had named Arturus as my heir. The three of us were involved in this decision. If the wrong choice was made then Rheged itself could fall.

Gawan went to the pitcher and the bowl. "When we have washed, brother, I will speak with my son, alone if you would."

I nodded, "Aye, that would be right. For this does not bode well." I went to the second bowl and filled it with water from the pitcher.

Arturus did not move but looked from his father to me and back. "I am my own man, Warlord. I should make my own decisions."

Shaking my head, I said, "Did you not hear your father, Arturus? He will speak with you alone. The decisions we make here are weighty ones. You are not just a squire who soon will be an equite. You are the heir of the Warlord. What we do here will echo into eternity." I pointed south, "Wyddfa and the tomb of Myrddyn lie close to here. I for one, will not make any decision until I have slept. If Myrddyn does not come to visit me I will be surprised." The words I had heard on the road flickered in the back of my mind. He had foreseen this turn of events.

I saw Arturus clutch at the wolf clasp on his cloak. Even my headstrong nephew still feared Myrddyn.

I washed and, after shaking the dust from my clothes left them. The ladies were no longer in the hall but the King was and he had a jug of wine, "Come join me, Warlord." He poured us a goblet of wine each. "That was unexpected. It was as though four of us did not exist to those two young people."

I nodded, "The word we would use is *wyrd*. I know that you are Christian and do not believe such things but the connection there was strong. It seemed to me that the two are drawn to each other. It may not end well but I cannot see what we can do to break this invisible bond."

"What does his father say?"

"Like us, he is not happy and he is speaking with Arturus. I am not sure it will do any good."

That evening there was a strange atmosphere as we ate. He had invited his leading warriors. My senior equites, Llenlleog, Kay and Bors, also attended. Daffydd ap Miach had been invited but his family had originally come from close to the stronghold and he had asked if he could visit his former home.

Queen Heledd had seated Arturus and her daughter as far away from each other as it was possible. Even so, they kept glancing in the direction of the other. I knew that they would be using their thoughts to speak with each other. The Queen could do nothing about that. Her elder sister Heledd looked most unhappy. She had known that her parents were trying to arrange a match between her and Arturus. Her younger sister had stolen Arturus' heart. I could see that she thought it unfair.

The King and I were seated alongside Gawan. The King shook his head, "I said that I wanted a match with Arturus for one of my daughters but I thought it would have been Heledd."

"I have spoken with my son. He will have Gwenhwyfar or he will have none. I fear that if we do not accede to his request he may take matters into his own hands."

I shook my head, "Then his life would be ended for every door would be closed to him."

Gawan was silent and then said, quietly, "There is still Constantinopolis. Gwenhwyfar might be the thing which keeps him here."

I was not happy. I did not like to be held to ransom like this. Was Arturus bewitched? Certainly, Gwenhwyfar had more confidence than was normal in a girl of her age. I turned to glare at him but his eyes were fixed on the Welsh Princess.

"I confess, Warlord, that a marriage of Gwenhwyfar to Arturus would solve a problem for me. I can think of many suitors for Heledd but Gwenhwyfar is another matter. She and your nephew seem to have an understanding already." He lowered his voice, "My wife might be unhappy but then she is often thus."

I remembered the conversation I had had with the King about his heir. His was not a happy marriage. I stared at the ceiling as though seeking inspiration.

Gawan, sensing my thoughts, said, "Brother, sleep on it. We are close enough to Myrddyn that, if he chooses, he can speak to us and, perhaps, Arturus." He turned to the King. "You will have your answer in the morning."

It deferred a decision and I nodded. We went to our chamber and I began to undress. I could not bring myself to speak with Arturus. His behaviour was not that which I had expected. Gawan spoke to him normally as though there was no discord. He was a wizard and could dissemble. I was a warrior and could not. He was his father and, more importantly, he knew his son's thoughts before he spoke them. It made life easier. He handed me a chalice of wine. He put a few drops of a potion into it. "This will help you dream and to sleep. A man makes poor decisions when he is deprived of sleep."

Arturus said, "Uncle, this is meant to be. I love the maid. I know that she will be wild but I believe that is a good thing. I need a strong wife and I know before I have even held her hand that she is strong. Our children will be strong and powerful."

I drank down the drug-infused wine, "I hope so but I have reservations. Let me sleep on it. Myrddyn spoke to me when I saw Wyddfa. Perhaps he will convince me."

The draught worked and I fell swiftly asleep.

I was in a black world. I had been in such places before and they did not frighten me. It was as though I was being prepared for the Otherworld. That would come soon enough. The darkness grew lighter, faintly at first but growing stronger. As it grew brighter it became orange and then red. It was the flame of a dragon and it hurtled towards me. I could not move and I knew that the dragon would burn me to a crisp. The flame died and the dragon walked closer to me. Bizarrely I saw its heart beating. It was a steady beat which I could hear in my head. Then I saw its face. Its face resembled my brother's. I saw Gawan in the dragon's features. Then it changed to become Arturus. The dragon was my nephew. Then the dragon opened its mouth and flames leapt forth towards me. They did not burn me. They passed over and, when I turned, I saw behind me a horde of Saxons. They were burning, melting before me. When I turned around all that was left was the heart of the dragon. It was still beating. As I stepped towards it I found that my feet were in water. The closer I came to the heart the deeper was the water and currents began to suck at me, dragging me beneath the water. The heart was swept away. It disappeared and with it, the water. I was alone once more. I opened my mouth and shouted, 'Myrddyn! Do not forsake me! Where are you?' There was no answer.

I sat in silence in the darkness but I could still hear the heart of the dragon beating before me. Then I realised that it was my own heart which was beating.

'Myrddyn! Do not forsake me! Where are you?'

My heart began to slow and my eyes grew heavy. I had had no answer. Just before I fell asleep a voice came to me. It was inside my head and it was Myrddyn's. 'I have answered you once and my answer is still the same. This is all meant to be. He will choose well. It may not be your choice, or his father's but it will be the right choice.'

The last thing I remember before waking was the sound of oars in the water and sea birds in the air.

Gawan was looking down at me and Arturus looked terrified. Gawan held a goblet. It was ale this time. I drank and it soothed my throat. "I was shouting?"

Arturus nodded and Gawan said, "Screaming. Did you get an answer?"

"I am not certain. Did you not see?" He shook his head. "It was hidden from me."

I told him what had happened and he frowned. "This tells us nothing of our dilemma. Was there nothing more? This dream is of a life after our death. This is a foretelling of the future."

"He said he had told me before." I pointed to Arturus, "Arturus has made the right choice." I shook my head. "I still cannot see it but…"

Arturus looked delighted. "Then I can marry the princess?"

Gawan looked at me. His shoulders sank in resignation. "If the King agrees then aye!"

The King was at the gate when we emerged from the hall. We wandered over to him. He smiled, "I know we are Christian but there is something reassuring about the close proximity of the mountain. It makes me feel part of this land."

I nodded in agreement, "I grew up under its shadow. I miss it more than you can know for my father lies entombed beneath it. It has great power. The spirits of the dead spoke to me."

He sighed and turned to Arturus. "Has the madness gone, young Arturus? Or do you still wish to marry Gwenhwyfar?"

"I do, King Cynddylan, and my father and uncle have agreed to support me."

The King looked from my brother to me and back. He saw our expressions and knew that Arturus spoke true. "Would it were that easy. The Queen is opposed to it."

Gawan said, "Do you mind me asking why?"

"Gwenhwyfar was a difficult child and when she became a young woman she became impossible. She and her mother have had many arguments. Her mother favours Heledd."

I shook my head, "Then I would have thought she would have been pleased to get rid of her."

"No, for that would be my youngest child winning and that would never do." He sighed, "I am King and I will make the decision. The alliance will strengthen us. King Cadafael is a weak king but he has men in his court who would take this little kingdom from me. Powys is richer but this one is closer to my heart. Come let us bear the news. There will be two women who will be unhappy and one who will be overjoyed."

As we headed down the ladder I asked, "And when would you have the wedding?"

"As soon as it can be arranged. I fear the battle we have just fought will be nothing compared with the battle between my daughter and my wife. The sooner you are wed, Arturus, and can take my daughter to Civitas Carvetiorum the better."

Gawan turned to the King, "I would say marry now but I know that my wife would like to see our son married. We can be back here in four days for we could return by sea."

"Then I will see the Bishop of St. Asaph and arrange it for five days from now."

He was correct about the reaction. His wife flew into a rage and began pointing a talon at Gwenhwyfar and screaming that her daughter had bewitched Arturus. Heledd just wept. Gwenhwyfar grinned at her mother which just incensed her even more. I felt sorry for Arturus. The joy of knowing that he would have the bride of his choice was spoiled by the screaming Queen and the fact that he could not do what he wished and throw his arms around her.

King Cynddylan ended the storm by raising his voice, "Silence! I am King and my word is law. The pair will be wed in five days' time. If you cannot arrange the wedding, wife, then I will get our steward to do so. Should I invite guests or will you do that?"

The Queen subsided. This was an opportunity for her to show off her finery and her jewels. I saw her calculating and weighing up the trade-off of losing to her daughter and getting rid of the irritant. "I am Queen and I will arrange it." She turned and smiled at Gawan, "Will your wife be attending, lord?"

"We will be leaving now to return as soon as we can."

The Queen beamed for she had a partial victory. Gwenhwyfar's face fell as she realised that Arturus would be going and she would be at the mercy of her mother and sister. Families were complicated affairs.

Chapter 8

As we headed north, Daffydd ap Miach joined me when Arturus rode with the squires at the rear of the column. My nephew had much to tell his brother in arms. When he became Warlord, he would lead them into battle. It was right that they shared in his joys too.

My captain of archers looked nervously from Gawan to me, "My lord, you know I visited family?" I nodded. I saw him take a deep breath. In all the time I had known Daffydd he had rarely spoken of anything other than his trade. "It concerns the Princess Gwenhwyfar." We waited for him to continue. "Some is gossip and rumour. I will not repeat that but the Princess ran off a year since. This is fact for the King had all his men hunting for her. They found her in a cave on the eastern side of Wyddfa. She was with a witch, one of those who did not convert to Christianity. They brought back the princess and had the witch buried alive."

I looked at Gawan. If there was the power of the spirits involved then he should have known. He nodded. "I sensed power in her but I saw it as raw and untamed. I thought it just a relic of her heritage." He looked at Daffydd, "The rumours and gossip, they were about her parentage?"

"Aye lord." My captain of archers was not surprised for he knew Gawan's powers well. "It is said by those with nothing better to do than to chatter like magpies that a young Hibernian warrior, some say a prince, was shipwrecked and came up the river for help. He stayed a month. It was when the King was away fighting his enemies around Powys."

Gawan said, "It is the hair and the features. She has her mother's beauty and yet she does not look like her sister or her father and then there is her hair. I believe the gossip for it would explain much. It would explain her mother's attitude towards her daughter."

I turned to Daffydd, "Thank you Daffydd. I can trust your discretion. We would not wish Arturus to hear of this."

"Of course, lord. I had to speak."

"And you did right." When he had gone we spoke quietly about the choices we had before us. After a morning's discussion, as we neared the river by the old Roman fort of Bremetennacum, we decided that there was little to be gained by telling Arturus what we had learned. Her parentage was not her fault and she would either tell or not tell him why she ran away. Gawan would use his powers to try to unravel the mystery.

As we dismounted he said, "Now I know why Myrddyn told you what he did. I do not think that Gwenhwyfar will be easy to live with but I believe that she has been sent to serve a purpose. As yet I cannot see it. If Myrddyn wishes it then it will, in the end, help us. But the river flows a long way before it reaches that sea."

While our horses drank and we ate I spoke with Llenlleog. I could see that he had been curious about our conversation. "Is aught amiss, Warlord?"

I smiled. He was not what the women in the town square at Civitas might call nosey but he had a little of the wizard in him and I knew that he was genuinely intrigued. "Gawan and I were speaking of the changes which the fiery princess will bring to our land."

"Your nephew is smitten, Warlord, that is obvious and she is enamoured of him and yet..." He looked uneasy.

"Speak."

"To me, this seems like a volcano. I have never seen one but I know from those who have seen the ones in Italy and Greece that they are brooding and silent. They bubble and they hiss. When they erupt you have no warning. That is what I see in this liaison. They are obviously in love but that does not guarantee peace."

"Like Gawan you have powers; do you see harm?"

"I see change and men our age never like change."

"Thank you Llenlleog. You are a good friend." I looked south. "The world has changed since my father led the alliance of warriors who defied the Angles and the Saxons. Now we fight alongside some of them. We cannot go back and change the world into one we like. We must make the best of what we have. Myrddyn told me that this was good. I have to believe him. If he was wrong then our whole world is based upon a lie. We are getting old Llenlleog. Any change is an unwelcome one for us.

Arturus will lead and I believe he will have someone at his side who can help him."

Gwyneth was the one who was most overjoyed at the news. The fact that her son would be marrying a princess made up, a little, for the fact that she was not living in Constantinopolis. She was a little annoyed at the haste and the fact that we would be leaving less than a day after we had returned. She wished to impress Queen Heledd. She wanted more time to have dresses made. However, she knew she would have to forego that. It was a small price to pay for a bride for her son.

We were lucky that our ship *'Gwynfor'* was in the river. Her captain, Daffydd ap Gwynfor had been cleaning her ready for the new trading season. We would not be able to take as many people as Gawan's wife wished. It was not as big as Gwyneth would wish. I left Llenlleog to command in my absence and allowed Arturus to choose the four equites and squires who would come with us. He chose Agramaine, Pol, Llewellyn and Griflet. The rest of the passengers would be Gwyneth's ladies and servants. She seemed to need a great number.

We left on the high tide and headed west. We had to use oars to navigate the first stretch for the wind was from the north and west. It would help us when we sailed but it prevented us from using the sails to reach the sea. With so few men on board Gawan and I had to take an oar. *'Gwynfor'* was not a galley. The oars were sweeps intended to turn and manoeuvre the ship. Had we had time we would have organised horses to pull us to the sea but we knew that the King had set the date and we had to be there.

Gawan grinned at his son, "Well Arturus you have the sons of the Warlord pulling on oars like galley slaves just to take you to your wedding. I hope you appreciate the sacrifice."

It was said with humour but Arturus was serious as he answered, "Aye, father. I know what you and my uncle have done for me and I hope that you do not think I am ungrateful. I do not think that my bride will give me an easy life but she is meant for me. Myrddyn has told me all. My wife to be has no secrets from me. All of this is…" he smiled, "*wyrd*."

"Does this mean you are forgetting your White Christ? Are you returning to the old ways?"

In answer, he said, as we pulled on the oars, "There are many versions of Christianity, Warlord. If you go back to the teachings of Christ and read the originals, as I did in Constantinopolis, you will see that Rome and the priests have changed the message. We believe in spirits and the one you call the White Christ became a spirit. There is not as much difference as you might think. Many who become priests try to make the world and the church fit their vision. I know what I believe."

Captain Daffydd shouted, "Take in the oars. Thank you, lords. The wind will take us now. Loose sail!"

Agramaine pulled up a bucket of estuary water for us to cool our hands. Gawan said, "Then you did not spend all your time in the east enjoying yourself."

He laughed, "No father. I did study. I became a better warrior and a better man. I became a Christian not because of what the priests said but because of what I read. Christ cared for the poor and the ones who could not defend themselves. That is what grandfather did. It is what the Warlord does. We owe a duty to the land but we also owe one to the people who live there; all of them. It matters not if they are Saxon, Welsh, Hibernian, Jute or Angle. We fight those who would use the sword and the spear to rule. That will be my quest. Your quests, uncle, showed me how we ought to be in the future. We will never have many equites. Let us use them as you do, wisely. A couple of equites, squires and archers can make sure that simple farmers, shepherds and herders are able to carry on with their lives without fear of attack, slavery and death."

Gawan put his arm around his son. "Then your extended absence was worthwhile, my son. You have learned and you will be the leader to inherit the land of Rheged from my brother."

I left father and son for they had much to say. I had no children left, not in this world, I had Rheged as my child and I went to the landward side of the ship to watch Rheged as it slipped by, Gawan was right. All of this was meant to be. Rheged would be safe, for a while at least. As I saw the ring of peaks which surrounded the heartland of Rheged I knew that one day it would fall. Myrddyn had told me that but Arturus was a promise of a different Rheged and that was good. My hand went to Saxon Slayer. The sword had come to me to bring light into a dark world. It had been hidden for a long time but the spirits who watched over our land had chosen the right time to bring it forth from the earth. When my time came I would see that it was returned to the earth from whence it came. Its light would be extinguished but its return would herald a new dawn.

Once we left my coast we would be in open waters. We would be on seas which could be dangerous. Our ship was a good one but she was slow. She was tubby and she laboured like a cow about to calve. Daffydd had good lookouts. It was getting on to dusk and we were halfway to the island of Ynys Môn and the mouth of the Clwyd, when the lookout shouted, "Two ships to the west." There was a pause. "I think they are pirates!"

Daffydd's lookouts were experienced. If they said there were pirates then there were. The captain shouted, "Full sail. We will blow the sticks from her!" He put the steering board over so that we had the wind astern of us. The Hibernians who followed would also have the wind but our ship had just had her hull cleaned. It might make a difference.

I shouted, "Warriors get your weapons.! Women get into the cabin." There was a small cabin at the bow of the ship. It would be crowded but they would be safer there. "Gawan you and Arturus guard the women. The rest with me." I saw Griflet's squire, Tal, picking up his shield. "You will not find that to be of any use. Use a dagger with your sword."

Agramaine joined me. "If we had but six archers we could hold them off."

"But we have not and we make do with what we have. This will be a test of our skills for we dare not wear mail. If they gain a foothold on our ship then we are lost. Hold the men here by the mast and I will go to speak with Daffydd."

"Aye Warlord."

Daffydd was alternating looking astern and at the sail. "If we can survive until dark then we might lose them, Warlord. I know the waters around our coast better than they do. We can take them towards the shifting shellfish sands. We are shallow draughted."

His voice suggested that he was more in hope than expectation. "If you can isolate one of them and let them try to board we might be able to discourage them."

"Aye, I will try!" He nodded to his crew, "These are good lads and they have bows."

When I reached the mast Gawan was there. He had two small pots. "I have made a small fire of wood chips and coals in this one and oil in the other. If they close with us then have one of your squires throw the oil and then a second the candle. If we can burn them…"

"Aye. Agramaine, have your squire and Pol's ready to hurl them. They are strong. Near to their mast would help."

The two Hibernians were closer now. I could see the warriors at the bows. They were six hundred paces apart. Whichever way we bolted one would catch us. Almost half a mile behind us it would take some time for them to draw closer. I drew Saxon Slayer and my long dagger. Both were sharp and both had tips. The Hibernians were wild warriors but they had poor weapons. Some would board us with cudgels. Nasty, vicious weapons, they were crude and hard to use effectively on a ship. However, if they traded blows with their swords then their blades would bend or break. We had to retain our resolve and trust in our skills and our weapons. We all wore leather jerkins. Our mail was wrapped in cloth and below the decks. Salt air did it little good. Leather was protective and kept out the wind better than cloth. It would have to serve as armour.

When they were less than two hundred paces from us they had closed to within one hundred and fifty paces of each other. Daffydd ap Gwynfor chose his moment well. He put the steering board over to sail due south. Although it would bring us closer to the westernmost pirate we would have more speed for it would be from our quarter. Our captain was trying to give me all the advantage he could. The manoeuvre took them by surprise and they reacted slowly, allowing us to gain a length or two. When they did turn one was quicker than the other and they were no longer sailing side by side; the one which had been to the west of us was ahead of the other.

I knew now which ship would attack us first and that made things a little easier. Our small ship had ropes which the crew called stays and sheets. The Hibernians had the same. They were a weakness for if they were destroyed then the mast and sail would be at serious risk of falling. They could also be used for support so that we could fight along the rail which topped the sides of the ship. As our ship rode higher in the water then this was an advantage. It was only a slight advantage and we would be outnumbered but it was all that we could do. I heard the Captain order his crew to ensure that they were armed. All of them had a seaman's knife and most had a bow. The knife was a wickedly sharp blade but it would be of little use save in close combat. The first mate was issuing hatchets, hand axes and short swords. We might be taken for ransom. They would be killed or taken as slaves!

It was a race and the Hibernians had oars as well as a sail. They were catching us. I saw that they were coming along the same side as the steering board. That was a sensible move from the pirates. If they could disable the steering board then the ship would be theirs.

"Come, we will go to the Captain. We will be his sword wall. Squires, you watch our backs and when they are close enough throw the pots at their mast. We will try to buy you the time to enable you to do so." I had chosen two squires who were known for their strength but if it was the Hibernian's bow which struck us then they would have to throw the pots further.

I used one of the backstays to pull myself up onto the rail. I placed my feet well apart and balanced myself. Looking astern I saw the leading Hibernian had a prow filled with warriors. All were half-naked. They had breeks and that was all. I glanced down the ship. Gawan and Arturus were at the cabin watching. If my equites fell they would have to race the length of the ship and try to repel the enemy. If we five could not do that then I doubted that they would. The crew of the ship were behind my squires. They would fight and die hard. The battle would be won or lost in that first contact.

The wild men from the west were screaming and hurling insults at us. They were building themselves up for an attack. The first ones over knew that they would face just five warriors. The five of us were standing on the rail. One or two arrows sailed over but the pitching decks and the precocious wind made accuracy impossible for the poor bows the Hibernians used. It was a nuisance more than anything. I saw Griflet bat away an arrow as it came towards him. It was as though it was a summer fly, an irritant rather than a threat. Daffydd's crew used the mast and stern to send their arrows at the Hibernians. Without even a leather jerkin some of their arrows found flesh.

The pirate ship came closer and closer. Its consort was four lengths behind. If they disabled the ropes which held the steering board then they would attack from the other side and we would be overwhelmed. I watched Daffydd ap Gwynfor. His eyes flicked from the pirate to the sails and back again. He was the only one without a weapon in his hand. He was about to make our ship a weapon. The pirate ship was almost upon us. The warriors at the fore were ready to jump. Daffydd did something I would never have been able to do. He judged the move with the steering board to perfection. He made a slight move away from the Hibernian and even before the pirate had reacted he turned back on our original course. The six warriors who were at the prow leapt as they saw our hull within leaping distance. One made our ship but the other five all fell between and beneath the two ships. As the hulls came together, briefly, two men were crushed between them. The warrior who made the prodigious and successful leap which landed him on the rail found Saxon Slayer in his middle. With a surprised look, he tumbled over the side and into the water.

The deaths of their brothers in arms infuriated the pirates. They began screaming even louder. Their captain changed his course to move parallel to us. More men were lining the sides of the ship. He would place his bow closer to the mast.

"Spread out, equites. You two squires fill in the gaps."

Daffydd had done all that he could and now it was down to our swords and skills. Night was falling fast now. The coast had disappeared into a grey murk. Captain Daffydd would know where we were. Behind us, the sunset made the sails of the two pirates sinister silhouettes. I saw the pirate come closer. If we turned away we would lose way and the second pirate would close with us. Daffydd did the only thing he could. He turned towards the pirate. We were a bigger, stronger ship. He trusted to his vessel. When we hit it, the pirates standing on the rail lost their balance. The ones who held on did so with both hands. Our crew threw hatchets and hand axes. I saw a Hibernian's head split open and he fell backwards. I slashed my longer sword in an arc. It tore through the guts of one pirate and into the forestay. It parted with a twang. My four equites were in their element. The pirates were struggling to hold on and our weapons were longer. The two squires who did not have pots joined in with their swords and seven pirates fell. There were many more waiting but they had to pull themselves up. I swashed my sword and they reeled away. I sensed something behind thrown over my head and knew that the oil pot had been thrown. When the second one flew I prayed that the spirits would guide them both and that the flames would catch.

Despite the fact that ships sail on water covering the hulls, their decks and masts, not to mention the ropes, are bone dry. Fire and flames are their greatest enemy. I heard a crash as the oil-filled pot broke. A pirate threw himself at our ship and his left hand grasped the rail at my feet. One of our crew brought down his axe and severed the hand. He fell screaming between the hulls. Just then the second pot struck. The two squires had done well for they must have landed close by each other. The flames flickered and then ignited. They raced up the mast. The wind from astern fanned the flames and I saw them catch the sail. The sail was tinderbox dry and the flames seemed to dance and race up it. Daffydd moved the steering board away from the pirate. We lost a little way and the second pirate came a length closer. It was a wise move for the severed rope and the burning mast and sail suddenly crashed down the length of the pirate ship. The whole vessel seemed to catch fire at once. I saw men hurling themselves in the sea. The crashing mast stopped the ship and Daffydd was able to put our steering board over and head south. The second pirate could not catch us for he had to sail around his stricken consort. The sunset was replaced by the burning pirate. We headed into the darkness of the coast.

I jumped down and saw that Bedivere, Pol's squire, had a cut across his left arm. Gawan was already fetching his leather satchel to heal him. All the rest had survived. The crew cheered for they knew how close we had come to disaster and death.

Gwyneth and her ladies came forth. They saw the flaming ship. She came up to me, "We watched through the slats in the cabin. We could have died. The Lord saved us."

I shook my head, "Your husband saved us with his pots of fire. Those men who attacked us were followers of the White Christ." I held the wolf clasp from my cloak in my hand. "If any saved us other than Gawan then it was the Allfather and the spirits."

She turned, tight-lipped and returned to her ladies. I had not said the right thing.

We sailed all night and, as dawn broke, saw Wyddfa ahead of us and the mouth of the Clwyd. We had to wait for high tide. The river was wide enough all the way to Rhuddlan but we dared not risk grounding her. The fight with the pirates might have weakened her hull already. The wait gave us the opportunity to clean the blood from her decks. We had been lucky and I had made a mistake. I had not brought archers. I could take nothing for granted. With enemies all around us then I had to be prepared for any and all dangers.

We had been seen bobbing in the estuary and the King himself was at the wooden quay to greet us. There was a pair of priests with him. From their attire, they were the Abbot of the monastery at St. Asaph and the Bishop. I found myself clutching the hilt of Saxon Slayer. My father and Asaph had been friends. Gwyneth and her ladies left the ship first followed by Arturus and Gawan. Normally it would have been me who would land first but now I was the least important of the guests. I busied myself with Daffydd. "We will be here for a day or two at least. Do you wish to have the ship hauled from the water?"

He smiled, "You read my mind, lord. We smacked that ship hard and *'Gwynfor'* is no longer a young lady."

By the time we left the quay was empty. My equites and I left together. The crew and the squires carried our chests. We were coming to a wedding but we had our war gear.

The hall had been well prepared for the wedding and we all had accommodation. I did not have a chamber to myself but shared a small hall with my men. It suited me. I wished to return to my home as soon as possible and the less I had to do with this ceremony the better. The wedding would be held in the wooden cathedral of St Cyndeyrn in St Asaph. It was not far to travel but I was always uncomfortable in these Christian edifices with the ceremonies conducted in a language few understood.

The King had laid on a feast the night before the wedding. His lords and chiefs were in attendance. He had invited King Cadafael but he had said that he was not ready to travel at such short notice. Patently an untruth the alliance had clear cracks! I was the guest of honour but all the attention was on the young couple and their parents. It suited me for I was able to observe the men alongside whom I would be fighting should war come again. They did not inspire me with confidence.

Beli ap Llewellyn looked to be the most promising of them. He was younger than the King and he wore good mail. More importantly, he looked like a lean warrior. The others like Gruffyd ap Cyndeyrn, Owain ap Owain and Daffydd ap Mordaf looked like overweight chiefs with a greater opinion of themselves than I had. Those men we had trained for Cadwallon had died with their King at Hagustaldes-ham. They had not been replaced with warriors of the same mettle and the warriors who surrounded Gwynedd had a lesser threat facing them. Potentially the whole of the land to the south of us could easily fall to an aggressive enemy. I could hold on to Rheged but not the rest of the land.

Gwenhwyfar and Arturus, however, appeared to be genuinely in love with each other. Myrddyn had known more than we had. I was not sure it would be an easy marriage for they appeared to be too similar to each other. Time would tell but time was not something I had in abundance. My equites apart, everyone was very drunk. Gwyneth appeared to be happy and that was something to be applauded.

As Gawan and I helped to put some of the squires and a deliriously happy Arturus to bed I asked him, "Will this all end well, brother? I see little in this alliance to benefit us. Cynddylan's lords are weak. We might end up having to support him rather than him coming to our aid."

He nodded, "I agree but I can see little that we can do about it. Myrddyn and the spirits are happy. The couple is patently well suited. This is all planned, brother and we will just have to live with it. I am no Myrddyn and I cannot see far into the future. Like you, I do not think this bodes well but we trusted Myrddyn as did our father. We can trust him a little longer, eh?"

With that depressing thought in my head, I retired but I slept little. I did not dream but my mind was filled with pictures of the land being ravaged by war. The peace created by my father might well become a distant memory.

The wedding went well in that no one in the church objected. Even Queen Heledd seemed happy although Princess Heledd looked unhappy and sulked and the sun shone. The couple were married in a Christian ceremony which I did not understand. I am not sure that many did. My nephew understood Latin but his bride did not. He had to constantly prompt her. As was the tradition in this part of the land the couple retired to a specially made bedchamber after the ceremony and all waited outside while the couple entered. The guests then left for a further feast but I decided to head down to my ship and speak with Daffydd. I wanted to leave as soon as I could.

He and his men were busy working on the hull when I arrived. They were coating the repaired strakes with pine tar. There were many pine forests around us and they had made a great quantity. It never went amiss.

"We can leave tomorrow?"

"On the afternoon tide, aye lord."

I was disappointed. It meant we would have to travel at night. I did not wish to risk pirates again. "We will have extra guests. You had better rig up a shelter for the servants. They will not all fit into the cabin."

"I have done so already." Daffydd was wise. "Something troubles you, lord?"

I waved a hand, "This land. When our fathers lived on the island of Mona we had a time of peace and a place of plenty. I fear that this will become a debatable land."

"The people will survive. My family still lives on the island. They are raided and they lose both property and people but they endure. What they all have is a memory of a good time when the Warlord ruled and they believe that those days will return. Civitas Carvetiorum is hailed throughout this island as the palace of safety."

"But not with me as Warlord."

"Do not be hard upon yourself. The wars and the plague took many. Our people are not as numerous as they were. We need time to build."

"You think that this marriage will help?"

"It cannot do other. We know that Lady Gwenhwyfar can be wild." He laughed, "My family on the island spoke at great length about her but she looks like a queen and she is fey. She has powers. They will grow together." He smiled and lowered his voice, "Warlord on the voyage out to Constantinopolis and back I spoke at length to your nephew. He has a good heart and he would be as you are. Fathers always worry that their sons will not be what they wish them to be and the simple fact is that they will not. They become new men, different men. They change and adapt. You are not his father but he is as a son to you. He will be a good leader."

I would have to be content with that. I felt as though I had let down my father by losing what he had won. I determined that I would make, Carvetitas as my stronghold was known amongst my equites, as a place of strength to which any could come. The rest of the island might suffer but not my home!

Chapter 9

The voyage home was, mercifully, incident-free. Arturus and his bride giggled and laughed the whole time. There was nowhere for them to be alone and so they huddled and cuddled on the deck. We left in the late afternoon and they stood watching the sun setting in the west. When darkness came they went towards the prow and watched the flickering lights to the east where tiny communities eked out a living by the sea. With the women occupying the cabin the rest of the deck was littered with bodies of those asleep or trying to sleep. As Warlord I felt duty-bound to walk the deck and ensure that all were comfortable. I could do little even if they were not but it was the least I could do. I had just checked that Gwyneth and her ladies were comfortable and stepped out onto the deck when Gwenhwyfar and Arturus appeared.

"Uncle, my wife would have a word with you."

"Of course. We stepped into the lee of the cabin where the wind was not as strong and we could speak.

She began by stretching up and kissing me on the cheek, "This is to thank you for allowing this to take place. I know that you could have forbidden it and I am grateful that you did not."

"Arturus is the nearest that I will have to a son. It is natural that I wish the best for him."

"And you have heard that I am a wild child who ran off with a witch. You fear that I will enchant Arturus."

I smiled, "I believe that he is enchanted already."

Arturus said, "And I know about the witch, Morgana. My father is a wizard; why should I fear a wife who may be a witch."

She poked him playfully, "I am not a witch. If I were I might turn you into a toad. Morgana just told me of my past. She said that I had powers. She intimated that Myrddyn and my mother had lain together."

I laughed, "I was with Myrddyn longer than you were alive, child and I can attest to the fact that he never went near to your mother."

"Even when he worked on his tomb?" Arturus' mind was as sharp as ever.

For the first time doubt crept into my mind but then I dismissed it. "You do your mother a disservice talking about her thus."

"It was she spoke to me about it first. She kept saying that she had made a mistake when I was conceived and my wilful nature was her punishment." She shook her head, "I had nothing to do with my birth! How could I be a punishment?"

"And are you a Christian?" I held up my hand. "For myself, I care not but Arturus is a Christian."

"You can be a Christian and believe in the spirit world."

I shook my head, "Do not try to argue that case with a priest. I agree with you for my brother is wise and has explained it to me but do you believe it Arturus?"

"I have to, Warlord, for I can read my wife's thoughts as she reads mine. I am not the youth who came back from Constantinopolis so full of himself. I have changed."

I suddenly spied hope. "Then Gwenhwyfar, I wish you and your husband well. You will be as safe in Civitas Carvetiorum as anywhere and my equites will protect you. When I am gone to the Otherworld it is Arturus who will lead them."

She squeezed my arm, "Do not be in a hurry to get there, Warlord. I wish to get to know you."

She was an enchantress. I felt myself falling under her spell. It was as though the wild child we had first met had suddenly become a woman and that she had powers now that she did not know of earlier. A wind came from the south and made me shiver. Was this good or was it ill?

When we arrived back we were greeted by the whole settlement. Arturus and Gawan were both popular. Gawan's wife was taken with the young beauty her son had married. Denied daughters of her own the two got on well. That was a relief to Gawan for Arturus would be away for half a moon every three moons and he did not want conflict in our halls. It also helped that Gwenhwyfar was overwhelmed by the civilised stronghold that was Civitas Carvetiorum. It boded well.

Arturus' bride also seemed to have an understanding of the ordinary folk of our town. She took pleasure in walking the streets with her two ladies and speaking with those that she met. She was kind and she was generous with both her coin and her time. Morgana had taught her skills and she was able to offer advice on illnesses which women had. Sometimes they did not feel they could speak with Gawan and Gwenhwyfar was a kind listener. This was not the wild child of whom we had been warned. Myrddyn was right, yet again. She became popular and when her skills as a healer were discovered then she was much sought after. The witch who had given her shelter had taught her and developed her natural skills. Perhaps that was another reason her mother and she had not got on. It was something she did not understand.

Now that we were back from the wars, our world could return to what passed for normal. Our quests resumed and we added, for we now had more equites, a second quest to the north and the borders of Alt Clut. We had an ally there who was closer to us than any. If we could stop Oswiu from encroaching there then so much the better. We also had to plan for Arturus' elevation to the order of equites. I left that in the hands of Llenlleog. I had much to occupy my mind. We had more messengers from both Penda and Cynddylan in the months following the wedding. King Penda used the boar symbol and Cynddylan used men who were known to Gwenhwyfar. We learned that the Bernicians had fled north but now had a line of defences along the Hwmyr. It was in the land of Deira and that had been King Oswiu's. He had now been proclaimed King of Northumbria. The fact that he had his strength in the south made our lives slightly easier.

After the last message from the King, I sat with Gawan. Arturus was still enjoying the company of his wife. He was diligent when he performed his duties but he no longer spent every spare moment with the squires. He was closeted with his wife as often as possible.

"And King Penda is happy with the gathering of an army upon his borders?"

I nodded and sipped the wine. A ship had sailed from Constantinopolis. Our copper and iron were highly prized for their purity. Arturus and Gwyneth had made good contacts in the port as well as in the court. "He is for he wishes a final battle.

When Oswiu is dead then King Penda can take the last two independent kingdoms. He will be High King."

"And then we will have to watch out."

"I think not, brother. I have never tried to gain a kingdom, merely save one. King Penda has no desire for our land. He wants flat farmland which yields him rich crops. He told me so and I believe him. I looked into his eyes and saw no deceit."

"That is what he says now but when he takes Northumbria he will look at Rheged with greedy eyes."

"Then we will fight him!"

Gawan laughed, "Of course, you will."

Daffydd ap Gwynfor had also been back to the Clwyd. He had been to collect more of Gwenhwyfar's chests. While there he had sailed to his former home and spoken with his family. What he had told me had been disturbing.

"There is something else. Daffydd heard of the Clan of the Snake." I had Gawan's attention. Having killed our last living relatives both of us sought vengeance. "They have resurfaced in Wessex. They have acquired ships. They have four of them and they are using the land of Wessex to raid the seaways. Cenwalh, who was King, has fled. Some say he is hiding with the Jutes on their island but it cannot be confirmed. With King Penda now ruling Wessex, the Clan of the Snake has managed to create their own domain. When Penda has dealt with Northumbria then I can see him ridding his land of these barbaric men but for now, we have a danger to the south and west. It is said that he also uses some of the rivers in the heart of Gwynedd to raid ships bound for the northern waters. That is too close to home. I would not like to see those savages let loose in my land again."

"Then I will have to use my powers." He hesitated and then, sighing said, "Gwenhwyfar has powers. I feel stronger with her here in this stronghold. If she aided me then we might be able to detect the Saxons."

"That is a risk and I am not certain your son would approve."

"I can ask him. It will take all of my powers to see into their dark hearts. They have powers themselves. If they have ships then they can avoid your equites. I cannot see how we would defeat Saxons in ships."

I drank down the wine and smacked my lips. It came to me. "Constantinopolis has towers along its walls. Do you remember brother?"

"Aye, but how does that help us? We have towers here on our walls."

"Think bigger; think the land of Rheged. We need towers on the coast and along the Eden valley. The wall already has them."

"And who will man them, brother?"

"That is the good part. We ask those who live close by to build the towers and to keep watch. We tell them what to look for. This way we could spot an enemy coming up the coast and be ready to meet them in battle. It also gives them a refuge should they be attacked. Our land is rich in stone. Let us use the stone as a weapon." Gawan did not appear convinced. "Gawan, we know from my father's time that it is very easy to lose a land. We have fewer men now to protect more people. The people must help themselves. We have made a start for all the men who live in Rheged can use weapons. This would be good training for the boys and youths."

He smiled, "Perhaps you are right. How would we tell them what we need?"

"That is simple. The equites and squires who do not go on a quest this moon can ride and visit with those who live on the coasts and the High Divide. It will be good for the men of Rheged to see equites."

Surprisingly my equites were all in favour of the idea. They also saw the benefits of riding among those they protected. Kay summed it up succinctly, "One day, Warlord, we will have to fight alongside these men. If you know a man before you are his shield brother then you will fight better together. Our equites can advise them how to build the towers and to man them."

I took Arturus with me and we rode to the wall. We had refortified Banna. There were ten of our archers there. The two of us rode east. We had the easiest task of all for the Roman Wall stood and there were fragments of towers all along it. We chose the best of those that remained and sought out the men who lived closest. The fact that the Warlord asked them to seemed to imbue them with a greater sense of responsibility. We stopped when we reached the site of the battle where King Cadwallon had perished, Hagustaldes-ham. We saw no sign of enemies. We had been away from home for ten days. Our horses were tired and I needed a bath. We headed to be home.

We left Pen Rhudd after speaking to the headman there and then headed south. The route I took was not direct. I would ride south to Aelletün and see if all was well there. We would spend the night and then head back to my bathhouse the next day. The men who lived in the place with the terrible memories might appreciate a visit from the Warlord to reassure them that they were not forgotten. I thought the idea came from my own head. I was wrong. The spirits guided my thoughts.

We were just a day away from home close to the head of the Long Water when we both smelled death. I had fought for many years and recognised it. Arturus was relatively young but he knew it for what it was. We both drew our swords. The smell of death was human. That might well attract animals. Wolves still prowled the high ground of Halvelyn. A wolf disturbed whilst feasting could be a vicious enemy.

There was a line of trees on the lower part of the hill next to the road and I knew that there were rocks and rough ground behind. I waved Arturus to the left and I went right. As we brushed through the trees and bushes, magpies and crows took flight. I saw the bodies. It was Galeschin, one of my newer equites, and his squire Ywain. I recognised the wolf clasp on their cloaks. They had been butchered. Their heads were on spears. Galeschin's mail had been taken and both men's hearts had been removed. Their weapons had been taken too. Of their horses, there was no sign.

Arturus almost whispered, "Who could have done this?"

"I know not but the torn-out hearts fill me with foreboding. Galeschin and Ywain were given the task of speaking to those who live north of Shap." I dismounted. I regretted riding in with our horses. We might have ruined any tracks that had been left. It could not be helped. I looked around. Our men had not come through the treeline. The nearest break was fifty paces north of where we stood. I walked back to the gap. The hoof prints were obvious now. I followed them. As I neared the ambush site, for that was what it plainly was, I wondered why the men had left the road. What had induced them to ride off the beaten track? I walked further up the slope. As I did so I spied a piece of dead ground. When I stood and looked down I saw that there were many prints. Their attackers had waited here but what had drawn Galeschin here? I kept walking and saw that the ground dropped away. Then I saw how my young equite had been lured. The body of a young woman lay at the foot of the small cliff. Her lower body was bloodied. I knew what her fate had been. Perhaps she had been forced to shout and that would have drawn in Galeschin. Galeschin was a young equite but he was capable as was his squire. As I walked towards Arturus I saw blood spatter and deeper footprints. I signalled for Arturus to bring the horses and follow me.

The footprints went to a jumble of rocks some fifty paces above the road. Arturus had to dismount rather than risk damaging the horses. I saw, as I approached, that the stones which had appeared to be natural had, in fact, been moved. The moss on them was not even. Sheathing Saxon Slayer, I moved five of them. A tattooed arm fell out. It was a Saxon; it was the Clan of the Snake. Arturus and I uncovered the bodies and found eight of them. My men had died hard and taken enemies with them. They had been buried not out of respect but to hide their presence from me.

"We have enemies loose in our land. We must track them."

We mounted our horses. "How many will there be?"

"I know not."

He pointed to the skulls on the spears, "We cannot leave them."

"We will return and bury them with honour and the girl I found but first we find where they are. Do you wish more of our men to die? More of our people to suffer?" He shook his head.

We had not ridden over this ground and I soon spotted the hoof prints. They were riding double and the hoof prints stood out. Once we were on the road we would lose them but as the road led through Aelletün they would have to leave the road or risk the wrath of my men who lived there. Despite the fact that we had left our dead unattended I would not rush the chase to return to them. This was too important. I, therefore, kept a close watch on the side of the road once we reached it. "Arturus ride to the left. If you see a hoof print then let me know."

"Aye Warlord. How many do you think there are?"

"They are riding double which means at least four and I have seen the footprints of men beside them. I do not have the time to examine them but I am guessing at least ten."

After a pause, he said, "And there are but two of us."

"We are equites and unlike Galeschin we know that there are enemies abroad."

There was another pause and Arturus said, "You think he made a mistake do you not, Warlord?"

"Is that you reading my mind, son of the wizard, or are you using your warrior's brain?"

"Neither. I know you now, Warlord. I have watched your back since I returned to become a man. You strive for perfection in all things. It is what set you against Gwenhwyfar when first you saw her. She was not perfect and that is what you sought for me."

It was uncanny for he was right. I was never satisfied with anything that I did. I held up my hand. "Here, Arturus, they left the road!"

I dismounted to make certain that I was correct. They had left the road but they had dismounted when they did so. They were trying to hide from pursuit. I led Copper and walked along the prints. After forty paces they became deeper again as the Saxons had remounted. I looked up to try to divine their purpose. Just ahead of us was a huge rock which locals called Old Toothless for in the late evening it resembled a toothless old man. There was a track which went around it and then passed to the north of Halvelyn. It headed west and not south. Had these Saxons come by ship and, if so, were there others loose in my land? We were set on our course and we would have to follow it.

I waved Arturus over and explained what I had discovered. "Fortunately, there are so few people living between here and the Round Water that they can do little harm. They will have to camp soon. The track they follow has some dangerous places. They must have come east along this road to have known where to leave the road."

"I see neither track nor trail."

"That is because they are not on it yet. It begins some mile north and west of here. When we find it, unless I miss my guess, they will head along it to the west. They are returning to their boat." We had our spears with us and I slid mine from its leather bindings and nodded to Arturus. He did the same. A spear was the weapon for hunting men on foot, not a sword.

The angle that the tracks approached the trail confirmed my suspicions. The path twisted and turned so we would not be able to see them and they would not be able to see us. Had they taken the tracks to the north or south of this one then we would have been clearly visible to each other. We watered our horses at each bubbling stream we crossed. We let them graze on the grass. We would not catch these Saxons before dark if at all. They had a lead but they were going at the speed of men. The blood I had seen on the leaves of the bush when we had left the road told me that at least one of the Saxons was wounded.

Heading west meant we travelled towards the fading light. When it became too dark to travel I sought shelter. I spied a shape to the side which looked like a hut. I dismounted and, with spear held before me, walked towards it. I had not heard Galeschin's horse neigh but I was taking no chances. A dog growled. The fading light showed its eyes and as I looked closer I saw bared teeth.

I lowered my spear and dropped to one knee. I held my hand out and said, "Good boy. Good boy."

My use of familiar words seemed to have an effect and he came closer. As I stroked its fur my hand came away bloody. It had been wounded. I stood and drew my sword. I pushed open the door and entered the hut, I almost tripped over the bodies of the shepherd and his family. "Arturus, fetch a flint."

The dog began to whine and lick one of the bodies. The hut was a traditional one. It was made of stone and was round. There would be a fire in the centre. I made my way there and, putting my hand down felt the warm ashes. The fire had been lit that day. I felt around until I felt kindling. I had just laid the fire when Arturus came in. I heard his sharp intake of breath as he almost tripped over a body. "Go and see to the horses. Make certain that the door is closed and hang your cloak over it so that no light can be seen. Secure the horses behind the hut. Bring our bags in."

"Aye Warlord." His voice was filled with unasked questions.

The door closed and I took the flint. I was in complete darkness. I had to do things by feel. Myrddyn had taught me how to do this. He had made me practise finding things in the dark. When we had entered Din Guardi it had been an invaluable skill. The spark struck the wood shavings I had placed around the kindling. I blew on them gently and the red flames began to eat into the dried twigs. The leaves on them flared and ignited others. I added a couple of larger pieces of wood and when I was satisfied that it was alight I stood. What I saw turned my stomach. There was a shepherd who had been dismembered. His chest had been torn open. His wife and daughter had been abused and despoiled. I could do little for them. I did not want Arturus to see them. It was a horror which would live with him his whole life. I carefully moved the bodies and body parts to the side of the hut away from the bed and covered them with a cloak. I then turned my attention to the dog.

It was a shepherd's dog. They were common on the fells. It was a golden-brown colour. It resembled a fox save that the ears were not erect. I saw that it had been struck a glancing blow by a spearhead. The wound was a long one along its back. It must have been defending the family. I took my water skin from my side and poured a little into one of the family's wooden bowls. The dog lapped it eagerly. While it drank I poured some on the wound. As the firelight grew I saw better. I wiped away the blood and unmatted the fur. It was a clean wound. It was on its back and it had not rolled in dirt to poison the wound.

The door opened and Arturus came in. He was careful to avoid light spilling from within. "Give me the vinegar and honey. We will sleep here this night."

He saw the cloak covered corpses, "The family?"

I nodded, "They were butchered and we are closer to them than I thought. The bodies were not cold when I moved them. The Saxons are, perhaps, five miles or so ahead of us."

"Why did they not stay here?"

"These Saxons have planned well. The further west they camp then the shorter their journey. They will have headed east when they came and remained hidden. They will cause mayhem on their way back for they know where there are isolated farms. We will just rest for a couple of hours. Nights are short at this time of year."

While he prepared some food, I tended to the dog. He must have known I was trying to help for even when I used vinegar to cleanse the wound it did not snap. I smeared honey on the wound. It would stop the wound from becoming dirty and would help the healing process. At least it did with humans and horses. Perhaps it was the same with dogs. We needed the dog. The spirits had saved it for it would be able to track the Saxons and give us a warning when it smell them. I took out some dried venison and fed it to the dog.

Arturus had found a pot and some vegetables. He had made a stew. We had not eaten since we had left Pen Rhudd at dawn. We were starving. We left enough in the pot for the dog to eat and to lick it clean. As we lay down to sleep the dog came to curl up close to me. I smiled, "We shall call this dog Warrior for it has the heart of a warrior." As I stroked the sleeping dog I remembered my father and uncles telling me of a dog they had which had hunted Saxons with them when they were little more than boys. It was *wyrd*.

I woke myself when it was still dark. The dog stirred when I did and rose stiffly to its feet. I went to the door and opened it. I slipped under the cloak and went to the side of the hut to make water. I heard the dog as it did the same. I went around the back and saw that the horses were both well. It was as I came back to the entrance that I saw, across the valley below us, a pinprick of light. It had to be the Saxons. We were close. I went to the door and said, "Arturus, rise!"

I brought the horses around and we saddled them. We had to hurry. Once dawn broke then the pinprick of light would disappear. We had to get as close to them as we could before dawn came. Darkness would hide us for this was a steep-sided valley. I fed and watered the dog again. We had to look after him and I swallowed down some water and then chewed on dried venison. We headed west.

The sheepdog, Warrior, looked much better and loped alongside us. He sniffed as we hit the trail and I saw his ears prick. He had the scent of those who had hurt him and killed his shepherd. We took it steadily for it was still dark. The pinprick of light flicked, disappeared and reappeared. Men were moving before it. I kept glancing from the trail to the light and it soon became obvious that the Saxons has come this way. It was confirmed by the dog. Dawn came slowly, almost insidiously. Halvelyn acted as a block to its rays. I saw them shining on peaks to the west of us. The campsite of the Saxons was still hidden in darkness. The path twisted and turned down the contours of the steep-sided valley. At one point Arturus' horse sent stones skittering down the path. To rush would be fatal. We reached the bottom and forded the bubbling mountain stream. Warrior leapt from stone to stone and was barely wet. We had just begun to climb when the light disappeared. They had extinguished it. It did not matter overmuch as we were less than a couple of miles behind them.

As we climbed, we were in the darkness of the bottom of the valley but the sun gradually spilt down the western valley side. I spotted the horses with the two riders on each of them. I counted eight other warriors. I could not be sure of the exact numbers but they were within sight. We could see them but Halvelyn protected us and we were in darkness.

The fact that we could see them and they, I hoped, would be unaware that they were being pursued, gave me hope. We reached their camp at the fourth hour of the day. The sun was up and the day would be hot. Two of their men had died. We found the stones covering the graves. My equite and his squire had taken many with them. I was proud of their sacrifice. I realised that they were taking the hard route. It was over the emptiest and roughest part of Rheged. I knew the place they were heading. The Romans had had a fort at Parton. It was on the coast and was a good harbour with ten or so families. They had taken the port. I had a hard decision to make.

"Arturus, you must ride north to Carvetitas. I need every archer, squire and equite at Parton. They must pass across the high ground and along the Flat Water and thence to Parton. It is the only place close by where they could moor a ship unseen. That is where they are headed."

"Warlord, I cannot leave you alone! There are twelve men ahead of you!"

"And two of us cannot hurt them. They cannot make Parton without another camp. They have but two horses. I can watch them and I can slow them down. Have Llenlleog come down the coast it will be quicker and easier than the route they must take."

"They are not worth the life of the Warlord!"

I smiled, "Then, squire, as your last act before you become an equite, see that I do not die! Now go. I have the dog!"

He looked at me and nodded, "Stay safe Warlord!"

"You are not ready to fill my boots Arturus. I will be safe."

As he headed north I dug my heels into Copper. This was a true quest. I did not think it was my time to die but if it was then I was ready. Arturus would soon be ready and Llenlleog was more than capable of making the right decisions until he was. I would not let my father down. My life meant nothing. Rheged was all.

The ground was rough and undulating. There was no chance of seeing those I pursued. They could not see me and I could not see them. This was a narrow pass which led across one of the emptiest parts of Rheged. I knew not what the peaks were called to the north of me only that men would not willingly scale them. I knew then that the dog had been sent by Myrddyn to help me. I might still die but the dog would give me a warning and I would take Saxons with me. We twisted, turned and climbed during that hot day. When I spied hot horse dung I slowed. I was catching them. Warrior's ears were constantly pricked. Darkness would be my ally. I stopped and ate some dried venison and drank water. I shared my food with Warrior. Copper drank from the stream and cropped the grass. We continued west.

I was too old to be riding for so long but I dared not stop. As the sun began to set I slowed. They would light a fire. This was remote. We had not passed any habitation since the farmhouse of corpses. We dropped down below a ridge and, as the sun set before me I saw their shadowy silhouettes on the skyline and then they disappeared. They were less than a mile away. I slipped from my saddle and walked Copper. My horse needed rest. Warrior had become agitated over the last mile. He knew the killers were close. I gave him a piece of venison and stroked him.

"Stay by me!"

I could almost smell them. They were that close. When I detected the smell of burning wood, I stopped. They had made camp. I looked around and found a dell close to a stream. I walked Copper there and tied her to a tree. There was water and there was grass. I had not yet decided what to do. Myrddyn would tell me. I ate and I drank. The dog was the problem. I gave him some venison. "Warrior, stay." I pointed my finger. I repeated, "Stay!"

He took the venison and lay down. I hoped he would obey. I took out my sword and my dagger. I did not need my helmet and my wolf cloak was dark enough to hide me. I left the trail and walked over the rough ground to find their camp. I heard them before I saw them. They were arguing.

"All this way to kill two warriors! It was a waste. We lost too many warriors!"

"Lang Seax has led us well. We are richer and we have good weapons. We killed more than two warriors and we enjoyed their women. Life is good. If Lang Seax thinks that this raid is worthwhile then who are we to argue."

"We should have brought more men. This land is ripe for the plucking."

"It is but we have but four boat crews. When we have six then we can strike. Be patient. Lang Seax will rule this land one day."

I crept forward on all fours using the bushes and rocks for cover. I was approaching from the darker, eastern side. and saw their fire and their sentries. They had two of them. They were on opposite sides of the camp and well away from the fire. These warriors knew their business. I sat beneath an elder bush and I waited. They would sleep. I counted twelve of them. I was confident that I could kill four and still escape. This was not the work for Saxon Slayer. My sword was too long. I slipped my dagger out and held it while I waited. The two horses were tethered to a tree. I heard them moving restlessly. They could smell me. It neighed; that alone showed the stress it felt. Its master had been killed and it forgot its training. One of the sentries walked over to them and smacked one. "We need you for but another day and then you die. I like horsemeat." The horses stamped and there was another hard slap.

Saxon Sword

The two sentries came together and talked. They were just twenty paces from me. They were slightly higher than I was. Their camp was on a small flat area and the ground fell away. Hunkered down I was below their eye line and invisible. I needed them to separate before I could strike. I had to be silent and swift.

"I must have eaten something bad when we stayed in that shepherd's hut or perhaps the bitch we killed cursed me. I have the worst gut ache!"

"Aelle, you always have a gut ache! You eat too much!"

I heard a laugh, "I like my food. Besides hunting men and staying hidden means you eat when you can! Creeping across this land and avoiding these horse warriors is hard on a man's need for good and plentiful food."

"You are right there. Hiding for seven days and working east was not easy. These warriors of the north are hard to kill. Their mail is like the skin of a wild boar. The ones we slew were young but they had courage. Even though struck many times they fought on."

"Aye and the bows were useless against them. The arrows just bounced off. Lang Seax will need more than six crews if he is to conquer this land."

"True but think of the power he would wield if he did. Oswiu and Penda would both vie for his favour. We would have the smallest kingdom and the greatest power."

A voice from the fire said, "You cannot watch and talk!"

They moved apart and I saw my chance. The fire they had built up silhouetted them. One moved to the other side of the camp. The one on my side came towards me. I did not think he had seen me. He clambered down the smaller boulders and rocks to the flat ground just four paces from me. I was hidden behind a bush but he was not looking for me. When he dropped his breeks then I knew what he was here for.

I slipped out of my hiding place. He had his back to me and I heard the hiss of his water and then the sound of him beginning to empty his bowels. The smell was vile. At least one of his hands would be occupied. He was using his other to rest on his spear. The noise of his water and straining masked the sound of my feet on the turf. I put my hand over his greasy mouth and pulled back sharply. At the same time, I ripped my dagger across his throat. The blood sprayed. I laid him face forward against the rocks and took his sword, spear and knife. I moved further to the right for there was a better place to hide. Two large rocks had fallen and a third had made a roof. I slipped in. The camp was above me to my right. If they knew where I was then I was trapped but I had watched the two sentries and seen their movements. They had not come near the three rocks.

The second sentry was on the far side for a long time and I feared that I might have to search for him. Then I heard the sound of his footsteps above me. "Aelle, where are you? Tol will have you gutted if you are asleep!"

There was, of course, no reply.

"Is it the gut ache?" There was concern in the voice and I heard him slither down the gentle bank. "Is that you over there?"

He appeared in my eye line. He was heading for his dead friend. I rose like a wraith as he passed me. He must have sensed me for although I made no sound he turned. I put my left hand across his mouth and lunged with my dagger. I hit him so hard in the throat that the blade appeared out of the back of his head. I lowered him to the ground and took his weapons. Placing the bodies together I took the rope they used to secure their breeks. I headed back to the place I had hidden between the rocks. I jammed the two spears so that their points were the height of a man's stomach and then I tied one of the ropes between two small bushes which flanked the path the sentry had taken.

I hurried along the side of the camp, keeping low. I took in that the men were spread around. One man slept by the horses. Reaching the far side of the camp I used the two swords and the other rope as a second trap. As I finished tying off the rope a wild thought entered my head. The ground fell away to the north and west towards the Flat Water. The large tarn was so named because the ground around it was flat. There were farms there. If I stole back the horses then I could ride down the slope and return to my own camp by riding around the peaks. It would take me half a day but they would have to move more slowly for they would not have the horses. It would take a day for them to reach Parton and that would involve running. It was worth the risk.

Saxon Sword

I worked my way around their camp. The horses became restless as I neared them. The Saxon who slept close by them heard them. "Quiet! Cannot a man sleep!"

I paused and saw that they had hobbled the horses. I would have to free them before I could escape. I used the horses for cover and walked upright towards them. I stroked the mane of Badger, Galeschin's horse and, slipping down cut the ropes which bound him. I moved to the other horse, Strider. As I stroked him he whinnied.

The man who lay close by rose. Rubbing his eyes, he said, "I'll teach you!"

He had not seen me. He stood and raised his arm. I rammed the dagger into his open mouth. He gurgled and died. I barely managed to catch him. Strider obligingly shifted out of the way and I laid him down. I cut the last hobbles and sheathed my dagger. The Saxons had discarded the saddles and so I slipped onto the back of Badger and held Strider's reins. I began to walk out of the camp. I walked around the edge of the camp close by the two dead sentries. There was more turf that way and fewer stones. Inevitably one of the hooves dislodged one of the stones and it clattered down to the rocks below. I held my nerve and kept walking until a voice shouted, "Aelle! Stop the horses from moving."

It was the rising sun behind me which was my undoing. False dawn had crept unseen into the sky and the sudden flaring of the new day silhouetted me.

"Wake!"

I dug my heels into Badger and the two horses took off down the pass. The Saxon camp had been well chosen for it was on the highest part. It meant that the two horses could open their legs. The Saxons who were running down behind me would not catch me. I heard a cry and a shout as one of them tripped on my trap. I slowed down the horses to conserve them. The pass twisted north and around a rock. I was hidden from view. We descended rapidly and as we neared the flat ground and the first of the farms ahead I spied a path to the south. I was on the horns of a dilemma. I needed to get back to my own horse but I could not leave the farmer and his family to the Saxons.

I rode onto the farm and banged on the door. "It is the Warlord rise! There is danger!"

I heard noise within. Our farmers used huts with just one door. It opened slowly. A frightened-looking man with a short sword stood there. He recognised me, "Warlord!"

"There is no time for words. A warband of savage Saxons is less than a mile away. Take your family and flee south. Use this horse."

All of our farmers knew the dangers of a warband. "Quickly, do as the Warlord says!" He had a wife and three children. His son held the reins of the horse as his wife and two daughters clambered on.

"I will try to lead them away. Warn your neighbours. My equites are coming and these are heading for Parton! Raise the alarm. Make noise!" I needed the rest of those who lived around the Water to be safe. I could not warn them all.

The farmer waved as he ran after the horse, his son and his family. I wheeled Badger around and rode back up the pass. I had almost reached the trail to the south when I saw the Saxons. They were still running down the trail towards me. Drawing my sword, I galloped across the rough ground to the path. One of the Saxons, seeing that I was within a hundred paces of them tried to take a shortcut. It ended badly and he tumbled down across the rocks. When he rose, I saw that one arm hung awkwardly from his side. He was hurt. The rest did not follow. They headed down the trail towards the farm. That was one family they would not get. They had escaped the savage Saxons.

The path I took was not a good one. It was narrow and I had to pick my way along it. After an hour of tortuous climbing, I spied their camp. It lay more than six hundred paces from me and below me. I chose a route which would take me to my own camp. That added another hour to my journey and the sun was higher in the sky when I reached Copper and the dog. I gave the dog some venison and water to Badger. Wearily I mounted Copper, tied a halter to my saddle and, leading Badger, rode towards the Saxon camp. I counted on the fact that they would be desperate to get to their ship and would have hurried down the trail.

Warrior growled as we neared it. Someone was still there. I drew my sword. I saw the Saxon. He had his back to the rocks where I had hidden. He had run into the spears and been gutted. He was barely alive. Warrior continued to growl as he approached. The Saxon gave me a wry grin as I dismounted. He spoke Saxon, "Do you come to have your dog eat my guts?"

"It is what you deserve for what you did to the shepherd and his family."

He laughed and was wracked with pain. "You think they were the only ones, horseman? The people paid for the deaths your horseman caused us. When Lang Seax brings all of our men then your people will truly know pain."

I had been watching him and saw his hand sneaking around his back. He must have had a dagger there, one of the wicked weapons called a seax. Even as I raised my sword and pulled it back Warrior leapt and fixed his jaws around the hand. The effort was too much for the Saxon who expired. I patted the dog's head, "Good boy. You have had some vengeance, at least." I took the Saxon's seax and stuck it in my belt.

I rode down the trail towards the farm. It was still intact but there was no sign of the farmer or his family. Riding around the Flat Water I saw no sign of the Saxons. I reached the end of the valley at noon. Some armed men appeared from the woods there. They were my people. "Warlord, we heard you were abroad." The leader pointed west. "The Saxons went that way." He held up a head by its greasy locks. It was tattooed. "We found this one with a broken arm. They had left him. It is one less savage to worry us and pays in part for what they did."

"What they did?"

He nodded, "Ten days since a larger warband came through and they killed Radgh of Asby and his family. Six children were in the family."

"This is the same warband. How far ahead of me are they?"

"No more than two miles. We were scouring the woods for more of them when you came by."

I handed them Badger's reins. "We will come for this horse when they are dead."

"You seek them alone?"

"No, I have my equites heading to cut them off at Parton!"

I contemplated leaving the dog with them but he deserved to be there at the end.

I found them four miles from Parton. My equites and archers were on the far side of them barring their escape. The survivors had found a small island of land between two small streams. They had chosen the best place they could find for their defence. It mattered not. They would all die. I reined in to the east of them. I drew Saxon Slayer and raised it. My equites, half a mile from where I sat began banging their shields with their swords. I heard the Saxons singing. It was their death song. I lowered my sword and Daffydd ap Miach ordered his archers to loose their arrows. There were too few Saxons to make a shield wall and one by one they died. Some took five arrows to succumb but eventually all lay dead. I rode down and crossed the stream. Warrior walked up to them and sniffed. Then he cocked his leg and gave them the final indignity.

"Take their swords and then burn them. The rest will be in Parton."

Llenlleog nodded, "We saw their ship. We did not enter the village. We remained hidden and hunted these. Geraint found them."

Leaving some archers to burn the bodies we headed west. We saw a column of smoke spiralling into the air as we drew close and we saw the Saxon ship rowing away from the shore. They had fled. What they had left was heartbreaking. Every man, woman and child, had been butchered. Even the village dogs had been slain. Warrior put his tail between his legs and his ears down.

Llenlleog shook his head, "This is my fault. We should have come here before we went to catch the warband."

I shook my head. "They would have been dead already. The fire was to cover their tracks. I fear that there will be many such atrocities across the land." I told him what I had discovered.

He shook his head, "You took a mighty risk, Warlord. There was no need."

"You have fewer men to kill and if I had not recaptured the horses then they might have reached here even quicker. Besides, it is done now. We learn from this and we move on. I now know that our plan for the towers is even more urgent. This Lang Seax is building up his forces. He wants Rheged."

"Then he will have to fight us to get it, Warlord."

Part 3

The Battle of Winwaed

Chapter 10

The dog stayed with us. He had no sheep to protect and so he protected Copper and me. From that day forth he came with us when we went to war. He proved to be a sentry without compare. Sleeping at my feet I was never surprised for Warrior always woke me with a growl when anyone approached.

The attacks on the isolated farms ensured that all of us worked hard to keep a good watch until the towers were built. Our quests discovered eight farms and isolated hamlets which had been destroyed by the warband. It frightened me. Gawan, Arthur and I sat in my hall one late summer evening discussing it.

"It is my fault Warlord. I am no Myrddyn."

"Brother, he was a wizard pure and simple. You are a warrior and a wizard."

Arturus said, "We should use my wife's skills." We both looked at him. "After we returned she said that she had sensed some disaster in Rheged."

Gawan asked, gently, "Perhaps that was because the news of the warband was known by then, do you not think?"

I thought he might have taken offence but he had grown into a man. Soon he would be an equite and it was reflected in his bearing. "No, father. I know her thoughts. She genuinely felt unease. Now she will tell me if she senses any disorder in the land. She is completely happy here in Rheged. She has told me that she feels as though she has come home."

The more I thought about it the more sense it made. Her father did not come from Powys. "Then I am doubly happy that you chose her as your bride."

He smiled, "And she is with child. You will be a grandfather soon, Father."

"Will that affect her powers?"

"I know not. We shall see."

Saxon Sword

"Until the towers are built then each quest will continue." We were now restricted to just seven days in Carvetitas. It was fortunate that we had King Penda's horses for we would have worn the others out. We had also ensured that no equite and squire rode alone. Galeschin's fate had been a warning to us all.

We made Arturus an equite. The ceremony was quite simple but the oath each equite took before the assembled warriors was binding. Each equite swore to protect his brothers and Rheged in equal measure. Arturus became one of the Wolf Brethren. At the same time, two squires were also sworn in. Mine was Pelas ap Tuanthal. His father had died protecting me and I was honoured to have his son. Arturus had Kay's son, Ban ap Kay. I felt sorry for the two of them. They had two of the most important equites in Rheged to protect. At the end of the ceremony, I gave him King Oswald's sword. Few had seen it since the battle with Oswald and Oswiu. All were impressed; none more so than Arturus.

Gwenhwyfar touched the hilt. Most women would have shied away from the weapon but Gwenhwyfar was different. She closed her eyes. "This sword has had a Christian spell put upon it. I can sense it." She opened her eyes and we all waited. "If I put a spell of the Mother upon it then it will be twice as powerful." She took the sword and scabbard from her husband and went with Gawan. They returned sometime later. She handed the sword to her husband and they retired.

We all gathered around Gawan, eager to hear what had happened. He shook his head. "It was I who felt like the acolyte. It was like watching Myrddyn. She is a confident witch. Myrddyn was right, brother, she will be the saving of Rheged; for a time, at least."

We had an extra seven days without a quest for our squires needed to get to know both us and our animals. In Pelas' case, he had to win the approval of Warrior. Our squires now faced greater danger. Gone were the days when they tended the horses and watched the equites fight. Now they would be as likely to fight as their masters. The seven days of training and bonding would be crucial.

At the end of the training period, we rode abroad. Agramaine and Llewellyn were with Arturus and me. Their squires would be invaluable in ensuring that Ban and Pelas did not make too many mistakes. We might forgive them but often mistakes could be fatal. Galeschin had discovered that.

Our quest took us east. We would go beyond the Eden valley and Shap. We would enter the land of Deira. King Penda had sent me a message. He intended to move north to his northern borders when summer came. That was nine moons away but he wished to know the state of the land close to the High Divide. I knew why he was worried. Deira was a small part of Northumbria. There were more Angles north of Eoforwic than south of it. Daffydd ap Miach insisted upon sending eight archers with me. Llenlleog also complained for, once again, the Warlord was putting himself at risk.

"Galeschin discovered that you do not need to be in the land of the Angles to be in danger. The Clan of the Snake could use their ships at any time and they could destroy any of the equites we sent to the coast. All of us are now in danger, Llenlleog. The days when Rheged had a ring of allies around her borders are a thing of the past."

He grudgingly accepted it. I knew why he was disturbed. He would have to stay in Carvetilas with Gawan to protect the families of my equites. I know that he had a problem with Gwenhwyfar. He found her not only beautiful as did all of my equites, he found her dangerous for she had powers he could not control.

As we headed east I sensed a change in all of my men. Normally they chatted and bantered as we headed towards our borders. When we reached our borders then they became more vigilant. The attack by the Saxons now made them look around as soon as we headed along the Stanegate. Arturus was particularly nervous. He had left a pregnant wife at home. "We ride to Hagustaldes-ham and then head south, Warlord?" I nodded, "That is Bernicia."

"I know. It is why we have archers and Warrior. There are no strongholds close to the High Divide. Din Guardi is on the coast and Eoforwic is well to the east. I wish to see if they have reinvested Stanwyck. If they have then it will tell me that they are a direct threat to us and not the Mercians."

"Lord Lann and his brothers came from there, did they not?"

"They did. It is not far north of Eoforwic. King Penda's scouts can give the King a better picture of the land around Eoforwic. The King needs to know the state of Bernicia."

We camped at the abandoned fort of Vercovicium. There was now a tower here. One of the turrets from the Roman fort had been repaired using stones which had fallen from other parts of the wall. There was a farm close to the fort and the farmer and his family manned the tower.

Ceryn had eight children including five sons. He was pleased to see us arrive. "We watch during the day, Warlord. It means we have one pair of hands less on the farm but if it can warn us of danger then so much the better."

"You have a pony too?"

We had given a pony or a horse to each of the men who used the towers for us. It was partly payment for their work but it would enable us to learn of danger quickly.

"We have and we have repaired the door on the turret. We keep food and water in there. If an enemy comes we can survive for a few days. If help has not arrived by then we would be dead anyway. It buys us a little time. He looked east, "We are the closest people to the Angles, Warlord. I hope that men could reach us if danger came."

"All that you need to do is to reach Banna. There are archers there. They could be here in less than half a day. Can all your sons ride?"

"Aye lord."

"And they have weapons?"

"Not all lord."

I waved over Pelas, "Fetch the knives and swords we took from the Saxons. Let Ceryn choose weapons for his sons."

As he went off Ceryn looked relieved, "Thank you, Warlord."

"The men we took them from had neither mail nor helmet else we could have let you have them too."

"We can all use bows but a sword or a knife is handy."

When we left, the next day, they were in a stronger position. My archers had repaired the second gate to the milecastle so that an enemy would have to break through two gates to get into the tower. It would increase the chances of my archers reaching them. Arturus had also suggested that, as they had a stone fort, they could light a signal fire. The archers at Banna would know sooner of the danger.

Ceryn's tower was the last one. We headed down the Roman Road wearing our helmets and with spears at the ready. The archers had strung bows and arrows ready to be nocked. As noon approached we were heading down through the woods to the Tinea and the bridge at Hagustaldes-ham. There was no fort here but there was a Roman bridge and it could be defended. I sent the archers ahead to scout it out. It was late afternoon when they returned. It was with the news that the bridge was defended. It was just a mile ahead. We had three choices. I could return home. I could find another way around the defenders or I could rid myself of the problem. I had already decided what to do but saw a good opportunity to ask for the opinion of my equites and to see how far Arturus had come.

"Equites the bridge is contested."

The three equites were not as experienced as Llenlleog, Kay or Bors and it was a little unfair of me to ask. Arturus rose to the challenge. "If we did not have archers then I would have said the prudent course of action would have been to ford the river further west. We have archers and we can use them without risking ourselves too much."

I saw the nods from the other two. That had been my logic too. "Then that is what we shall do. We will ride with the equites to the fore. Archers, stay well back and listen for my command."

"Aye Warlord."

We donned our helmets and took our spears from our squires. I waved my spear and we began to trot towards the bridge. We emerged from the trees and I saw that the ground sloped down towards the town. The bridge was almost thirty paces beneath us. The town began fifty paces from the bridge. Our archers had been seen and the Bernicians were hurriedly making a barrier to bar our progress. I saw a thegn giving orders. There were thirty or so men. Only ten or twelve would be true warriors. The rest would be the fyrd. They would be armed with good swords and have metal tipped spears. We halted a hundred paces from them. They had bows and they loosed arrows at us. They were hunting arrows and we held up our shields. The tips could not penetrate the leather covering and they fell to the ground. Behind me, I heard my archers as they laughed. The thegn shouted something and the archers stopped. One of them ran back to the town.

Agramaine said, "I am betting he has gone to fetch slingers."

"And you may be right." Slingers could hurt us more than the archers. "Archers!"

My archers galloped forward and threw themselves from their horses. They had trained their mounts to stand still when their reins were dropped. That way we did not need horse holders. The Saxons were slow to react. They were standing in a loose formation. Their shields were not held up and they were not expecting arrows. Our archers could nock and release so quickly that it was like a blur. I did not know how they did it. There were just eight archers but they each sent three arrows so quickly into the air that the first had struck before the Bernicians even realised that they were under attack. One struck the thegn on his helmet. It did not penetrate but it knocked him to the ground. Four arrows found flesh. Even as they hurriedly and belatedly formed a shield wall I shouted, "Charge!" I trusted my archers not to hit us. They would continue to loose until the last moment.

As we rode, boot to boot, I saw more of the Angles fall to the arrows my archers sent. The thegn rose and pulled his shield tightly to him. He was shouting orders but it was too little and too late. The warrior next to him was killed when a plunging arrow found bare flesh near to his shoulder. I watched the blood arc and spray over the thegn. We were closing rapidly now. Five of the thegn's oathsworn remained with him. Three had metal helmets and two leather ones. Their shields all bore his sign, a blue diagonal cross. Six of the fyrd bravely stood but others had fled. As I pulled back my arm two more of the fyrd took to their heels. I rammed my spear at the throat of the thegn. He had a collar of mail but it did not cover his neck. It was a difficult strike but Copper gave me a smooth ride and I took the chance. He lifted his shield but he must still have been stunned from the arrow for the shield rose slowly. All it succeeded in doing was driving the spear head into his left eye. He was dead before I could withdraw my spear. Arturus' spear hit a shield and then the right shoulder of an oathsworn while Agramaine and Llewellyn managed to spear their enemies in the gut. Pelas ap Tuanthal showed his heritage for his spear took the last of the oathsworn and the fyrd ran.

I saw that they had fetched the slingers from the village but when they saw that their lord was dead they thought better of attacking us and left. The villagers were fleeing east. There were other thegns there and they would seek shelter with them. We did not wait for my archers but galloped through the small town. There was a monastery there and I saw men fleeing for sanctuary. We reined in before the church. A priest stood defiantly there. He held a cross before him as though it would ward us off. I dismounted and threw my helmet to Pelas ap Tuanthal. It was too hot to wear! Even though harvest had passed the weather was unseasonably warm. I had sheathed my sword when the men had fled and I took off my leather gauntlets. The priest began chanting a prayer in Latin.

"Save your breath priest you will not frighten me. Who was the thegn I slew?"

He looked at me as though he did not expect me to speak his language. He stammered, "Egbert of Hagustaldes-ham."

I nodded, "Had they not barred the road then the men who stood against us might have lived."

He frowned, "You are pagans. It is every Christian's duty to stand firm against you! King Oswiu and his men will hunt you down when they return to this land."

I smiled. He had given me information he did not intend. I exploited it. "I thought that we had not seen many warriors in the land. Why I could come here with less than a hundred men and capture it all."

He rose to the bait, "You could not for Eoforwic, Stanwick and Din Guardi are well garrisoned. When the Mercians are defeated then our King will turn his attention to the abomination which is Rheged."

I tried another ploy, "So long as your King still hires mercenaries like the Clan of the Snake then I know that he does not have enough Northumbrians to fight me."

"They are swords for hire but they serve a purpose. They die in place of our warriors. You will be defeated!"

Saxon Sword

I took a silver coin from my purse, "Here priest, say a prayer for your thegn. He was brave. Foolish and misguided, but brave!"

I turned to join my equites. "We will stay in the thegn's hall this night. There should be food and it will be more comfortable." The nights were longer and colder now. Winter would be upon us soon enough. The archers had brought the swords, helmets and mail. We now needed all that we could scavenge. The more we had the less was available to the Northumbrians.

We walked our horses. Warrior's head darted from side to side as he looked for a threat. I took some dried venison from my belt and threw it to him. Arturus asked, "Why did you ask questions of the priest and tell him so much?"

"I told him nothing yet he told me much. We have to send a message to King Penda. The enemy are hiring mercenaries. It may come back to haunt King Oswiu but for the moment it is a real threat to King Penda. They have a huge army waiting for the Mercians. With their strongholds fully manned they do not expect Northumbria to be invaded."

"But the King of Mercia has Welsh allies."

"In which case, we will still win for mercenaries only fight for gold and with the hope that they will be rewarded again after the battle is won. The Clan of the Snake shows that some mercenaries who come here seek a better opportunity to gain riches and power. These mercenaries hired by Oswiu will either threaten his kingdom or seek their own. They are the danger for us."

Arturus looked west. He was thinking of his wife. When we had discovered the shepherd and his family the shock on his face had shown that he had changed. He was a married man. He was about to become a father. He had seen men butchered in battle but he has seen little of the devastation caused to families.

I said, gently, "You are thinking of a life in the east are you not? It would be safer than here."

He nodded, not surprised that I had done what his father had and read his thoughts, "Aye but the sea voyage would be as dangerous as staying here. Perhaps more perilous, for a wooden hull is not as good as a stronghold." He had a sudden thought.

"Where is the lair of the Clan of the Snake? It cannot be in Mercia nor Wessex. We should have questioned them before they died."

"They would not have told us. I will ask Daffydd to ask other captains. Six Saxon ships would be difficult to hide."

The next morning we headed south. The day was grey and a chill wind came from the east. My wolf fur kept me warm. The Dunum had just one Roman fort and that had been at Morbium where it had guarded the bridge. We called Morbium, Roman Bridge. I had not heard of it being occupied but we would ride there for it lay close to Stanwyck and to the place whence my father had discovered Saxon Slayer. There would be Angles living closer to the sea but they would be small isolated communities. We would head to Morbium and then see the defences at Stanwyck. If we could capture one of the Bernicians who defended it we might learn more.

The land between the Tinea and the Dunum was full of small hills and steep valleys. I was reassured to have with me Daffydd's archers. The land, however, was free from warriors. It was getting closer to winter, we needed our cloaks at nights, but normally thegns would be hunting. This was the time of year to cull the animals in the forests and lay in a store of food for the winter. Their absence was worrying. We reached the land north of Roman Bridge close to dusk for the days were now shorter. The archers reported that none guarded the bridge and so we picked our way south to the old abandoned fort.

I could not help gripping the hilt of Saxon Slayer as we approached. Once we crossed the river then we would be near to the farm which one of our ancestors had farmed and where he had buried the sword. The old fort had been the place where his curiosity had rewarded him. I can remember him telling me as we had camped close by here when I was but a squire.

'I saw that they had destroyed anything in the fort which had been useful but I also saw places where the soil was in mounds, as though something had been buried. I found a charred piece of wood which had a pointed end and I began to dig away at the nearest pile. Once I got through the grass and weeds it became quite easy and I felt a thrill as my wood struck something solid. I was encouraged to dig harder. The wood was no longer helping

me and so I took to using my hands to clear away the dirt. I found a wooden box. The top had started to rot but it was still quite solid. I made a hole down the side of the box and reached down. I found a leather handle and I pulled. I strained as hard as I could and I was about to give up when, suddenly, it sprang up and out at one end. I dragged it clear. There was no lock and I pulled at the top to open it. I have to admit that I was excited. What treasure would I find within? When the lid finally popped open I was disappointed. After I removed the sacks covering the contents I saw that it was filled with nails and shoes the Romans had used. My father had said they were called caligae and the Roman soldiers had used them.'

I smiled at the memory. Hearing his words in my head made it seem as though he was alive. He had shown me the places he had excavated the metal treasure. We always looked for such mounds when we discovered a new fort. It had been many years since we had done so.

The old fort was familiar to me and I led my men to the half-wrecked building which had housed the officers. There was a wrecked stable block but as it still had a roof we used it anyway. The horses would have some protection from the cold. The Angles had built their village further upstream. The first ones who had come had feared the ghosts of the Roman soldiers. We lit a fire. We would keep it going all night for it was cold. The wind had picked up during the day and we were grateful for the walls which offered shelter. We would keep a watch on the bridge during the night to ensure that no word of our presence was sent to Stanwyck and then we prepared our food.

I took out the sword and held it on my lap. Arturus and the others had never been here and I told them the stories my father had told me. They were like children rapt in the wonder of them. I retold them the story of my father's discovery of Saxon Slayer. I never tired of telling it for it was a sign that a warrior and his weapon could live long after his death.

"He and his brothers had buried their family and they were at the ancestor's farm, not far from here when they dug for what they hoped would be weapons. His brothers, your uncles Raibeart and Aelle, were disappointed but not your grandfather, Arturus. He told me the story, many times. *'I lifted the sacks carefully already knowing what would be beneath. I saw more sacks but this time they were wrapped around objects. The first one was long and I almost held my breath as I peeled back the oiled rags. The pommel told me that it was a sword and the fine jewels told me that it was not the sword of a common man. It was the sword of a mighty warrior, a lord or a king. As I unwrapped the blade I heard the gasps from my brothers. They had not been expecting such a treasure but I had. The scabbard was leather with strange runes and markings upon it. Holding the scabbard in my left hand I withdrew the blade with my right. The light from the setting sun in the west caught the silvery blade and it seemed to shine.'* His voice was always the same when he told the tale. He had made a sacrifice to Icaunus and been rewarded. The sword had been sent from the past to fight the enemies of the present."

"And what of the future, Warlord? What happens then?"

I looked at my nephew. "The sword must never fall into the hands of our enemies. If I fall in battle then you must take it, Arturus."

He nodded and we sat in silence. Their eyes were on the mystical blade. Agramaine said, "And if you are alone when…" He did not finish the sentence. It was bad luck to speak of a warrior's death.

"Before I die, Agramaine, I will hide it. Our ancestor did so. One day one of those who come after us will find it."

Arturus asked, "How can you know, Warlord?"

I smiled, "In the same way that the Christians believe in their White Christ, I believe it will be so." I waved a hand above me. "Myrddyn watches us. His voice speaks to me in my head. It is all *wyrd*."

We left before dawn had broken for I wanted to be close to Stanwyck while it was still dark. We had to pass the long deserted farm of my ancestor but I would not disturb it again. My father had taken all that he needed and it would not do to continue to disturb our ancestors.

Stanwyck had been built long before the Romans had come and dominated the land. It was a shadow of the stronghold it had been but, as we sheltered in the woods, a mile from the ramparts we watched dawn break and saw the light shine on the newly built wooden walls. It was defensible again.

Agramaine said, "That would be hard to take, Warlord."

"We need not take it. However, it poses a problem for King Penda. If he comes north to conquer this land then he would have to have his men bleed on its walls. Eoforwic would be as hard to take. King Oswiu has learned how to fight. Llewellyn and Agramaine, you stay here with four archers. If any messengers head north then take them. Arturus and I will do the same for the road south. If we find none then we will rejoin you on the morrow and head home."

We had a long loop to ride to reach the road which headed to Eoforwic. I did not think that the others would find a messenger. The journey to Din Guardi was a long one. This was the wrong time of year to send a message across the land. A ship could more easily sail up the coast. Stanwyck was the western defence. I hoped that there would be traffic.

We reached a spot where we could watch the road a short time after dawn had fully broken. We tied the horses and then spread out to watch. We had been there but a short time when we heard the sound of men approaching. It was a thegn with twenty men and they were marching from Stanwyck. There were too many for us to attack. We would reveal our position. They were singing as they came. The song was a marching song and showed that they were in good spirits. This was not the army we had defeated by Oswald's Tree!

We settled down to wait patiently as they headed down the road. A wind came from the east. It would herald snow. It was the wrong time of year for it to settle but it was a warning that we needed to get home as soon as we could. Just after noon a flurry of snow made the road white. When it stopped the road was invisible. It was not deep but the icy wind stopped it from melting. One of the archers, Beli, waved to me. He had seen someone approaching from the south. We drew weapons. Our four archers each nocked an arrow. The snow muffled the sound of their hooves but there were two men on horses. The snow suddenly came again from the north and the east. The air itself became white and the two figures pulled their cloaks tighter about themselves. They would soon be in the warm and safe.

We needed them alive. The snow and the wind would make our archers less accurate. As we were a mile or so from the hill fort and with the snow still falling I took a chance. Drawing my sword, I said. "Step out before the horses. They will stop. I want these as prisoners." We were fortunate that the riders were not confident. The slippery road was treacherous and they were walking with their heads looking at the ground immediately in front of them. It allowed Arturus, Pelas and Ban to step out unseen. The horses stopped and reared. One of the riders fell from his horse and cracked his head. The other drew his sword. Two arrows struck his back. My archers had been protecting me. It was annoying but I could understand why they had done what they had done.

"Search the body and then take it and hide it in the woods."

My archers ran up. Dai said, "I am sorry, Warlord. We could take no chances. Captain Daffydd would have our skins if aught happened to you on our watch."

I nodded. "Tie the wounded man to a horse and fetch the other animal." I looked up at the snow laden sky. "The snow will cover our tracks. We will head back to the rest."

It took us longer to get back to the place we had left Agramaine and the others. Despite our furs I was chilled to the bone. I made a decision. "We will ride back to Morbium. We need a fire and we need to question this messenger."

The wind began to veer from the east as we headed up the road. When it was no longer in our faces it was a relief. The snow began to ease and I saw that there was less of a covering closer to the river. We crossed the bridge as the snow turned to sleet. We dismounted inside the fort and helped the unconscious Angle from his horse. We had found, on the dead one, a metal token. It matched the one we found on the unconscious one. They had learned from King Penda and used it to identify men who were trustworthy. Whatever they knew was important. There was nothing written down.

We lit a fire and Arturus and I sat on either side of the messenger. Head wounds are unique. If a man has a cut to his body then, by and large, it can be healed. A head wound often has no sign. The man had been wearing a helmet and so there was not even a bruise to be seen beneath his long lank hair. We ate and we waited. I had seen this before. Men had head wounds which did not kill them straight away. They slept, sometimes for days and then slipped silently into the Otherworld. I wondered if this would be such a case.

Arturus had dozed off when I felt a movement. Warrior growled, waking Arturus. I held up my hand and the dog became silent. The Angle's eyes opened and he stared at me. "Who is there and where am I?"

I clutched the wolf clasp on my cloak and answered him in his own language. "You are safe in the hill fort. We drove off the horsemen but your companion is dead."

"Aethelfrith was my brother." He suddenly winced and then, waving his hand before his face said, "I cannot see and my head hurts. I beg you put me closer to the fire for my feet are frozen."

His feet were just the length of an arm from the fire. He was dying. I did not have long to question him. "I am Egbert of Hagustaldes-ham. What is your message?"

He smiled, "God has sent you to me for it was you I sought. King Oswiu wishes you to bring all of the warriors from the north to Eoforwic at Hrēðmonath. We go to bring devastation to the pagan Mercians. We have a holy banner from the monks of Holy Island!" He gave sudden shake as though wracked by pain. "Ale!"

We had no ale. "I will have some brought. Tell me…"

"How did my brother die? Has he been buried yet? I …"

Suddenly his head lolled to the side and blood began to ooze and trickle down his nose. He was dead.

I shook my head, "I did not like deceiving a dying man. I have to save Rheged and that means making sacrifices."

"He had no wound, Warlord, how could he die?"

"See the blood coming from his nose. I have seen this before. His spirit was strong. He delivered his message. We have to ensure that King Penda knows this. No matter how many men he thinks he will have to fight there will be far more. They are emptying the north."

We buried the Angle in the Roman cemetery. He would be with other brave warriors. Arturus said he had not confessed before he died and his spirit would not go to heaven. That did not seem fair to me. We headed home the next day. The snow had ceased and was replaced by sleet and snow. It made even the Roman roads treacherous and added half a day to our journey home. We met Llenlleog and a patrol of equites by Shap.

The leader of my equites looked relieved to see me. "You are days late and we were worried." He saw the two extra horses. "I see that you have found the Angles."

"We found some and, more importantly, we found information. We have much to do."

Chapter 11

Winter came upon us rapidly. I did not trust to the roads and so I had Daffydd ap Gwynfor take me to the Dee. I could sail to within a few miles of Ethelbert of Tatenhale's hall. I took with me my new squire, Pol and Griflet with his squire. With ten of my archers this time we were prepared for an attack at sea. It would be a much shorter journey than the one to Dogfeiling. Arturus was happy to stay at home. His wife was now entering the last few moons of her pregnancy. He rarely stirred from her side.

Before I left Gawan spoke with me. "We know where Lang Seax is. He has taken over part of the land of Gwynedd. Our ships' captains have spoken with other sailors who have warned them to steer clear of the Welsh river mouths. Cadafael is a weak king. He has allowed the mercenaries to take over the Afon Mawddach."

I looked at him in surprise. "That is where we found the blue stones. *Wyrd.*"

"He is clever. His ships can attack the vessels which ply those waters and yet, by heading through the mountains he can strike at the heart of Mercia. It may be that he wished to conquer Gwynedd and not Rheged."

I smiled, "Do not try to fool your brother. You have dreamed and know that he wishes me dead and Rheged for his own. This venture in Gwynedd is just an interlude. He is building up numbers and he is now a near neighbour. We will need fighting ships of our own."

Gawan nodded, "This is the wrong time of year to build them but come the new grass and we will."

"And did you dream my death?"

There was the slightest hesitation and then he smiled, "No brother. You will return for there is a battle to be fought. We do what we can and the rest in the hands of others. We do not have great numbers any longer. While the Angles and the Saxons wax, we wane. The glory days of Rheged are gone but we can hold on to what we have. You have done much already. The towers and the men who are trained to defend their homes will ensure that no matter what happens Rheged will survive. It will be a glorious, golden memory which will light the dark days ahead."

I laughed, "Gawan, you are getting more like Myrddyn each day. You talk in riddles and depress me beyond belief but I will take each moon that we survive as a blessing."

We left on an evening tide a moon before Yule. At this time of year there was more than twice as much night as day and it was fortunate we had but sixty miles to sail. I was tempted to use the cabin but decided against it. I wanted to scan the horizon. The last time we had sailed these waters we had come very close to disaster. As what passed for dawn broke I saw the sands to the east of us. They stretched for miles and made this one of the emptiest coastlines in our land. It was not until we reached the Maeresea that we would find clusters of huts and people. The winds were from the northeast still and our journey was not as quick as it might have been. We reached the river leading to the old Roman fort a short while before dusk.

Thegn Ethelbert had done as he had promised. There were twenty men in the fort. Although the gates were barred I was recognised and admitted. His gesith, Edgar had a few horses and he gave them to us so that we could continue to Tatenhale. The crew of our ship and most of the archers stayed in the fort. It was a hard ride through an icy dusk to reach Tatenhale. It was late when we arrived and we had to bang hard upon the gates. Even then the sentries brought a light to ensure that we were who we said we were.

The thegn was apologetic. "I am sorry, Warlord, but we have been plagued by rogue warbands."

I looked at him sharply, "The Clan of the Snake?"

He shook his head. "They have raided the Maeresea and the land of Dogfeiling but so far they have left Mercia alone. It is King Cadafael. He is a weak king. He is afraid of the Saxons who bully him and force him to allow them sanctuary. He thinks they will protect him but they will not. Lang Seax is building up his army. He has many new members of the clan and some wear mail. Not all fight half-naked and are tattooed. He wants numbers. I sent two of my men as spies to find out where he was based. I received their heads and hearts. We are in the dark."

"But he is not the major problem?"

"No, for he does not bother us directly. King Oswiu has put a bounty on any Mercian head brought to him. Thegns and gesith bring greater rewards to the bandits. These are not warriors. They are small bands of desperate men. We have caught and killed ten such bands but they ambush our warriors and our thegns. We dare not travel abroad save in large numbers."

I gratefully drank some of the warmed ale his servant had brought me. "This is a cunning plan." I told him what I had discovered. "With Gwynedd no longer an ally and Powys and Dogfeiling having to defend themselves from these attacks it seems to me that King Oswiu has the upper hand. Thegns are not easy to replace. He is taking your leaders. When you fight him, he may not have the numbers which King Penda does but he will have the leaders and that will prove crucial."

"Your warning helps us. If he musters at Hrēðmonath then we have time. Perhaps we can persuade King Cynddylan to aid us."

I was not certain. It was the early hours when we retired. We had had much to talk about. King Penda trusted his Eorledman and he trusted me. If he listened to our advice then there was a chance that Oswiu could be defeated. If not then the battle would a long and bloody one.

We returned to our home safely and reached it in time to enjoy the celebrations for Yule. Winter had gripped the land and we had to cease our quests. Now that I knew King Oswiu's plans I was more confident that he would not be sending raiders to our lands and if Lang Seax tried to raid us he would have the land to contend with. Coming in summer had been one thing but winter made the mountains impassable. Many of my people would be cut off for the whole winter. They were hardy and knew how to prepare for winter.

My home was busier now. Gwenhwyfar had brought ladies to serve her, there were four of them, and we also had more servants. In an ideal world we would have had halls for Gawan and for Arturus but we shared the hall built by King Urien. I struggled to find a place to be alone. I know that many thought me lonely but I was not. I missed my father, my family and Myrddyn. When I was alone I could close my eyes and I could speak with them. I think some thought me mad as I sat with a goblet of wine, my eyes closed and a smile upon my face.

It was one such occasion when Gwenhwyfar entered silently. The first I knew was when a cool hand was pressed upon my forehead. I opened my eyes with a start. She smiled and said, "Close your eyes, Warlord, and let me help you." She smiled and I felt myself drowning in the deep blue pools that were her eyes. "Arturus' father is a half wizard. I have more powers than you can possibly imagine and the child within me makes me stronger. Until she is born let me use them to ease your pain."

"A girl?"

She put her finger to her lips. "Do not tell Arturus. Let it be a surprise for him. Now close your eyes."

She stood behind me and placed her two hands on the side of my head. She began to murmur an incantation but I could not understand the words. Perhaps there were none for it was almost hypnotic and I felt myself falling asleep.

Suddenly I saw Aileen's face. My wife was inside my head and my mind. She spoke. **'Husband, you are troubled. I have not long with you but you must know that you could have done nothing to prevent my death. It was meant to be. Arturus is the future. Our children and I were sacrificed so that you could make him a great leader. Myrddyn told me. We are all proud of you. Gawan helps you but Rheged is what it is because of you. We have a place for you when you come to the Otherworld.'**
There were so many things I wanted to say but it was though I was struck dumb. Then the vision went and Gwenhwyfar took her hands from my head. She looked tired.

"I am sorry I did not have the power to help you longer. I can try again in a few days."

I stood and I put my arms around her and hugged her, "Thank you. Just to see my wife's face and hear that she had forgiven me...."

Gwenhwyfar shook her head, "The witch who took me in told me about the plague. It killed many. It was not sent by the Mother. It came with the priests from the east. It was their curse. Our people are stronger now. The plague will not return."

"Sit. I have not had much time to talk with you."

Saxon Sword

She suddenly looked older and wiser than before, "And I fear that we will not have many more opportunities."

"You have dreamed my death?"

She shook her head but it was to hide her eyes so that I could not see the lie there, "I will have a baby to care for and then I shall have another and he will be a boy. It is my first, Myfanwy she will be called, who will change the future. Women can affect change more than you think Warlord. Myfanwy will fight not with her sword but her blood and her spirit. Her child will wield a magical sword."

"Saxon Slayer?"

"Saxon Slayer's time is now and was the past. In the future there will be another. The blood of the Warlord will flow through her veins and she will have my magic too. The enemies of our people will overlook her. Many men will die but only one woman needs to live to ensure that our people prosper." She stood, "You are tired. Drink your wine and then sleep. I promise that you will enjoy your dreams."

I sat before the fire and drank the wine. It tasted better than any wine I had ever drunk and I wondered if she had used a potion. Then I slept. And I dreamed. My wife and my family lived. My father was there with them. I could not hear them but I saw their smiling faces and I recognised the joy. The dream was a joy. The Otherworld was not a place to be feared.

Myfanwy was born at the start of Sōlmōnath. The cooks baked cakes both sweet and savoury to celebrate and the whole town was filled with joy. I thought it touching that they had named her after my daughter or perhaps it was a name Gwenhwyfar liked. I did not know but I was touched. Arturus did not mind that it was a daughter and Gwyneth was ecstatic for she had just had one boy and no daughters. After the birth Gwenhwyfar kept hold of the child until I entered. I could see Gawan's wife and Arturus were desperate to hold the babe but Gwenhwyfar waited for me and she handed the swaddled child to me. That was unusual. There was a meaning to it that I could not discern at the time.

"You have no grandchildren, Warlord. Myfanwy might make up for that. Speak to her and tell her your hopes."

Gawan gave a knowing smile but Arturus and Gwyneth looked confused. I looked down into the pale blue eyes of the red headed baby. To my surprise, she stared back at me.

"Speak Warlord. This child is special."

I felt foolish but I spoke. "Myfanwy, you are a lucky child for there will be three of us who will be as a father to you. This land of Rheged is yours to care for. Through your veins runs the blood and the spirit of the Warlord. I will not be here when you are grown but my spirit will watch over you always. When I am dead close your eyes and you will see me. Listen and you will hear me." To my eternal delight, she smiled at me. I put a finger towards her and she grasped it. I gently kissed her cheek.

Gwenhwyfar smiled, "Now I will have my child back for she wishes to suckle now."

Gwyneth was shocked, "Will you not have a wet nurse?"

"A wet nurse for the child who will save Rheged? I think not."

As Myfanwy hungrily drank I thought back to the words of Myrddyn. The old wizard had been right. The coming of Gwenhwyfar was as important an event as my father finding the sword.

I had purpose once more. Now that we knew when we had to assemble I could organize the horses and weapons that we would need. We had to await the message which would tell us where we would meet but I suspected that would be Tomworðig. I was closeted with Gawan and Llenlleog for many hours each day. Arturus was allowed time with his daughter and wife. Gawan was also happy with the power which Gwenhwyfar had within her. He did not resent her superior powers. Myrddyn had taught us both that the Mother gave those women who followed her cult greater powers. We both knew that the witch who had trained Gwenhwyfar had been priestess of that cult. She had been the sacrifice to enable her acolyte to come to the aid of Rheged. Even whilst he was in the spirit world Myrddyn watched over Rheged. It was as though he was not dead.

We had few maps of the land around the Humber. We knew a little about Lindum, the major Roman fort and the road which led to Eoforwic but the rest was largely conjecture. We had never travelled that far east before.

"There will be swamps." We both looked at Gawan. In answer to our unspoken questions he jabbed a finger at the crude maps. "It stands to reason. When the Romans came Lindum was almost at the sea. Now ships cannot travel there for the sea is moving away." He shrugged, "The gods have not finished shaping this land. We know that at its mouth the river is as wide as a sea. That means that it is a powerful river and will be spread out with tributaries and streams feeding it. The land around the borders is flat. It will be swamp."

He sounded a little irritated. I smiled, that was like Myrddyn. "So, it is swamp."

"And that means that your horses will be at a disadvantage. They like hard ground. You will not be able to manoeuvre. You need to persuade the King, when you see him, to allow you the freedom to move around the swamps and the streams."

In the end we discovered that we were wrong and we had done King Penda a disservice. A messenger arrived ten days after Myfanwy was born. He handed me the boar token and then spoke. "Warlord, King Penda would have you meet him at Stanwyck."

Even Gawan had not expected that. "Stanwyck?"

The messenger nodded, "Aye Warlord. He is marching north. King Oswiu and his family are north of the Tinea at a place called Iedeu."

I looked at Gawan who quickly took the map that Old Oswald the priest had made for us. "It is remote, brother. Is the King certain?"

The messenger smiled. "He has his own spies Warlord. He sent them north when he received your message from the Eorledman. The Northumbrian armies are still in their winter camps. He intends to pass through them. He would have you and your men take Stanwyck and hold it for him."

Llenlleog said, "That would be hard, Warlord. We would not be able to use our horses."

"We did not use them at Din Guardi either." I turned to the messenger. "We can do this. We will await you at Stanwyck."

My renewed energy after my talk with Gwenhwyfar was rewarded. We were ready to ride within two days. The ground was hard but the ice which gripped the land would make a good surface for our horses. We would be able to reach Stanwyck within two days. I knew that they would not be expecting us. I saw that Arturus was torn between wishing to serve with me and being with his wife and new born child. I made it easy for him.

"I need someone to stay here and guard my land. I will be taking most of the men. You would not want your child exposed to danger."

"Then I will stay but this will be the last time I do not ride at your side."

I was relieved. "That is a promise!"

Gwenhwyfar came with her babe to see us off. Arturus held his arm protectively around her. She looked serious. She held the babe so that its blue eyes pierced our spirits, "Myfanwy here are your grandsires. They go to do battle with the Angles. They are great warriors. When you grow remember them. Tell your son of them for they have laid the foundation stones for a future kingdom here in Rheged."

I kissed her on the cheek and the babe on the forehead. I felt power surge through my body.

Gwenhwyfar smiled, "The power of the Mother will be with you, for a while at least."

Gawan did the same and then embraced his son, "Watch over your family, my son."

"I will and we would have you return safe and whole!"

Arturus did not know but his wife, father and uncle did; we would not be coming back. This would be the last time I would see my family. I drank them in like a heady wine. I burned their faces in my mind.

I rode Star. Copper was getting old and it was still winter here in the north. We left and headed along the Roman road which ran by the wall. We knew that we had destroyed our enemies at Hagustaldes-ham. There were none at Roman Bridge, Morbium. We could approach Stanwyck from the one direction they would not expect it; the north!

This time we were not a handful of men. I had every equite save Arturus and most of my archers. We numbered more than two hundred and fifty warriors. We also had twenty servants with the tents and the spare weapons. We were travelling in winter and we would not fight nature as well as our enemies. I noticed Gawan looking around him as we headed east.

"You seem interested in the land, brother. At this time of year, it is but a bleak white world."

Enigmatically he said, "And that is why I stare for I have never travelled it at this time of year. It is beautiful is it not? The animals and the trees all sleep beneath the icy white blanket and that I find remarkable. The Mother will wake them all and within a few moons it will be green and full of life. We need it to be bleak so that it can be reborn. Out of the dead white land comes life." He waved a hand behind us, "The same will be true of Rheged. When we are gone the land will die but it is an illusion. Out of that death a seed will grow."

I lowered my voice, "You speak of Myfanwy."

He smiled, "Arturus' wife is powerful. She is, perhaps, as powerful, in her own way as Myrddyn. She is stronger than Arturus and yet it is he who will be remembered. I have spent many hours with Gwenhwyfar and even now she is here." He tapped his head.

I felt a little betrayed. I had thought that I had been the only one with whom she had confided.

Gawan reached over and put a gloved hand on mine, "Brother do not be angry. I spoke to her as one mystic to another. She spoke to you as the defender of Rheged. What you do will echo through eternity."

We camped at Hagustaldes-ham. There was no one to stop us. The monks in the monastery kept their doors barred but we left them alone. I wondered if they would send a message to King Oswiu and then I realised that he and his family were at Iedeu in secret. As we sat around a fire warming ourselves I asked, "Why has King Oswiu gone to Iedeu?"

"I have heard that there is a monastery there. The messenger from King Penda seemed to think that the Angle was trying to prepare for war through contemplation."

Kay snorted, "A waste of time. The only way to prepare for war is to practise war!"

Perhaps he was right. Had the spirits lured King Oswiu north to enable us to have the final victory? If King Oswiu was dead then the Mercians would rule the land. The White Christ would be finally defeated.

Chapter 12

Geraint and my scouts reported that the garrison at Stanwyck were within their walls. They had seen little sign that they had left during the last month or so. There was hardened virgin snow. It boded well.

I sent Bors and ten archers to cut the hill fort off from the south. They would light no fires despite the cold for, when we attacked I wanted it to be a surprise.

We camped to the north of the hill fort deep in the trees. The servants used the tents to mask the fires that we would use. We needed hot food for we would be attacking. The days were still short and when we rose, the next day, I wasted no time in scouting out the ramparts. I went with Tadgh, Llenlleog and Gawan. We wore no mail but had, instead our wolf cloaks. This was the time of wolves. As we had rode along the wall we had heard their howling. This was a wolf winter. It was harsh and the wolves were desperate for food. They would risk their greatest enemy- man. If a sentry did see us he would take us for prowling wolves. I did not intend to be seen.

The tree line ended just two hundred paces from the first of the ramparts. There were two sets of ramparts and three ditches. When the hill fort had been repaired they had not built two sets of palisades as the builders had originally intended. They had just used the inner one. It meant they needed fewer sentries. It was a mistake. Tadgh pointed down to the stream which ran along the eastern side of the fort. It was frozen and would not be a barrier. We would be able to cross it easily. We could hide in the ditches and rise to scale the walls. The wooden walls were as high as a man on the back of a horse. We would not need ladders. We could use our shields to boost warriors over the top. It would be a task for our squires. Once they were over the top then they could open the gates and we would flood in.

We headed back to our camp and I spoke to the equites and Daffydd. "We rest during the day and we leave just before dusk. As soon as it is dark I would have us move towards the ditches.

When we get back to the camp I will tell all what they need to do."

Daffydd ap Miach was unhappy that it was the squires who would be risking their lives. "Warlord, my archers are good with knives! Let us do this."

"This war will need your archers later. The squires must become warriors sooner rather than later. This is *wyrd*. Let the squires become blooded."

We had servants to watch the horses and the camps. We headed south, through the woods to the ramparts. There was a moon, if was a wolf moon. It seemed as though it burned in the sky. As we peered to the ramparts Daffydd said, "The light is good enough for our archers. They will see us if we move in large numbers."

I nodded, "We have time. Let us see their routine."

We saw that they had six sentries and they patrolled a section some hundred paces long. They had a fire burning at each corner of the wall. It must have been in a brazier and set upon the earth rather than the fighting platform.

Daffydd said, "I have seen enough, Warlord. Let me go and clear one section. Then the squires can come. They will have an easier task."

"Very well." Twenty of my archers scurried down the slippery slope. I turned to Pelas, "Take the squires. We will follow."

The archers and the squires were lighter on their feet than we were and they were faster. They reached the outer rampart before the sentries had returned from the warmth of the brazier. Inevitably it was our weight which was our undoing. We had armour. The squires and Archers did not. Bors and Kay crashed through the ice. As the four sentries on our side of the walls turned Daffydd's archers sent their deadly arrows into them. One cried out as he fell.

"Bors, Kay and Pol, take half the equites and help the squires. The rest of you with me. We shall take the gates!"

Inside I could hear the sounds of alarm. The other sentries ran around the ramparts to see what was amiss and three of them died by arrows for their trouble. I ignored the wall and ran over the rampart and down into the ditch. It was slippery at the bottom for the water there had frozen. Llewellyn slipped over. I

Saxon Sword

just ran and, mercifully, did not fall. I knew that the men inside would have to get from the hall to the walls. They would either have to waste time grabbing a shield, helmet and weapon or come as they were.

When we reached the gate, there was no one above us. I turned. "Form a shield wall. We will batter this gate down." The bridge which led to the gate was four men wide. Llenlleog, Griflet and Llewellyn flanked me. Others formed behind. I shouted, "One, two, three!" We ran at the gate. There were twelve of us and we were mailed. The gate creaked and cracked. "Once more and it will fall!"

I heard the sound of combat as my squires scaled the walls and began to fight the defenders. This would be a test of their skills!

"One, two, three!" We ran and when we hit it this time it shattered and cracked open wide. Running into the flat area where my great grandparents had lived I looked for Angles. I saw men fighting on the ramparts but there were none close to us. I spied the warrior hall. Raising my sword, I ran towards it. The thegn and his warriors burst out. They had donned helmets and leather armour. They hefted shields and swords. We were together and, as they came out of the hall piecemeal, they were not. I held my shield before me and raised Saxon Slayer. I did not pause for an instant. I ran at the thegn who emerged exhorting his men to kill the pagans. He had leather armour and I had mail. His sword smashed into my shield and mine swung down to hack across his shoulder, into his collar bone and then his neck. I pushed his body away and turned to slash the next Angle in the back. My backhanded stroke shattered his spine. The Angles were desperate to hurt us. They poured from the hall and the buildings. They had a bigger garrison than I had expected.

Three of them ran at Kay as he descended the rampart. The dunking in the cold water must have slowed him. Even as he slew one the other two hacked at his legs. He killed a second but the third rammed his sword up into his middle. Kay brought his sword around and took the Angle's head but the damage had been done. Kay sank to his knees and I could see that he was mortally wounded. I had no time to look longer for six Angles burst out of the hall. Llenlleog ran to my side and Agramaine hurried to help me. I had a cold anger within me. Kay was one of my oldest equites. He needed vengeance. I blocked an axe on my shield and, dropping to one knee, rammed my sword into the guts of one Bernician. As I flicked it out I sliced into the side of a second who thought I had not seen him. I stood and punched my shield into the face of a third. As he reeled backwards I swung my sword to take his head. The six were all despatched and I ran to the hall. Inside were merely women and slaves.

I turned and shouted, "Rheged!"

From around the ramparts came answering shouts. Daffydd and his archers were now on the inner rampart and the wolf moon helped them to pick off the isolated Angles who fought on. It was a large hillfort and it took us until dawn to ensure that it was clear of enemies.

I saw Bors lead ten equites towards a shield wall of Bernicians. The thegn knew his business. Bors and the equites smashed into them. The spear which stabbed into Bors' side was not meant for him. It was just unlucky. The wound half turned him as he slowed. The thegn saw his chance and he swung his sword at Bors' shield. Bors was slow, thanks to the wound, and the blade bit into his shoulder. The warrior next to the thegn rammed his sword into Bors' middle. It was a mortal wound but Bors just roared. He smashed his shield into the face of the thegn and then took the head of the man who had stabbed him. As the thegn tried to rise Bors took his sword in two hands and fell, dying, into the chest of the thegn. Their resistance crumbled and my men fell upon them.

There had been more than one hundred and fifty defenders. King Oswiu intended this to be a bastion. We had lost Kay and Bors. The dousing in the frozen stream had been their undoing. Four squires had died but we had the fort and we had their food. After repairing the gate, we piled the enemy in a pyre beyond the ramparts and burned them. Our dead we buried, with honour in the centre of the hill fort. When we left, we would burn the halls as a memorial to our brave dead. Llenlleog, Gawan and I stood by the two graves. "I shall miss those two, Warlord."

"As shall I, Llenlleog, but I shall see them sooner than you!"

Gawan said, "And now we wait for King Penda."

Llenlleog nodded, "Fear not Gawan. We can defend this better than the Angles did and besides they do not know we have taken it!"

This was the first time Gawan and I had been in the hill fort. I knew that he was sensing the spirits of our grandparents. Our father had told us that the boys had buried them close by their hut. With no marker there was no way of finding them. While our men made the hill fort safe, secure and comfortable Gawan and I walked around it. This was too far from our land to make it our own but I admired its construction. When first built it would have been impregnable. The three ditches and two rows of palisades with offset entrances would have been a death trap for any attacker.

Gawan was in reflective mood. He had been quiet since we had left our home. "It is strange that we should begin this campaign here. It is where our father started his war against the Angles."

I shook my head, "When he led his two younger brothers and killed those who slew our grandparents he would have been little more than a youth with neither training nor skill. How did they survive?"

Gawan and I had reached the westernmost part of the walls and he looked towards Rheged, hidden behind the great divide. "They were chosen; the Warlord was selected by the spirits to hold back the tide. The knife in his back ended that dream. We had a brief moment when a golden world returned and then…"

"Yet Myrddyn seemed hopeful."

Gawan turned, "What I have learned in my dealings with Myrddyn is that he sees beyond time. We see each battle, victory and defeat as important. He saw them as interesting moments in time which would shape the future. He saw the future." He smiled, "I was wrong about Gwenhwyfar. Myrddyn was right because he saw the future. When I dream I dream a world half seen through a thick fog. I believe that Gwenhwyfar has far more powers than I." He looked at me sadly, "Her words, when we left were goodbye. It was not a farewell it was an ending."

I had sensed it. "I know but we are men and we are warriors. Whatsoever happens is *wyrd*. I have come to learn that. We walk in footsteps laid down by others. We have to follow them where they take us; even if we like not the destination."

Llenlleog and the others could not understand our sombre mood. They put it down to the deaths of Bors and Kay. "They died as warriors. They were happy in their deaths."

"And what of their sons? Ban son of Kay and Geraint son of Bors are both in Civitas Carvetiorum. When we return with the news of their father's death, what will they think? I know that when the Warlord fell I took little comfort in the fact that he knew he was going to die and that he had sacrificed himself for Rheged. I just saw my father lying murdered."

My words set men to thinking and the hillfort was a quiet place for six days as we awaited King Penda. When he arrived, he brought a mighty host. He had Welsh allies but neither king had come with him. He had a warband from the East Angles. In all he brought thirty warbands. With our men we had more warriors than when we had fought at Oswald's Tree.

King Penda took me to one side as soon as he arrived. "I thank you for your news. Had you not sent it then I would not have been able to put this plan into action. Knowing that the majority of the Angles were gathering at Eoforwic meant I could catch King Oswiu unawares."

"You are fortunate that he went to this Iedeu."

"I have known of this for years. He and his brother used to go the monastery for two moons, after Yule. They spoke with their God. I knew that they kept their army close by. This time he has mustered his army at Eoforwic. All that Oswiu has is his personal guards. He has but one warband. We can defeat him and make this land ours! Your scouring of the north and the fact that you took this one obstacle to us has given us this victory. You are, truly, the Warlord!"

His confidence and optimism were infectious. I could not see how we could lose. My horsemen would ensure that he did not escape north. Yet Gwenhwyfar's farewell still brooded in my mind.

Before we left we pulled down the palisades and, placing them on the hall, made a pyre. Our men who had been killed had been buried close to the hall. Their graves would not be despoiled. We had lain them in their armour with their weapons and they would enter the Otherworld as warriors.

It would be a two-day ride to Iedeu. King Penda's route had meant that the army gathered at Eoforwic had no idea that they had been outwitted. The empty land to the north of us allowed us to move freely. We camped at Hagustaldes-ham.

King Penda came to me, "Now is when we need you and your mobile warband. I need you to ride north of Iedeu and prevent any from fleeing. You need not attack. Just ensure that they cannot flee. There are woods to the north of Iedeu and the road passes through them. You will be able to observe their hall from there. I need Oswiu and his family alive."

I looked at him in surprise. "Why not just kill him?"

He shook his head, "Then another could become King of Northumbria. This way I make him swear allegiance to me. I will be High King. The East Angles and the Welsh have agreed to that already!"

"Is that why they did not send their kings?"

He frowned. He had thought of almost everything but not that, "We do not need their kings. We have their men. They follow me."

As we headed north I thought of the weakness in King Penda's plan. Less than half of the army was Mercian. He had fifteen warbands and mine on whom he could rely. We still did not know the make-up of the Anglo-Saxon army. The rumour was that there were mercenaries as well as warbands. I regretted not sending Geraint and Tadgh to scout out the enemy. We could have done so while we had waited for King Penda. Such oversights can often be fatal.

It was a long hard ride on frozen roads. We crossed the river which ran by Iedeu south of the hall at a small ford. Tadgh had found the hall and we skirted it at dusk. We would be hidden but even if we were not then they could do little about it. We reached the woods just after dark and we made our camp. We could, had we wished, have attacked and captured the hall. There was not an enormous camp of men. I spied but twenty horses and the camp fires of a single warband. This was not my war, this was King Penda's war. I would follow my orders.

King Penda would come the next morning. He wanted King Oswiu to see the thirty warbands he had brought. He wished a bloodless victory. We had a hard, cold night. We rose at dawn and mounted. The archers would be used if we needed them. I hoped that the sight of our banners, horses and mail would deter any escape north. King Penda came with a flurry of horns and drums. His banners and standards hung stiffly in the cold, early spring sky.

The Bernicians reacted quickly. I saw over a hundred men march from the hall and array themselves before the monastery. They were going to sacrifice themselves to allow their king and his family to escape. Horses burst from the small palisade. There were forty warriors and another twenty who looked to be the King, his family and his priests.

"Forward!"

We emerged from the woods and the Bernicians slowed down. I waved my sword to the right and left. My men spread out to form a huge circle. There was no way out. The forty warriors rode at us. They had ordinary saddles and spears. More importantly these housecarls of the King were used to fighting with the earth beneath their feet. The thegn who rode at me tried to use his spear as a lance and he punched it at me. It hit my shield and he fell backwards. I swung my sword at the Angle behind him. His spear wavered over my head as he tried to thrust and keep his saddle. My sword hacked into his shoulder. Then I was through the warriors and I found myself facing King Oswiu, his queen and his son, Ecgfrith.

"King Oswiu, I would happily slay you but King Penda has asked me to spare your life. Surrender or die. Those are the only two choices." I saw him look behind me. I, too, turned. The warriors who had not been slain had fallen from their horses as they tried to fight like equites. My squires had spears at their throats. "He said nothing to me about sparing your men. Would you like your hearth-weru slain too?"

He shook his head, "I surrender to you, Warlord." He turned his horse and led his party back to the monastery and hall. Ahead I saw that the warriors they had left had all been slain. Their deaths had been in vain.

King Penda had wasted no time in occupying the hall. Even as we dismounted and led the captured Bernician King and his family inside he had seated himself upon his throne. He smiled; it was a cruel smile. "King Oswiu, you are my captive. Thank you, Warlord. Once again, I am in your debt. You shall be rewarded for this."

I nodded but inside my head I was angry. I did not want a reward. I wanted safe frontiers. I wanted Oswiu and his family dead. King Penda was correct there would be another King but not one as powerful as Oswiu. He was descended from Edwin, who was now a saint. His brother had been martyred too. Any pretenders to the thrones of Deira and Bernicia would have to fight each other gain the thrones. While they did that we would build up our strength again. Had Myrddyn and Gwenhwyfar seen this?

"Do you want, King Oswiu, to be crucified on a cross as your brother was?"

Gawan said, quietly to me, "I thought he was dismembered and hung from the branches of a tree."

"He was but I think King Penda is making a point."

King Oswiu did not answer. "I am in a generous mood this day. I have lost few men and here is my decision. Your son, Ecgfrith, will be taken to my hall at Tomworðig. He will be surety for your compliance with the rest of my commands." There was little reaction to this punishment. Ecgfrith would be well treated. It was a common practice. "Secondly you will bow your knee to me and acknowledge me as High King of Britannia, Lord of the Saxon kingdoms!"

King Oswiu glared at King Penda. He had no choice. If he did not agree then he and all of his family would be killed. I knew, from Arturus, that a Christian did not believe that a promise made to a pagan had any meaning. King Oswiu would break his promise as soon as he could.

King Penda had not finished. He knew how this game was played. "Finally, I have thirty-one warbands. You will give me thirty-five boxes each filled with one thousand pieces of silver or its equivalent in gold."

For the first time that elicited a response from King Oswiu, "That is all of the treasure in Northumbria! I will have to strip every church to find it."

King Penda smiled, "I know. Do you agree or shall I let the Warlord have his way and slay you and your family?"

This time King Oswiu turned to me and he glowered at me. Hatred oozed from his eyes and his mouth as he said, "I agree but know this, pagan Warlord, my brother sought to have you killed and he failed. I swear that I will not fail and you will die upon my orders."

I spoke for the first time too, "And know this, King Oswiu, that once I return home I will bring an army and I will hunt you down like the dog you are."

King Penda frowned, "But not until we have the treasure and we are all back in our own lands, eh Warlord?"

I nodded and smiled, "Of course, King Penda."

King Penda took out his sword and made King Oswiu swear his allegiance on the sword. King Penda smiled and turned to Prince Peada, "Now my son, there are horses for you and Prince Ecgfrith. There is a warband of two hundred men. They will escort you back to Mercia."

Even Peada was surprised, "Now, father?"

"The sooner the better."

Ecgfrith had a brief moment to say goodbye to his parents and then he was whisked off. King Penda was clever. They would be in Mercia before the army which was in Eoforwic knew of the disaster.

"And you, King Oswiu, had best give orders for the treasure to be collected. You have half a moon!" He turned to me and said quietly. For your part in this there will be two chests. You have earned it more than the others."

"Thank you, King Penda."

After they had gone I saw that one of the leaders of the warbands was a Deiran. Œthelwald of Deira was a claimant to Bernicia. Now I saw King Penda's plan. He was threatening King Oswiu. If he failed to live up to his side of the agreement then King Penda would replace him.

Now that a battle was unlikely I sent a quarter of my equites and squires, led by Llewellyn, back to Civitas Carvetiorum.

Arturus would need them. We settled into the monastery. We ousted the monks.

That night Llenlleog was in good spirits. "We will have treasure to spend and King Oswiu will not have the services of mercenaries."

Gawan shook his head, "This is worse. Those mercenaries will seek pay from somewhere. Perhaps they might choose to take it from us."

Llenlleog laughed, "There are easier targets than us, Gawan. Do not be such a pessimist. This has gone well."

He was right. It had gone well. Too well.

Chapter 13

The chests arrived within ten days. King Oswald was keen to have the Mercians gone from his land. I did not think the Northumbrian king was finished with King Penda. I sent my share back to Rheged with Griflet, accompanied by ten equites and archers. I also sent back the servants. They would not be needed and it was unfair to risk men who were not warriors. I would have gone home but King Penda asked for my horsemen and archers until he had reached his borders. He wanted a mounted escort back to his lands but he did not need all of my men. Rheged did. The Clan of the Snake was still slithering around my borders. I now had half the force I had brought.

He gave his reasons for the request, "King Oswiu will do nothing but there is still an army of sorts at Eoforwic. There are eorledmen who seek power. One of those may raise an army and try to stop us. We have more than thirty chests of treasure. We are a tempting target." He saw the lack of enthusiasm on my face. As payment for your time you can have one more chest of treasure when we reach Tomworðig."

Having sent our share back home I agreed. The main reason was Gawan. I intended to go home with my men until he spoke with me, "Brother the spirits have set our feet on this path. Our fate is bound up with that of King Penda. We have no choice."

He knew something. The spirits had spoken. I agreed for my land was safe now with Arturus and Gwenhwyfar and I had sent half of my men back.

The ten days we had waited had seen a change in the weather. The thaw had come. The ice and snow melted. The warm winds came from the west and that meant that they were wet winds. The roads became a muddy morass as soil was washed onto the cobbles. It was not an easy journey south. My equites and squires had the saving grace that we were the vanguard. I still had one scout with me, Geraint. Along with Daffydd and his archers they were the best eyes and ears we had and they ranged ahead of us. Warrior of course, was my personal eyes and ears.

He growled at everyone who approached, save my men. That included a bemused King Penda.

I sent Geraint to scout Eoforwic as we approached it. The army had gone, they had dispersed. That did not reassure me as we had not seen men marching north. Where had they gone? King Penda was also concerned. He had expected them to try to stop us before we reached Eoforwic. The fact that they had not worried him. He kept the army together. At least he tried to do so. There were desertions. It was not a flood, it was a trickle but it unnerved the army. We had no desertions from the men of Rheged. I would not have expected that. We travelled for more than six days before we found them. They were gathered at the River Went. One of the northern tributaries of the Don, it was not an easy river to cross. They intended to dispute our crossing. This was the first river that they could do so. Although fordable it was a wide river and the banks would be slippery for men to ascend. The alternative was a detour west towards the High Divide. We had to fight them. That night we had a counsel of war where King Penda explained our course of action.

"The Warlord and his men will be on our left flank. The river is deeper there. They will find it easier to ford the river. The men of Powys and Gwynedd will be on the left with the men of the East Angles and Œthelwald of Deira. The Mercians will be in the centre."

As plans went it was a sound one. Our scouts had reported the enemy numbers and we outnumbered them. However, as we rode along the river bank to see for ourselves I saw that one of the warbands facing the Welsh, Angles and Deirans, was the Clan of the Snake. Lang Seax was here and he would take some stopping for his warband now numbered three hundred.

As we made our camp and prepared our weapons Pelas ap Tuanthal asked, "Warlord, we are the smallest of warbands and yet we face almost a quarter of their army?"

I nodded, "King Penda has planned well. They will not willingly fight us. We have archers and mounted men. The Northumbria's will relish fighting the Mercians more than us." I lowered my voice, "We fight tomorrow because it bars King Penda's route home. I want you to live after the battle tomorrow.

There is nothing here for Rheged. I have said we will fight and so we stay but I would rather head west and ride to Rheged."

Gawan had heard me and he shook his head, "Brother, it matters not. Our path is set and there is naught we can do about it. What will be will be."

With that depressing thought I prepared Star. Pelas had already seen to my horse but I had some old apples in my bag and I gave him one. I checked his hooves and his legs. He needed to be in perfect condition. We would be fording a river against men in prepared positions. It would not be easy and my horse might be my only salvation.

I sat with Llenlleog and Gawan by the fire and watched the flickering fires of our enemies. "At least the Clan of the Snake is not facing us."

Gawan said, "Not yet, Llenlleog, but the battle may be a long one. They have a blood feud with us. We have bested them twice. They will seek vengeance." He turned to me, "You and Lang Seax will have to settle this one day and only one will survive."

"My brother is right, Llenlleog. Whatever the outcome tomorrow, save as many of the equites, squires and archers as you can. Rheged will need them. I fear this alliance is ended."

Llenlleog nodded, "That suits me. I would rather fight on Rheged soil anyway. There we know who our enemies are. I do not trust half of the men we fight with!" His words were uncannily prophetic.

I went to bed but I did not sleep. When I had been in Constantinopolis I had heard men talk of hubris. They had explained it but until that moment I had not understood it. Now I did. King Penda had brought us to the brink of disaster. We were fighting a battle on ground our enemies had chosen and that was never wise. As I could not sleep, I heard the noise from further west. Fearing a night attack, I rose. When I reached the Mercian camp Eorledman Ethelbert was there. He was at the King's tent reporting to the King.

"King Penda, the Welsh have fled. They have headed west in the night. The other warriors there were asleep for the Welsh said they would set the sentries."

King Penda's face became red and it was not just the firelight. He was angry. His careful plan was unravelling before his eyes. "I knew they were weak! When we have dealt with Oswiu's men they will feel my wrath and I will boil Ecgfrith alive!"

I knew it was all sound and fury. It was for the benefit of his own thegns. More than a third of our army had deserted. Our right flank had been our strong one and now it was weaker than mine. There were just two warbands there and one was Deiran. Worse, they were facing the Clan of the Snake. I had fought them and knew that they would be tough men to beat in battle.

The King saw me, "Warlord you and your men are now vital. You must stop my attack in the centre being outflanked."

"It is your right which is in danger, King Penda."

He sighed, "Aye, that is why I have my best warrior there. Eorledman Ethelbert will be as a rock." He waved a servant forward. "Here is your chest, Warlord, have it now in case…"

I hefted it. It was not as heavy as the others we had sent home. This was another sign that the army was breaking up. Someone had stolen from it. Tomorrow would end badly

When I reached the camp, I took a decision. "Pelas ap Tuanthal, go and fetch Llenlleog."

Gawan had not been able to sleep. He smiled at me, "I read your thoughts brother. What you do is both wise and thoughtful."

"Let us see if Llenlleog and Pelas see it that way."

When Llenlleog arrived, he was still half asleep. My first equite had the ability to sleep standing up! "The Welsh have fled. I fear tomorrow will be a hard day. I wish you and your squire to go with Pelas here back to Rheged." I pointed to the chest. "We have more coins from the King."

Pelas looked at Llenlleog who said, "You send away your best equite when you think it will go badly? That does not make sense."

"It does for if I fall then you will be there as Arturus' guide. You are younger than I am and you can teach him that which I cannot. He needs to become a better equite and you are the best." He did not look convinced.

Gawan said, "There is nothing that you can do here tomorrow Llenlleog that a lesser equite can do. In Rheged you can watch over my son and his wife. You can ensure that Myfanwy grows and fulfils her destiny."

He knew how to obey commands and he nodded, "I will go but it is with a heavy heart."

Pelas said, "Let me stay Warlord!"

"You guard the chest Llenlleog will guard you." I clasped Llenlleog's hand, "Wolf brother I have been honoured to fight at your side. Look for me in the Otherworld!"

He nodded, "And I have done more than any warrior has a right to expect and that is because I followed the Wolf Warrior and Saxon Slayer." He turned to Gawan, "I will watch over your family as though they were my own. Come Pelas ap Tuanthal. We obey our lord!"

"Take the road due north and head over the High Divide close to Shap. If this goes badly tomorrow then there will be bands of men hunting us."

The three of them left. They walked their horses from our lines. It would not do to give the impression that we were fleeing.

After they had gone I woke my men and told them what I had done. "We fight today because I said we would. I wish I could take those words back but a man cannot do that. If I fall then leave. My body is unimportant. Rheged is all. I would have you fight for Rheged and keep the dream of my father and King Urien alive."

None answered but I could see in their eyes that they would not leave me. I could do nothing about that. I felt closer to them all in that moment than any man alive, save my brother. They knew that more of us would die the next day than survived and yet they still chose to follow the wolf warrior and his sword. In that moment I felt that the sword was almost a curse. It had caused my father's death and now the equites, squires and archers I led would also die.

Daffydd ap Miach who commanded the twenty-five archers who remained with me said, "Warlord, we are your oathsworn. That means we stay by your side until we can no longer pull a bow or draw a sword. If this is our last battle then let us make it one to remember. Forget these faithless warriors who flee in the night. We are the men of Rheged. We follow the last Wolf

Warrior. Even if we are to die then we will not be beaten. My son is at Carvetitas. He will follow in my footsteps. He will serve Arturus as I serve you and my father served yours. That is our way. We will be ready come dawn and the Angles will bleed!"

I was content. I had not deceived my men. I had told them that I thought we would die and they would still follow my banner. This was where I missed Myrddyn. He could see as clearly into the future as most men do in the past. My father had known the manner of his death but I did not.

I saddled Star myself. I would have no squire to pass me another spear. I put three in the scabbards which were on the right side of the saddle. I could hear movements and noise on both sides of the river as men prepared for the battle. I heard the splash of feet in the water further west. Was that Saxon scouts crossing or East Angles fleeing? The priests on the other side were chanting their prayers to their White Christ. Mercian thegns made pleas to the Allfather. Metal chinked against metal. Yet all was invisible. Darkness was all around. We were wrapped in night's cloak. And then it began to rain. A trickle at first it rapidly became a deluge. Daffydd's arrows would not be as effective. We would not have the range we needed. The spirits were not making it easy for us. The rain delayed the dawn. Grey murk replaced blackness and I saw the serried shields across the river. They were the men of Bernicia. I recognised some of their devices. They knew me and my men. There were two warbands. It was a compliment. They would outnumber us by more than two to one.

Our squires would need to charge with us. I gathered my horsemen together. I could rely on Captain Daffydd to tell his archers what to do. "We are few in number. If we spread ourselves out then they will defeat us. I will use our weight and concentrate our charge. I intend to punch a hole in the centre of their line. Agramaine will be on the far right and Pol on the far left. We will spread the rest of the equites amongst the squires. I will be in the centre. Remember our task this day is a simple one. We stop King Penda from being outflanked. If we achieve that then we have a victory."

I would not be fighting close to Gawan. I found him readying his horse. He turned and smiled, "I know, brother you come to say goodbye."

"Reading my thoughts again?"

"We both know that this will be a hard fight. It will be the last battle we fight. I could not have a better brother and remember that death is just the beginning. You and I have a journey to the Otherworld. No matter what pain we endure here all will be healed in the Otherworld. We are not Christians. We need no priest to say we are forgiven. What we have done is for Rheged and Myrddyn has promised us that there is a welcome waiting for us."

"I would tell you to ride home, Gawan, but you will not." I put my arms around him and held him tightly. I pulled his head forward and kissed his forehead, "Take care, little brother." I forced myself to turn away and to hold my emotions in check. My men needed a leader. I mounted Star and donned my helmet. The rain had made the red plume hang down. It looked bedraggled.

I found myself next to Garth and Gruffyd. They had only been squires for a year. I did not know them well. I could see that they were nervous. I smiled at them. "Remember that our spears can find the gaps between their shields and their armour. If they raise their shields then they cannot see you. It matters not where you strike them save that you draw blood. You do not have to kill with every blow. Your horse is a weapon, use it. Its teeth can bite and its hooves can kill. If we can break through their shield wall then all will be well."

They nodded. They needed to be confident when we fought. Bedivere's squire carried the dragon standard. Both were honoured for normally it was Llenlleog's squire who did so.

The rain, which bad briefly become a shower, now came down harder. Daffydd rode up to me. "I am sorry, Warlord, but our arrows can fly less than eighty paces in this murk."

"Then cross the river on your horses behind us. We will protect you and you can come closer to the foe to send your arrows over our heads."

He turned his horse and rode back to his archers.

Saxon Sword

The Mercians began banging their swords against their shields and chanting. I knew that it was to build up their own courage and to help them cross the river, reform and then charge the waiting Angles. Even so it did help to steel all of our men. The Welsh had deserted. Better they did so before the battle had started than when we were engaged. King Penda was no coward. He would lead his Mercians. They would attack first and when he reached the far bank then the two wings would follow. It was a good plan. The first horn sounded and the Mercians marched to the river. It was hard to see them because of the rain which pelted down.

I raised my spear, "Prepare to move!"

Daffydd and his archers appeared behind us. Their bow strings were still inside their seal skin pouches. It would keep them dry until the last moment. The King and his oathsworn were in the centre of the river. I did not see who commanded the Angles. It was not Oswiu for he was still in the north. They waited in three ranks. The mercenaries were all on their left flank leaving us with the Deiran warbands. The bank was slippery and I saw the Mercians struggle to reach solid ground. That should have been the moment for the Northumbrians to attack but they did not. They seemed content to allow King Penda and his men to form up. The Mercians were disordered as they struggled up the bank. Why let them form a shield wall? It made no sense to me. I began to hope and believe that we would win.

The Mercians formed three lines and then the second horn sounded. We moved forward. I glanced down the river and saw the men of the East Angles in the water. Œthelwald of Deira had not moved forward. In fact, he had withdrawn his men to a small hill which lay further north. He was not attacking. He was waiting to see which side would be likely to win. We were nearing the south bank when a Northumbrian horn sounded. Lang Seax led his clan and the mercenaries. Some had crossed the river. They must have been the splashes I heard in the night and they fell upon the flank and rear of the single warband of East Angles. They fell upon the Angles in the river. The one warband faced three. I forced myself to concentrate on what we needed to do. Our right flank would fall! We had to defeat those on our side.

We were in one line. Daffydd shouted, "Ready, Warlord."

Normally we would have taken our time but the longer we waited the less effective would be the bow strings. "Charge!" The damp ground would mean a charge at a trot rather than a gallop but we had to support King Penda. Already he was engaged with the Bernicians. Their blades and spears clashed in a deadly cacophony. I had my own battle. The arrows might not have been as effective in the rain but the first ones still flew two hundred paces and fell amongst those at the rear who did not have their shields up. Angles died! Even before we reached the shields another four flights had been sent into the enemy ranks. I saw the fall of arrows and knew that the range was decreasing incredibly quickly. Soon they would be useless.

Then we struck. I pulled back my arm and jabbed down with my spear. I was lucky. Even though Star did not have a firm footing the enemy had the same problem and as the Bernician who faced me stepped on to this left leg he slipped. My spear darted down and struck his neck I twisted and pulled. The blood arced spraying those around him. I urged Star on and his head reared above the Angle in the second rank. His jaws were open and his teeth looked terrifying. The Angle flinched and my spear found his stomach. The arrows had all been sent towards the centre, just ahead of me and I now reaped the reward. I was through their shield wall and I turned Star to head towards King Penda. I was attacking the side unprotected by a shield. Men tried to fend off my spear with their own but a spear is unwieldy at close quarters and I was striking down.

All was not going our way. I saw both Garth and Gruffyd pulled from their horses. They fought bravely but they were overwhelmed. I hurled my spear into the back of the warrior who was trying to take Garth's head. I drew my second spear. I saw that King Penda was beleaguered, "Head for the King!"

My equites and squires all followed me. Those at the rear were attacked by the warriors who had been on the far right. I heard Daffydd's voice above the mayhem all around us, "Archers, draw swords! Let us show them that we can fight as well as the equites too!"

A horse is the best vantage point to see the whole battlefield. With no enemies around me I looked west and saw that the East

Angles had been slaughtered. That allowed Lang Seax to lead his men up behind King Penda. The Mercian King was being attacked in the rear. To my right Gawan and eight equites had manged to get within thirty paces of the King.

I speared another Northumbrian who was too slow to pull his shield up and I shouted, "Gawan! Go to the aid of the King!"

I know not if he heard me above the clamour of battle or if he read my thoughts but whatever the reason he raised his spear and he and the equites began to hack their way through the Angles. We were now well behind the front line of the Bernicians. I saw their leader. If I could get him then we might still win this battle. Agramaine, Pol and Dai were the nearest equites to me. I saw that there were too many empty saddles. There were less than twenty equites left and perilous few archers.

"Let us take the Eorledman who leads them. If we take the standard then the rest might flee!"

"Aye, Warlord."

The four of us and their two squires kicked our horses in their flanks and rode towards the standards of Deira and Bernicia. Their attention was on the battle for it raged around King Penda and his standard. I saw Gawan and his five remaining equites as they fought their way to his side.

I forced myself to look at the twenty men we would attack. We were less than forty paces from them when they spied us. The thegn shouted an order and ten of his men ran at us with shields and spears. I still had one spare spear and so I hurled the one in my hand. It caught the Angle in the centre by surprise. My spear drove into his leather armour and pierced his chest. He fell and tripped the warrior next to him. I drew my last spear and as Star trampled to death the fallen man I stabbed down at a third Angle. I was through them and I left the others to be dealt with by my equites. The Eorledman had his standard bearer by his side. Two priests and three oathsworn were also with him. I was alone save for Warrior who still ran gamely next to me. This would be my death. I would die with Saxon Slayer in my hand but I would die. The odds were five to one. I hefted the spear and hurled it as I approached. The standard bearer had no mail. He had no armour. The standard showed a martyred St. Edwin. Perhaps he thought that would protect him. It did not and he fell, along with the standard. Behind me, I heard a cheer as the Mercians took heart.

Drawing Saxon Slayer, I rode at the oathsworn. The priests fled; their faith was not strong enough. The Eorledman had his sword drawn but his shield was around his back. As I neared them I pulled back on Star's reins and he reared. I slashed with my sword as his hooves hit one warrior. My sword struck the side of the helmet of a second. A spear was rammed up into my side. Warrior leapt and fastened his teeth around the oathsworn's neck They fell to the ground. Even as I pulled Star around the Eorledman had brought his sword down to take brave Warrior's head. He had died saving me. As the Angle with the bleeding neck rose I sliced across his neck with my sword. The Eorledman realised that he was alone and needed his shield. Even as he brought it around I hacked with Saxon Slayer. I struck his left arm, almost severing it. He looked up. His face was a mixture of shock and resignation. I brought Saxon Slayer from on high and cleaved his helmet and skull in two.

As I wheeled Star around I saw my two remaining equites riding towards me. Their squires were slain. I continued my turn and saw King Penda slain by Lang Seax. He raised King Penda's head to show what he had done. One of his men held up Pybba's head. It was the signal for flight. The Mercians ran. There was no logic to the direction they took. Some ran back towards the river while others tried to flee through the Northumbrians. Some of the Clan of the Snake had taken horses and were crossing the river to pursue them. The ones who stood the best chance were those who fled west. I turned to look for Daffydd ap Miach and his archers. I saw their huddle of bodies where they had made their last stand. Gawan! I looked back to King Penda's last stand. There was no sign of Gawan nor their horses. The Clan of the Snake must have taken them.

I dismounted and picked up Warrior's body. I laid it across Star's neck.

Agramaine's voice was urgent, "Warlord, we are lost! If we stay here then we will die too. We are the last three warriors of Rheged on the battle field. There may be others who have escaped. We should head south and then cut back north west."

Agramaine was right. I felt numb. In one battle more than half of the best warriors in Rheged had perished. Had Gawan fallen? Even as I turned Star to head south I closed my eyes and pleaded with Gawan to speak to me. Although he did not answer, strangely, I felt that he was alive and that gave me hope. I opened my eyes and we galloped through the Northumbrian camp ignoring the treasures which lay there. The most important treasure now was our lives. We had to get back to Rheged as soon as we could.

Part 4

The Clan of the Snake

Chapter 14

There was much confusion on the rain-soaked battlefield. We had horses. We were able to move faster across the boggy battlefield and the three of us slew Northumbrians to clear a path as much as anything. Small pockets of warriors fought on. All the leaders of the warbands lay dead, all, that is, save me and I had just two men left with me. I could not believe that all of my equites would have perished. I had seen few horses around the Mercians and none of them hasbeen the horse of an equite. We rode south until we had overtaken the last of those fleeing the battle. Some of the Mercians held up their hands and shouted to us, "Warlord! Take us on the backs of your horses!"

Agramaine answered for us, "You fled the field first! Let your legs take you home." It sounded heartless but if we tried to take them with us then we would all perish.

The trickle of survivors from the disaster that was Winwaed would take some time to reach home. Already King Oswiu would be hurrying south to join his men and to save his son from Peada. That was not our concern. We had to find as many of my equites as we could and get back to Rheged. We came to another river. I had no idea what it was called but we did not relish fording another river and so we rode along its northern bank which headed west. We had to ride slowly for our horses were tired. We had outrun the others who had been in the battle.

At what passed for noon on this rain-soaked day we found a dell by the riverside. The ground rose to the north and I spied, in the distance, some sheep. The willows by the river provided some protection from the rain. It was the right resting place for a brave dog. "I will bury Warrior here. It is a peaceful place and his spirit can watch over the sheep. He was a brave beast and he saved my life. When he followed me from the shepherd and his family I did not know why. Now I see that it is part of the

Allfather's plan. He saved my life and that has earned him a place in the Otherworld."

The ground was soft and we scraped a hole deep enough to bury the dog. Pol took some stones from the river bed and we laid them over the dead animal. We covered it with soil and I said, "Be free, Warrior. I owe you a life."

We took out some venison. I was not hungry but I knew we had to eat. Agramaine refilled our waterskins. As we ate he asked, "Does the Allfather's plan include your brother, Gawan, Warlord?"

I nodded, "Gawan knew that he would not return to Rheged just as I know." They looked at me in surprise. They were young equites. They had much to learn. "I know not where my path leads but I fear it is not to Rheged. We will head home but that may not be my destination."

Pol smiled, "Now you sound like Myrddyn and Gawan, lord! You are speaking in riddles."

I rested my head against the willow. "I do not think that my brother is dead. If he was then his spirit would be in my head and he would tell me so. When we went to Din Guardi he spoke to me there. I know not why he has not spoken to me but he is alive and I must find him."

"You would go back to the battlefield?"

"No, Pol, if he is on the battle field then he will be dead. As we fled I saw the bodies being stripped and I saw no equite to the west of us, at least none on a horse. He wore mail. All the wolf brethren will lie naked and despoiled on the battlefield. The victors will not leave them with mail on them." I touched the golden wolf clasp on my cloak. "We are richly adorned. This is the first time we have lost a battle and left our dead for the enemy. It sits heavy on my heart."

"Warlord it was not your fault that we lost."

"Yet we did and the cream of Rheged lie dead. All the equites, archers and squires were slaughtered. I now know that sending back the warriors I did was necessary. They could not have changed the battle and their presence in Rheged might save our home. They have Llenlleog to lead them."

"You think that the Clan of the Snake will head there?" There was fear in Agramaine's voice. We had seen what the Clan of the Snake could do.

"I know not. Gawan and Myrddyn were always here to give me advice. Now they are not and I feel that I am in a fog. We keep on heading home until I get a sign. Then you two will return to Rheged and I will end this quest."

"We do not leave you. If you are to die then there will be two equites who fall with you."

"And if I order you?"

Pol laughed, "That will be an interesting experience, Agramaine, refusing to obey the Warlord!"

We walked our horses for the rest of the afternoon. We had a long way to go and they needed our help. We kept heading north and west although with no sun our direction was ordered by the land. We guessed we were heading northwest. We walked up the young river valley. It became a stream. By night time we were on the eastern slopes of the High Divide. We had seen few houses for we had followed the river which had become narrower as we had climbed north and west. We were not on the roads. That made it harder for me to estimate where we were. We found a piece of ground which offered some protection. Rocks made a natural shelter from the wind. There was turf for the horses and so we stopped. The rain had stopped and so we risked a fire. Our clothes and cloaks needed to be dried. Using our cloaks to give us shelter we lit a fire. We waited until it was blazing and our soaked cloaks began to steam before we moved away.

It was when I was taking off my mail that Pol said, "Warlord, you are wounded!"

I remembered the last of the Eorledman's oathsworn stabbing me. I saw that the links on my mail had been pierced. Agramaine went for the vinegar and honey. Pol cut away the shift I wore beneath my padded vest. The white shift was soaked with blood. The blood had matted and when Agramaine wiped it clean with vinegar it began to flow again. He said, "Warlord, you are losing too much blood. I cannot stitch this. Pol, fetch a brand from the fire."

I nodded. He was right. Pol gave the brand to Agramaine and then we held each other's shoulders.

"Ready, Warlord?" I nodded. There was a hiss and then the smell of burning hair and flesh as he sealed the wound. The pain was excruciating and had Pol not been holding on to me then I would have fallen. The brand was placed back in the fire and my wound was covered in honey and a bandage.

We sat and watched our clothes and cloaks steam before the fire. "We will keep watch this night, Warlord."

I shook my head, "We are all tired. Our lives are in the Allfather's hands. We need our sleep and I think we have outrun any who might be pursuing us."

That night I dreamed. I saw Gawan's face but it looked to be in pain. He tried to speak with me but could not. All around him were the warriors of the Clan of the Snake. Each time I opened my mouth no words came out and then all faded to black.

Perhaps we were being watched by the spirits for we woke and all was well. I was stiff and my side ached when I moved but we were alive. The rain had gone to be replaced by grey brooding skies. Ahead of us the High Divide rose like a rocky wall. I spied a trail which wound up the sides. It was not a road but looked like a local trail. It had to lead somewhere and it was heading in the right direction. We walked our horses up the steep part to reach the trail. In the distance we saw smoke coming from isolated farms. They knew nothing of the battle and went about their lives as though nothing had happened. The undulating land meant we could not see them. When we reached the trail, we mounted. I saw that it was a cattle trail. Drovers used them to move cattle to market. I doubted that many had used them recently. The three of us scanned the horizon constantly. There would be warbands either seeking us or heading back to their own lands. Even the warriors of Mercia might prove to be an enemy. These were warriors without a leader. They might choose banditry now that their King and their chiefs were dead. The wind picked up as we climbed and I knew that we had to find a col or risk being silhouetted on the sky line.

It soon became obvious that if we were to stay on the trail we would have to risk being seen for the trail took the high level. We dismounted and hung our helmets from our saddles. We would make ourselves as small as we could. As noon approached we stopped in the lee of the hills. The wind was from the east and it was a relief to be away from its icy blast. We were eating the last of our venison when Star whinnied. Someone was approaching. We all drew our swords and stood, as one. We made a triangle so that we were back to back. If we were to die then we would sell our lives dearly.

Geraint appeared over a rise to the north of us. He had a bandage on his head and his arm was in a sling. He dropped to a knee, "Warlord! I have found you. I spied you five miles since and I have been following you. I am the last of your scouts."

We sheathed our swords. He looked exhausted; he looked almost grey. He had been hurt and he was exhausted. His horse was lathered. It could go no further. Pol took the weary mount while Agramaine and I began to tend his wounds. He began to speak as we cleansed his ugly wounds with vinegar. He barely winced at the pain. His arm had been laid open to the bone. Agramaine said, "This needs fire or he will lose it."

"See to it." The head wound looked worse than it was. He had suffered a blow from a metal weapon. "What happened to you?"

He shook his head as though trying to eradicate the memory. "I was with Daffydd ap Miach. By the time you charged our bows would send an arrow barely forty paces. He ordered us to draw our swords and charge. We used our horses." He smiled, "The Bernicians did not think we could fight as well as we could. When they began to hack our horses, he ordered Tadgh and me to find you and tell you that they were finished. Tadgh could not obey the order for he was hewn in twain by an axe. I did as I was ordered although it pained me to do so. The captain and his men made a circle and took many with them. As I reached the river I saw that they had all died. I could not get across the battlefield for there were too many enemies but the north was empty. That faithless Angle, Œthelwald of Deira, had led his men to join with the Clan of the Snake. They fell upon King Penda."

Agramaine had a fire going and he and Pol came over with water and some dried venison. "Eat and drink for you need it."

He shook his head, "I have more to tell you. The Warlord needs to know."

I nodded, "Get the fire hot so that the wound is sealed. Go on Geraint." I spoke gently for I could see that he was upset.

"The battle had spread out well to the west as men fled. Not all of the Saxons who had fought had died. They were pursued by vengeful warriors. I saw Eorledman Ethelbert fall. It was as I looked for a route around the battle that I spied Gawan leading equites to King Penda's aid. Pybba and the Mercian hearth-weru fought to the last around the King and his standard. The King fell to Lang Seax's long sword but our equites still charged to save him from butchery. Their horses were hacked and the equites and squires slain. It was horrible and terrible to watch. They took many of the Clan of the Snake with them but they died."

My heart sank. Gawan was dead. "How did Gawan die? Did he suffer?"

Geraint shook his head, "He did not die, Warlord. Lang Seax fetched him a blow with the flat of the blade. He was struck in the head and then he fell. I watched them bind him." He looked ready to pass out.

This was worse than the thought that my brother was dead. Agramaine said, "Warlord, his horse is out on its feet. If Geraint has ridden as far we must tend his wound and we must give him food. He will die else."

He was right and I nodded, "Geraint, you have done well. We will talk more when you have had food and you can order your thoughts. I must find a high place."

I walked to a large rock which was a hundred paces from our camp. I would be exposed but I no longer cared. If it brought the Clan of the Snake to me then I would have vengeance for my men and my brother. I stood on the rock and holding Saxon Slayer aloft and the wolf clasp on my cloak I closed my eyes and said, "Myrddyn, I know not where my brother lies. I need your help. I cannot leave and return to Rheged without knowing what has happened to him!"

There was nothing. The sound of the wind filled my head and my ears. Myrddyn had abandoned us. Then I heard the shrill cry of a hunting hawk and I looked up in the sky. Circling above me was a hawk. Then I heard Myrddyn's voice in my head, '*You will not return to Rheged. Your feet are now on a path which will take you to your death. The Clan of the Snake are heading home.*

They have wagons for their booty. Your brother lives, for a while, at least.' Then the hawk swooped and plunged to the ground. It rose and in its talons was an adder. It wriggled until the hawk's beak snapped off its head. I knew what I had to do. I had to take the head of the Clan of the Snake. I had to slay Lang Seax.

When I returned Geraint looked better. A little colour had returned to his cheeks.

"Myrddyn has spoken to me." My equites clutched their wolf clasps. "I must face this Lang Seax. He has taken Gawan and my brother is still alive. I believe that Lang Seax means to have sport with him and then kill him."

"He could be anywhere!"

"No Pol. He will be where he feels safe. He will be south of Wyddfa. There he has a stronghold and he has his ships. He will have more men there. Geraint has said that many of the Clan died. He will need his men. He has gold now. He will want more and Rheged will be where he gets it. To stop the Clan of the Snake I must cut off its head."

"There are just four of us, Warlord."

"No Agramaine, there is just me. I will do this alone."

Pol shook his head, "You would face a warband alone?"

"Geraint, how many of the Clan of the Snake survived?"

"They fought Mercians protecting their King and our equites, lord, more than half were killed or wounded. I knew that you would be south of the battle and I had to cross the Saxon lines to reach you. I found many of the Clan of the Snake dying on the road where they had been abandoned but Warlord, there are still more than a hundred of them."

I nodded, "Then I will kill them one at a time. I cannot leave my brother in their hands. Tell Arturus and Llenlleog what I do."

Agramaine said, "I am coming with you, Warlord. You shall not die alone."

"And I. We are equites."

"I am the last of the scouts. I will come with you."

"No Geraint. We cannot leave Arturus wondering what happened to his father. Would you wish Arturus to seek his father and take on the Clan of the Snake?"

"No, Warlord."

"We cannot save Gawan but we can stop them from hurting him before they kill him. Tell Arturus that if we do not return then we are dead and if we do return…" I shook my head, "that will not happen."

"And Saxon Slayer?"

"Saxon Slayer will die with me!"

We stayed with Geraint for the rest of the day and the night. We used the time to plan what we would do. I reasoned that as the Clan of the Snake were on foot we were quite likely to be ahead of them. They had to cross the Dee at Deva to get home and there were men there. Ethelbert had left an old warrior, Egbert, in command of a garrison of twenty men. If we could reach the fort before the Saxons then we had an opportunity to slow them down and inflict some casualties. The men of that part of the world had much to thank Ethelbert for. They would wish vengeance on his killers.

We parted from Geraint on the western side of the High Divide. There were no words left to say. We spoke with our eyes and our hand clasp. Geraint had to live else the last stand of the men of Rheged would not be told truly.

The plain ran all the way to the sea. The cloudy skies had given way to a blue sky. It was not warm but we could see a long way ahead of us. Our horses had had almost a day's rest and we were riding downhill. It allowed us to push them harder.

"Which way will they go when they have crossed the Dee, Warlord?"

"I think they will go the direct route, to the south of Wyddfa. If they go the easier way, the coast road, they risk being attacked by the Welsh. They might not fight for King Penda but a hundred Saxons passing through Dogfeiling might tempt them to action. Once we have his scent we will be like a hunting hound. No matter how much he twists and turns we will follow."

It was late when we reached the fortress. I knew that word of the disaster would not have reached them yet. The Queen and Peada at Tomworðig would know but the stronghold was three days hence. Egbert smiled when he saw us, "Do you bring news of King Penda's victory, Warlord? We are honoured to have such a noble emissary."

I dismounted and shook my head, "I am a harbinger of doom. Your King, your Eorledman and the flower of Mercia lie dead. They were betrayed by the Welsh and butchered by the Saxon mercenaries of the Clan of the Snake."

The old warrior's face fell. "I have lived too long. I served the Eorledman's father. I was in his hearth weru. He was a good man."

"Aye he was."

He had a shrewd mind. "Then what brings you here, Warlord, for Rheged is far to the north?"

"The Clan of the Snake have my brother, Gawan. They are heading home and I would stop them here. They have booty and the only way across the river is by this bridge."

"I have but twenty men."

"And I have three. We will be outnumbered four to one. We will lose."

He laughed, "You do not sweeten the medicine do you, Warlord?"

"We might lose but there may be a chance for us to rescue Gawan and to kill enough of them to stop them being a threat to you and your people."

He nodded, "For myself I do not mind but there are young warriors here."

I turned to look at the bridge. It was close enough to the walls for stones and arrows to be used as missiles. It was just wide enough for a cart or a small wagon. "If we blocked the bridge with trees then your young warriors could use stones and arrows from the walls. They would not be at risk. When they send warriors to clear the bridge then those of us who wish to could sally forth."

Pol said, "And if they swim the river?"

"They have booty. There is no one pursuing them. If they are able then they will try to clear the bridge. Perhaps, if Lang Seax sees me, he may decide to end the blood feud here."

Egbert was happy. "I will have the young men hew the blackthorn and hawthorn trees. They needed clearing anyway. If we tangle them together they will be hard to shift and they will tear their hands to shreds while they do so."

While they set about that I said, "It is a shame that the Romans built this to stop the Welsh. If the fort was on the other side of the river we would be able to guarantee that they would not escape. If they use shields then they can clear the bridge and escape us."

"Warlord you are using what there is. This is *wyrd*." Pol was right. There was no use in worrying about what we did not have. The road passed close to the fort and that would have to do.

The chopping and hewing went on into the night. We stabled our horses and prepared our weapons. Egbert had plenty of food and we ate our first hot meal in many days. It helped me to sleep soundly. That night, as I slept, Gawan came to me or at least his words did. I saw him not. I almost did not recognise his voice for his words were thin and reedy.

'Brother, I know that you are close. I can sense you. I am doomed to die, but you know that already and you are sacrificing yourself. They have taken my eyes and my fingers. They feared my magic. They have only left me my tongue so that they can continue to question me. I fear that this night will see them take my manhood. They have no honour and they punish me because Lang Seax fears you, Brother. He runs from you. He thinks that you pursue him. It is little enough but it may help. I know I am close to Wyddfa for I feel its power. I am close to death now, brother. The next time I see you will be in the Otherworld.'

And then he was gone. I woke with a start. They were close. I roused my two equites. "They are close. Let us find bows. It has been many years since I used one but our arrows may help to thin their numbers." They stared at me. "Gawan came to me in a dream. They are close. He has been blinded and tortured."

I needed say no more. It was some hours until dawn but if this was our last day on earth then we had eternity for sleep. We found the armoury. There were throwing spears as well as bows and arrows. Neither the bows nor the arrows were as good as the ones we used but they would have to do. The gatehouse was the closest place to the road and we took our weapons there. The original Roman Road had passed through the fort. The road which now ran around it was not Roman made. It was rough and it was ready. The bridge was a hundred paces from the walls but the road, separated by a double ditch was less than forty paces.

With the elevated fighting platform and our strength then we had a chance to use the throwing spears to good effect. The two young sentries looked at us as though we were mad. Not long before dawn we left the fort and took eight spears. We buried the shafts in the soil at the side of the bridge so that the tips were at groin height. Then we disguised them with ivy. For a day the ivy would remain green and appear as though it was natural. To get around the timber barricade they might try to climb the parapet. The first ones to do so would die. We had also found an old Roman buccina. We placed that on the fighting platform too. Then we hurried back inside.

As dawn broke Egbert brought the rest of the garrison to the walls. I told him what we had done and he nodded his approval. "I have eight older warriors who are willing to stand with the Warlord and his equites. With me that makes twelve any more would be unlucky."

I smiled, "That sounds a little like Christian talking."

"My wife is one. Let us say when I fight I follow the old ways but, in my home, I place my hands together. Today I am a warrior once more."

It was the fourth hour of the day when we spied them. We had all eaten and prepared ourselves for war. We heard the sound of wagons and I waved the men to hide beneath the parapet. I peered through the gap in the stone. The Saxons snaked down the road. Lang Seax rode at the fore and he was on an equite's horse. It was Garth's. I saw that he had taken mail. He was too big for it to have been Gawan's. It was the overlapping metal type. It was Pybba's. Tethered to the back was a shambling bloody figure. It was Gawan. He wore just the white shift and he was barefoot. There was blood around his middle and his hands had neither fingers nor thumbs. His nose and eyes had been taken. I wanted to fly from the walls and to kill Lang Seax there and then but Gawan was surrounded by ten of Lang Seax's warriors. I would be dead before I reached him.

They stopped when they were level with the gatehouse. Lang Seax glanced over. He saw the closed gate but appeared not to think it represented danger. He turned and shouted, "Some of you come and clear this bridge!"

It was what we had waited for. The twenty men who came did not bear shields; they left them by the cart. Agramaine said, quietly, "I have counted more than a hundred and twenty Warlord."

"Let us see how many we can kill with our first arrow shower." I peered again and saw the twenty men approaching the bridge. "Now!"

I had a bow and I aimed it at Lang Seax. The arrow was not a true one. It did not fly straight but still managed to hit his leg and drive into the side of the horse. He could not control it as it reared and he was thrown to the ground. Sadly, the horse protected him. He was on the wrong side for me to hit him. I flung the bow to the ground. Already the archers and slingers had killed ten Saxons. The men sent to the bridge ran back for their shields. I hurled a javelin and hit one Saxon who fell and brought down two others. As the two struggled to their feet they were slain too. One man reached his fellows who had all raised their shields.

Lang Seax's head appeared above the horse. Pol sent an arrow at him but it just struck the saddle. The Saxon shouted, "I thought you dead, Warlord. See your brother now. No longer the pretty little wizard he once was." He grabbed the rope and pulled Gawan towards him. He put his hand over his bloody sockets and said something to the warrior next to him.

Gawan shouted, "Rheged and the Warlord!"

The Saxon grabbed Gawan's tongue and slice it. I stood and hurled my spear. It was aimed at Gawan. I would put him from his misery. A fluke breeze diverted it and it sank into the side of the head of the Saxon who had taken his tongue.

Lang Seax laughed, "You will know where to find me Warlord for I will leave pieces of your brother for you to follow!" He was taunting me. He turned to his men and shouted, savagely, "Clear the bridge!"

Egbert said, "Warlord, he does not know how few men we have. If he did know then he would send them round to the other gates!"

I nodded and shouted, "Make them bleed. The more we kill here the fewer will escape!"

Saxon Sword

This time the Saxons had shields to protect their bodies but their legs were vulnerable. I threw another spear and it hit a shield square on. It must have driven almost through the willow boards. The warrior was struggling to hold up the shield and one of Egbert's men hurled a stone which hit him on the side of the head. The first two ran into the spears and fell mortally wounded into the river. They began to clear the trees but it was at a cost. Another twelve fell before they managed to remove them.

"Now it is our time. Pol, sound the horn. Let them think we sally forth with an army." Even as the buccina sounded I saw Lang Seax, using his horse as a shield, lead his oathsworn across the bridge. Those who had cleared the bridge joined them. The Saxon wagons were next and they had forty men to protect them. The gates were flung open and I led eleven men to attack them. The others on the wall targeted the drivers of the wagons. Those three had no protection and they died. When they did the wagons stopped, blocking the road. With my shield before me and a freshly sharpened Saxon Slayer held above me, we ploughed into the Clan of the Snake. These had no mail. My first blow struck across the chest of the leading Saxon. It bit deeply and blood spurted. I punched my shield at the man next to him and as he reeled I whipped my sword across his side.

A Saxon thrust his spear at me and it struck my knee. Pain coursed through my body as it tore into the bone. I punched him in the face with the hilt of my sword. As he lay on the ground I smashed my shield across his windpipe. The Saxons were organizing now. They had realised how few we were. Two of the Mercians fell dead and I believe we might have all been killed had not the younger warriors in the fort suddenly dashed out and, cheering, charged to reinforce us. Even so it was desperate. One of the Saxons had an axe. He had just used its edge to slay a Mercian and he back handed the head into my side. I felt something break. I brought my sword across in a wide sweep before he could reverse the weapon and took his head.

Agramaine was fighting three men. Two Saxons were between me and them even as I sliced into the Saxon's side Pol had slain one of the three. It proved to be his undoing for another Saxon axe swung and entered his spine. I threw myself at his killer. My sword drove all the way through his side. As I fell I kicked the legs from beneath one of the two men fighting Agramaine. As Agramaine slew the other I dragged my sword from the dead Saxon and plunged it up between the legs of the prone Saxon and into his guts. He died twitching and screaming. His screams seemed to act as a signal for the survivors, all fifteen of them to run to the river and swim across. They had had enough.

I crawled to Pol and cradled his head in my arms. He smiled, "I feel no pain, Warlord, but I am dead. I will see you in the Otherworld. I am sorry that I will not be with you when you rescue Gawan. Tell him…" His eyes glazed over and he was dead.

I stood. He had been a brave squire and a noble equite. Agramaine had tears in his eyes for they had been like brothers. "He gave his life for me."

I nodded. I saw that Egbert had but ten men left. The rest had died. "Egbert, your men fought like heroes. In these wagons is treasure. It is yours to use as you see fit."

"Do you not want it Warlord?"

"I need no treasure. We will bury our friend and pursue the enemy. In the unlikely event that we survive we will pick up Pol's horse. Until then care for it."

"Of course, Warlord, but there are but two of you. We slew many of them but, even so."

"We are the Wolf Brethren and we do not give up. My brother is being tortured. We will not stop until we find him."

Chapter 15

We buried Pol in the Roman cemetery of the fort. If was fitting. He was a Roman in all but name. He was buried with his mail, sword and shield. Agramaine tended to my knee and wrapped a bandage around my broken ribs. I now had three wounds and I knew that I would be slower. Agramaine had managed to avoid any wound and I would be more reliant on him. It was late in the afternoon when we crossed the bridge. We had sharpened our swords and taken spears from the armoury. I had seen more than fifty summers and I felt every one of those years. Our horses had benefitted from the whole day of rest and grain. We made good time on the Roman Road. We passed the bodies of two of the Snakes who had been wounded in the battle. They had been abandoned. We made almost twenty-five miles before we had to stop. It was dark and I did not want to risk an ambush. We found an abandoned hut and used it. We brought the horses inside. We could not risk going afoot.

After we had eaten, we had bread, cheese and ham which we had been given, Agramaine said, "Warlord it we do not catch them until they are in their stronghold then I fear our quest will be in vain."

"Then we catch them before they reach it. They have one horse. We can travel three times as quickly as they. I am guessing they are camped at the Roman Road. It is less than ten miles ahead of us."

Agramaine nodded, "We have whittled down their numbers but many more than twenty remain."

I smiled, "When we began they had more than a hundred and twenty. We take each step as it comes."

That night I woke. I had a pain in my heart. I thought I had been wounded. I could not understand it. When I felt my body, I was whole. What had the pain been? Was there some wound inside me? Had the axe done more damage than just my ribs?

We rose before dawn and left as the sun peered over the eastern horizon. I would have left in the dark but I feared tricks from the Saxons. When we reached the crossroads where the

Saxon Sword

road forked I saw the reason for the pain in the night. On a spear, ahead of me was a human heart. I knew that it was Gawan. My brother was dead. It was a message from Lang Seax.

As we buried the heart Agravaine said, "They will ambush us."

"I know but not yet." I pointed ahead, "This is a Roman Road. It is straight for many more miles and the hills are to the south and east of us. They will ambush us when we get into the rough country." I pointed to the soil. "This cruelty will come back to haunt Lang Seax. He thinks we follow him blindly. We do not. Thanks to Gawan and Myrddyn we know where his lair is. It is by the river of the blue stones. When we get to the rough country we leave the road and we will spring our own surprise." I knelt next to the grave. "This may be the only part of you that we bury brother but it is not out of disrespect. We will avenge you. That I swear."

We mounted and rode down the road. We did not wear our helmets for we wanted to see as far ahead as we could. They would have men watching for us. Lang Seax wanted my sword. More than that he wanted my head. They would be the weapons I used to destroy him.

We had travelled five more miles when we found one of Gawan's legs. It was hanging high in the branches of a tree which overhung the road. As we passed it I gripped the wolf clasp on my cloak and apologised to my brother.

We rode further down the road until we were a few miles short of where the high ground began. We went off the road and into the woods to the east. There would be shelter from any rain and we could make it more secure than being in the open by the road. We lit a fire and put water on to heat. Agravaine made a stew and busied himself around the campfire. I went into the woods and used some thin rope we had brought from the fort. Using my dagger, I cut some of the wild brambles and spread them around the outside of the camp. None of my traps would kill or even hurt the Saxons but if they came we would have warning. That was all we needed. We ate the food and, having made certain that the horses were secure, we laid down to sleep. We wore our mail. In my case it was too painful to remove. I had no intention of sleeping but I would, as Myrddyn had often said, rest my eyes yet remain alert. Agravaine and I had said all that we needed to say. Any further conversation would be just a means of filling the silence. We did not need to do that. We had our thoughts to occupy us.

I heard the Saxon trip not long after the fire had become a soft red glow in the dark. Saxon Slayer was close to hand and I gripped the hilt. A second rustle told me that there were at least two killers. My eyes were open and I was looking into the woods when I caught the movement. Despite my wounds, I was up on my feet at the same time as Agravaine. There were eight Saxons. We had made our camp so that we were on either side of the fire. It was at our backs. We would be looking towards the dark and the light would reflect off their faces. I slipped my dagger into my left hand. The four who came at me were confident. I was a greybeard. I had been wounded and they outnumbered me.

One was more eager than the others and he lunged at me with his sword. I flicked it away with my dagger and swept Saxon Slayer around to eviscerate him. A second saw his chance and lunged. I pulled back and the blade scraped along my mail. More of the links were damaged. My left hand slashed him across the throat. The other two were warier. They moved to my left and right thinking that if they both attacked I would be helpless. I had no intention of allowing them to dictate the combat. I feinted with my sword at the warrior to my right and even as he lurched back and his companion seized his opportunity to strike at my back, I was spinning around. The fire made him lose any night vision he had. I brought my sword around as I spun and although he tried to turn he was too slow and my sword slashed through his flesh and into his organs. I pushed his dying body towards his companion and I followed through. The dying Saxon stopped the last one from swinging his sword. I dropped to my good knee and drove my dagger up into his guts and thence his heart. He fell dead.

I turned and saw that Agravaine had killed the four on his side. He gave me a sad look, "Warlord, I am wounded." He had his hand pressed to his side and when he lifted it I saw that it was bloody.

"Sit they are all dead."

"There may be others."

"There will not." I grabbed a bandage from the leather satchel which lay by the fire. Perhaps I was gaining my dead brother's powers for I knew that we had killed all the enemies who were around us. I lifted off his mail. He had been stabbed in the left side. The blade had gone through and he was bleeding profusely. "Lie down and hold this bandage to the wound. I will build up the fire. I will have to sear it."

I threw fresh kindling and wood onto the fire and blew. The flames began to lick around the wood. As the fire grew I took the vinegar and honey. It was the last of the vinegar. I returned to Agravaine who looked pale. I wondered if he might pass out. I took the bandage from him and mopped vinegar along the wound. It would be painful. The blood was pouring. I hoped that there was no internal damage or else my healing would be temporary at best. I was not a wizard, I was not a healer I was a wolf warrior. I took the burning band, "Agravaine roll onto your side and put the handle of your dagger in your mouth."

"Aye Warlord." He sounded sleepy.

I had no time to waste and I sealed the wound. Mercifully he passed out and I was able to hold the brand there until the bleeding ceased. I waited until it had cooled and then applied honey. While he was asleep I fastened a bandage around him. I made it as tight as I could. He was still unconscious, or asleep when I had finished and so I put his mail back on. Then, as dawn was breaking, I went to the Saxons. They each had, around their neck, a snake amulet. They each had a gold coin as well. They had been paid by Lang Seax. My brother was right. He feared me.

Agravaine woke an hour after dawn. I made him eat. I would have ordered him to return to the Roman fort but I knew he would refuse. He smiled, as he mounted his horse. "This is my first serious wound, Warlord."

I nodded, "It was honourably earned."

As we neared the high ground I saw, in the rocks to the west, Gawan's right arm. It had been carefully placed so that I would have to climb and be exposed if I was to remove it. There would be men hiding close by waiting to ambush me. Behind it, I saw Wyddfa and that gave me hope. Myrddyn's spirit and that of my father were close by and watching me. I began to recognise where we were. I had been here with King Cadwallon when he had been a prince. I seemed to remember a hunting trail off the road. I wondered if my memory was playing tricks. Then, where the road began to climb I spied the track to the left. It was the hunter's trail I remembered. I remembered my dreams. I knew where we were.

I took the trail and dug my heels in to Star once we were in the trees. I knew that it would be agony for Agravaine to ride through such rough ground for my wounds were hurting too. It could not be helped. The end was almost in sight. Soon there would be no pain. At first, I thought that the trail would take us in a circle but then it turned back on itself and began to wind up around the hill. The trees masked any noise our horses might make and we rode until noon. We emerged east of the road. I saw the road winding up to the northwest. I knew where we were. This was the place I had seen in my dream. This was where the magical pool lay. This would be Saxon Slayer's last resting place. This was *wyrd*. We were less than ten miles from the tomb of Myrddyn and my father. Lang Seax would not know that.

I did not approach the road. The trail seemed to run parallel to it. I wondered if this had been used by the ancient people when they had attacked the Romans invading their land. Agravaine and I did not talk. Sound travelled. I knew that he was close for I could hear his horse. The afternoon was passing quickly. Would Lang Seax stop? Was he waiting to ambush me? The questions raced through my head and then, as the sun started to drop behind Wyddfa, I heard a voice in my head, it was Myrddyn. *'Hogan Lann you are close. The enemy are near. Remember the pool with the blue stone!'*

It confirmed what I had thought. We had found a blue stone in an underground pool. It was here in these mountains.

Donning my helmet, I said, quietly, "Draw your sword, we are close."

I took out Saxon Slayer and peered ahead. I caught a whiff of smoke. Someone was lighting a fire. We had no idea how many enemies faced us but I hoped that half of them were still waiting to ambush us. That way we had a chance. The trail made the difference. It dropped below the road and then climbed. I heard the voices of the Saxons above us. I dug my heels into Star and began to climb through the trees. I knew that the Clan of the Snake was close enough now that they would hear us but Star would be like a warrior. As I breasted the rise a Saxon turned from making water. My swinging sword was the last thing he saw. I spied Lang Seax. He was surrounded by four of his men. Another three were close to the fire. I rode at them knowing that Agravaine would be right behind me. Two of the three ran at me One had an axe. Star reared. His mighty hooves hit the axeman's companion in the head but the axe bit into brave Star's chest. Even dying he fought for me and his body fell on the axe man. I allowed myself to be thrown from his back and I rolled next to the fire. I saw Agravaine slay the third Saxon.

We had to be fast. I knew that the noise would attract the men at the ambush. I ran towards Lang Seax. He drew his long sword and hacked down at a body on the ground. He picked up Gawan's head and threw it at me. Two of his men ran at me while the other two ran towards Agravaine and his horse. I ignored the head and swept my sword at one of the Saxons. He blocked it and stabbed at me with his dagger. Even as my own dagger tore into the thigh of the other Saxon I felt the seax pierce my right shoulder. I saw Lang Seax lumbering towards me. The arrow wound in his leg had slowed him slightly. That evened things up a little. I swung my head around and headbutted the Saxon who had stabbed me. As he reeled I lashed across his throat. Even as he fell the Saxon I had wounded stabbed me in the side with his sword. I felt it scrape along bone. It caught and I stabbed him in the throat with my dagger. As he fell his sword was dragged clear. The pain was as bad as the spear wound to my knee.

Lang Seax saw the blood and thought that I was mortally wounded, "Soon I will have Saxon Slayer and then I will sail to Rheged and your land will be mine. I will be King! Your brother was just a wizard. When I kill you, there will be much honour and glory!" He laughed, "And the treasure you sent home will now be mine. You thought yourself so clever sending but three men with the gold Penda paid you! My men followed and they will already be on their way home with more horses and gold!"

"Kill me first and then boast!"

Saxon Sword

Lang Seax held his long sword in two hands. The sun was setting and I was silhouetted against it. He could no longer see the blood seeping from my wounds. He suddenly ran at me, a little lopsidedly, swinging his sword above his head to split me in two. I dived to my left and dragged Saxon Slayer along his thigh. It tore through the leather and blood spurted. I tried to get to my feet but I was slow. His sword came down for my head. It was my helmet which saved me. As I pulled my head away his sword caught on the metal which held my red plume in place. It tore the helmet from my head but it allowed me to get to my feet.

As I stood I saw that Agravaine's horse was dead as well as the last two Saxons but Agravaine was not moving. There were just the two of us left but, in the distance, I could hear the sound of the other Saxons. They had heard the battle and were returning to their chief. We were both moving slowly now. My sword had ripped a deep wound in Lang Seax's leg. Both his legs had a wound. I had no speed and little agility anymore. I had to use guile. I used deception. I bent over as though I could not breathe and he did as I had expected, he swung his sword at me. He expected me to either move away from the blade or not be able to move at all.

Instead of doing either of those things I stepped in closer to him. I held Saxon Slayer above my head. He would hit my sword and the power of the long sword might well force my weakened arm down but I had little choice. The blade hit but it was too close to him and my blade held his. I brought the seax I had taken from the Saxon in Rheged up under his left arm. There was no mail there. I felt the blade enter the hairy flesh and I pushed. Warm blood began to flow around my hand. I pushed and twisted. The seax had no hilt and my fist went into the hole I had made. I was close enough to him to see the moment of his death. My hand was almost inside his body and I gave one more push. The light went from his eyes and he fell.

I was exhausted but I could hear the sounds of men rushing to the aid of their chief. I sheathed my sword and taking the long sword rammed it between two rocks and I broke it. I dropped the hilt and ran to Agravaine. He was still alive.

"Come let us get away." It was a lie for I was dying but he had to have hope. I helped him to his feet.

"No Warlord, I am hurt. You escape and I will hold them off."

I shook my head, "No, Agravaine, this is the end. I will go and send the sword back to the spirits. Come with me."

"Go, I will hold them off as long as I can." His eyes told me that he was a dead man walking.

I clasped his hand, "I will see you in the Otherworld."

"I will be waiting."

I knew where the chimney of rock was and I headed up the trail. The sun was almost set now but there was enough light to see where I was going. The blood was pouring from my two wounds. As I recalled the pool was just above my head. I knew not where it was exactly and the question buzzed around my head, would I make it before I died or was caught? Below me I heard shouts and then the clash of steel on steel. A man cried out and there was more clashing of blades and shouts. There was a second cry and then a third and then silence. Agravaine had fallen. Each step was agony. I drew my sword and used it as a staff to help me up.

Suddenly I heard footsteps behind me. I turned. I was just int time to see one of the Saxons. My wolf cloak had hidden me and it was only when I turned that he saw my face. He was within two paces of me. I brought my sword across his neck. My blade bit deeply despite the fact that it had not been sharpened for days. I turned and hurried up the steep slope. I could barely get my breath and I felt blood flowing from my wounds. The Saxon voices told me that they had seen me. The pile of rocks ahead was a welcome sight. In my dream that was where the pool lay but footsteps behind brought another Saxon. This time, even as I turned, he rammed his spear into my middle. I had to use two hands to swing my sword. I hacked into his head. I pulled the spear from me. I saw entrails hanging down. I threw the spear into the dark and half ran and crawled to the rocks. I used my left hand to pull myself to the edge. Behind me, I heard footsteps. I did not have long.

I remembered Myrddyn's words, **'Remember this pool. It is the home of the sword. This is where it must lie.'**

"Father, Myrddyn, I have kept my promise. The sword will die with me until it is ready to be reborn." I dropped the sword into the hole. I heard it clang off the side and then there was a splash as it hit the water. I felt an excruciating pain in my back and I closed my eyes. All was black and then I saw four shadows walking toward me. They were men. Three were dressed in mail. It was my father, Myrddyn, Gawan and Agravaine.

My father held out his hand, *'Come my son, your work here is done. We have a place of honour for you. The sword is now safe until another comes to claim it.'*

I stood and all pain was gone. My wounds were healed. I took my father's hand and we stepped into the blackness.

Epilogue

Arturus' Story

We waited six moons for my father and uncle to return after Geraint arrived and told us of the battle and my uncle's last message. We still hoped that, one day, they would ride over the hill and back to our home. We knew they were dead when the Mercian, Egbert, sent us Pol's horse and a message that Lang Seax was dead. His messenger recounted the events of the battle of the Dee and the disappearance of my uncle and Agravaine. King Peada had sent men to hunt down the mercenary Saxons. They had found bodies a few miles from the wolf cave that was Myrddyn's tomb. The Clan of the Snake had left its lair.

We had also lost Llenlleog. When Pelas ap Tuanthal arrived back with his box of treasure he said that the three of them had been ambushed by the Clan of the Snake near to the Long Water. Llenlleog had led them up Halvelyn's side to draw them off. Llewellyn and I had taken the equites to go to their aid. We found Llenlleog's squire and their horses. They were dead and we found a trail of dead Saxons but we never found Llenlleog. It was as though the mountain had taken him. He had simply disappeared. We pursued the Saxons beyond our borders and slew them all. I placed their heads on spears at our boundary to mark that which was ours.

Rheged was bathed in sadness by our losses. We had many widows and orphans and we had lost our two rocks, the Warlord and my father. The gold we had been given and won meant that none went hungry but coins cannot buy fathers, brothers and sons. Only Gwenhwyfar seemed to be at peace. On the day that Pol's horse was returned to us and all hope left us she sat in my hall feeding Myfanwy. She reached over with her free hand and touched mine. "Husband, I have a confession to make. I have known of your father and uncle's deaths since they died. Their spirits came to me."

I was shocked. My wife had kept something from me. "But why did you not tell me?"

"You have many in your land who are Christian. You are Christian. I did not want them to know of my powers. You and I now have a duty to hold Rheged together for as long as we can. Until Myfanwy is a woman we will be the glue which holds Rheged together."

"How did they die?"

Her face clouded. "They died as warriors. They were both true to the end as were Llenlleog and Agravaine. Your grandfather trained his warriors well. The Wolf Brethren are all gone. The darkness is coming but your family has done that which was ordained." She put Myfanwy over her shoulder and rubbed her back to wind her. "As for you and me? We have a different adventure in our future but we will face that future together. The handful of equites you have will need to do that which more than a hundred did in your uncle's time. I must hold the people together and Myfanwy will be the hope of Rheged."

The next day I took Llewelyn and Pelas ap Tuanthal. We went with our squires and we rode to Halvelyn. We passed the empty shepherd's cottage where we had found Warrior. He had not returned and I guessed he was dead too. We left our horses there and walked to Halvelyn's peak. Standing there I raised my hands and closed my eyes. I shouted, "Spirit of Llenlleog, I know you are close, speak to me."

The wind answered me by whistling around my ears. I remained still. My only movement caused by the wind itself. I though he would refuse to speak to me for I wore a cross about my neck. I took the cross from my neck and held it in my hand. The wind itself seemed to speak to me. *'Arturus I am at peace. I died well even though I was alone. Rule this land well. Become the Warlord!'* Then the wind settled and became flurries of gentle air. I lowered my arms.

Ban asked, as we descended, "Lord why did you take off your cross? Are you no longer a Christian?"

I did not answer until we reached the horses. Then I put my cross about my neck again. "There are times when I will be a Christian but, in this land, there is an older force. If I am to be the Warlord then I need the land to aid me. I need the people to be behind me. I am no longer the golden child who returned from Constantinopolis full of himself. I have changed and I have grown. My father, my uncle and my wife have moulded me. I will be the last Dux Britannica. When we last equites die, we will become as my uncle, Llenlleog and my father. We will be legends who will keep hope in hearts which have little else." I mounted my horse, it was my uncle's, Copper. I stroked its golden mane. Drawing my sword, the sword my uncle had taken from King Oswald's hand, I raised it high, "This sword will light the darkness for as long as we shall live."

The five of us headed north to the last bastion of the old Roman Empire in Britannia, Carvetitas.

The End

Glossary

Anglo-Saxon months
- January, is Æftera Geola, or After Yule—the month, quite literally, after Christmas.
- February was Sōlmōnath, a name that derived from an Old English word for wet sand or mud, sōl; it meant the month of cakes, when ritual offerings of savoury cakes and loaves of bread would be made to ensure a good year's harvest.
- March was Hrēðmonath to the ancient Anglo-Saxons and was named in honour of a little-known pagan fertility goddess named Hreða, or Rheda.
- April was the Anglo-Saxon Eostremonath, which took its name from another pagan deity named Eostre.
- May was Thrimilce, or the month of three milkings.
- June and July were together known as Liða, an Old English word meaning mild or gentle, which referred to the period of warm, seasonable weather either side of Midsummer.
- August was Weodmonath or the plant month.
- After that came September, or Hāligmonath, meaning holy month, when celebrations and religious festivals would be held to celebrate a successful summer's crop.
- October was Winterfylleth, or the winter full moon.
- November was Blōtmonath, or the month of blood sacrifices.
- And December, finally, was Ærra Geola or the month before Yule.

Name-Explanation
Abbatis Villa- Abbeville –Northern France

Saxon Sword

Aengus Finn mac Fergus Dubdétach-Irish mercenary
Aelfere-Northallerton
Aelle-Monca's son and Hogan Lann's uncle
Aileen- Fergus' sister, a mystic
Aelletün- Lann Aelle's settlement
Alavna-Maryport Cumbria
Artorius-King Arthur
Banna-Birdoswald
-God of war
Belerion-Land's End (Cornwall)
Bilhaugh Forest –Sherwood Forest
Bone fire- the burning of the waste material after the slaughter of the animals at the end of October. (Bonfire night)
Bors- son of Mungo war chief of Strathclyde
Bro Waroc'h- one of the Brythionic tribes who settled in Brittany
Byrnie – mail shirt
Caedwalestate-Cadishead near Salford
Caer Daun- Doncaster
Caergybi-Holyhead
Cadwallon ap Cadfan- King of Gwynedd
Caldarium- the hot room in a Roman bathhouse
Carvetitas – Camelot
Ceorl- Commoner, ordinary soldier
Chonoc-salchild -Knock (Cumbria)
Civitas Carvetiorum-Carlisle
Constantinopolis-Constantinople (modern Istanbul)
Cymri- Welsh
Cymru-Wales
Cynfarch Oer-Descendant of Coel Hen (King Cole)
Dál Riata-land on the south west of Scotland
Daffydd ap Gwynfor-Lann's chief sea captain
Daffydd ap Miach-Miach's son
Dai ap Gruffyd-King Cadfan's squire
Delbchaem Lann-Lann's daughter
Din Guardi-Bamburgh Castle
Dùn Èideann -Edinburgh
Dunum-River Tees

Saxon Sword

Dux Britannica-The Roman British leader after the Romans left (King Arthur?)
Edwin-King of Bernicia, Deira and Northumbria
Eoforwic - York (Eboracum)
Erecura-Goddess of the earth
Fanum Cocidii-Bewcastle
Fiachnae mac Báetáin- King of Strathclyde
Fiachnae mac Demmáin - King of the Dál Fiatach
Freja-Saxon captive and Aelle's wife
Gammer- Old English for mother
Gareth-Harbour master Caergybi
Gallóglaigh-Irish mercenary
Gawan Lann-Lann's son
Gesith- Saxon chieftain
Glanibanta- Ambleside
Gwynfor-Headman at Caergybi
Gwenhwyfar- Guinevere
Gwyr-The land close to Swansea
Hagustaldes-ham - Hexham
Halvelyn- Helvellyn
Haordine-Hawarden Cheshire
hearthweru - King's bodyguard (the precursor of the housecarl)
Hen Ogledd-Northern England and Southern Scotland
High Divide- The Pennines
Hogan Lann-Lann's son and Warlord
Humbre (Anglo-Saxon) Hwmyr (Welsh) – River Humber
Icaunus-River god
Iedeu – Jedburgh
Ituna- River Solway
King Ywain Rheged-Eldest son of King Urien
Lann- First Warlord of Rheged and Dux Britannica
Lincylene -Lincoln
Llenlleog- 'Leaping one' (Lancelot)
Loge-God of trickery
Ladenses- Leeds
Loidis-Leeds
Maeresea-River Mersey

Maes Cogwy- Maserfield (the present-day Oswestry – Oswald's Tree)
Manau- Isle of Man
Mare Nostrum-Mediterranean Sea
Metcauld- Lindisfarne
Myfanwy-the Warlord's stepmother
Myrddyn-Welsh wizard fighting for Rheged
Nanna Lann-Lann's daughter, wife to King Cadwallon
Namentwihc –Nantwich, Cheshire
Nithing-A man without honour
Nodens-God of hunting
Oppidum- hill fort
Paulinus of Eboracum- The Pope's representative in Britannia
Penrhyd- Penrith, Cumbria
Penrhyn Llŷn- Llŷn Peninsula
pharos- lighthouse
Pol-Equite and strategos
Prestune-Preston Lancashire
Roman Bridge-Piercebridge (Durham)
Roman Soldiers- the mountains around Scafell Pike
Rhuthun -Ruthin North Wales
Scillonia Insula-Scilly Isles
Solar-West facing room in a castle
Spæwīfe- Old English for witch
Sucellos-God of love and time
Táin Bó- Irish for cattle raid
Tatenhale- Tattenhall near Chester
Tepidarium- the warm room in a Roman Bath house
Tomworðig- Tamworth (Capital of Mercia)
The Narrows-The Menaii Straits
Treffynnon-Holywell (North Wales)
Tuanthal-Leader of the Warlord's horse warriors
Vectis-Isle of Wight
Vindonnus-God of hunting
Virosidum- close to Middleham in North Yorkshire
Wachanglen-Wakefield
Walls of Brus- Wark on Tyne (Northumberland)
War shits- dysentery

Saxon Sword

Wrecsam- Wrexham
wapentake- Muster of an army
Wide Water-Windermere
Wyddfa-Snowdon
Wyrd-Fate
Y Fflint- Flint (North Wales)
Ynys Enlli- Bardsey Island
Ynys Môn- Anglesey
Yr Wyddgrug- Mold (North Wales)
Zatrikion- an early form of Greek chess

Saxon Sword

Historical note

There is evidence that the Saxons withdrew from Rheged in the early years of the seventh century and never dominated that land again. It seems that warriors from Wales reclaimed that land. I have used Lord Lann as that instrument. King Edwin did usurp Aethelfrith. Edwin was allied to both Mercia and East Anglia.

The Saxons and Britons all valued swords and cherished them. They were passed from father to son. The use of rings on the hilts of great swords was a common practice and showed the prowess of the warrior in battle. I do not subscribe to Brian Sykes' theory that the Saxons merely assimilated into the existing people. One only has to look at the place names and listen to the language of the north and north western part of England. You can still hear anomalies. Perhaps that is because I come from the north but all of my reading leads me to believe that the Anglo-Saxons were intent upon conquest. The Norse invaders were different and they did assimilate but the Saxons were fighting for their lives and it did not pay to be kind. The people of Rheged were the last survivors of Roman Britain and I have given them all of the characteristics they would have had. They were educated and ingenious. The Dark Ages was the time when much knowledge was lost and would not reappear until Constantinople fell. This period was also the time when the old ways changed and Britain became Christian. This was a source of conflict as well as growth.

It was at the beginning of the sixth century that King Aethelfrith was killed in battle. His sons, Eanforth, Oswiu and Oswald became famous and outshone both their father and King Edwin. Although Edwin became king he did not have the three brothers killed and they had an uneasy alliance.

King Cadwallon became the last great British leader until modern times. Alfred ruled the Saxons but no one held such sway over the country from Scotland to Cornwall in the same way that King Cadwallon did. He did this not by feat of arms alone but by using alliances. He even allied with the Mercians to ensure security for his land. His death saw the end of the hopes of the native Britons. They would survive but they would never reconquer their land. I have invented a Warlord to aid him but that is backed up by the few writings we have. Dux Britannicus and Arthur are both shadowy figures who crop up in what we now term, the Dark Ages.

King Edwin's life was saved by Bishop Paulinus who had been sent by the Pope to convert the Northumbrians to Christianity. The act made King Edwin order all of his people to convert. I have used Paulinus as a sort of villain. I have no doubt that the Church at the time thought they were doing good work but like the Spanish Inquisition a thousand years later they were not averse to suing any means possible when dealing with what they deemed pagans. King Cadwallon did convert to Christianity but still fought King Edwin. Bede, the Northumbrian propagandist, portrayed Cadwallon as a cruel man who destroyed the Christian kingdom of Northumbria. Perhaps that was because King Edwin became an early Christian martyr. History is written by the winners and the Anglo-Saxons did win, albeit briefly before the Norse and the Bretons combined to reconquer England in 1066.

The people of Brittany did arrive there as stated in the novel. I have obviously invented both names and events to suit my story but the background is accurate. They spoke a variation of Welsh/Cornish. There was a famous witch who lived on one of the islands of Scilly. Although this was in the Viking age a century or so later I can see no reason why mystics did not choose to live there.

The horses used by William the Conqueror at Hastings were about fifteen and a half hands high. The largest contingent of non-Norman knights who accompanied him were the Bretons and their horses were marginally bigger. It is ironical that the people of Britain came back to defeat the Saxons. It was a mixture of Briton and Viking (Norman) who finally conquered Britain. (*Wyrd*!)

The stirrup was unknown in Britain at this time. I can find no explanation for this. It strikes me that someone would have invented it. However, it seems they did not and so the Warlord and his men can't use the lance or the spear effectively. The impact of the weapon would have knocked them from the saddle. Charlemagne and his armies had the stirrup. That, however, was a century after this period in British history.

The battle of Hatfield took place on the River Don close to Doncaster. It was fought on a swamp in a bend of the river. It was in the early 630s. King Edwin was killed at the battle and the leaders of the victorious armies were named as Penda and Cadwallon. It marked a reversal in fortunes for the Saxons. They were forced to retreat further north and Eanfrith, the eldest of Aethelfrith's children became king of Deira. He was also killed by Cadwallon and Oswald became king. The kingdom of Northumbria would never be as powerful again until the Vikings conquered it in the ninth century. Bernicia and Deira emerged as minor kingdoms. King Cadwallon had a brief year of glory when he rampaged through the land of Bernicia. It was not to last.

The Viking name for Helvellyn was wolf mountain and there were many such animals there. Wolves were so prevalent in the north of England that William the Conqueror actually stipulated that his new lords of the manor had a duty to hunt and exterminate them. The last ones were only killed in the sixteenth century.

The change in King Cadwallon is attested to by Bede. Given that the priest was writing as someone who believed King Edwin was a saint we should perhaps take his testimony with a pinch of salt but Cadwallon was a Christian king. He said that King Cadwallon ravaged, *"provinces of the Northumbrians"* for a year, *"not like a victorious king, but like a rapacious and bloody tyrant."* The priest also said, *"though he bore the name and professed himself a Christian, was so barbarous in his disposition and behaviour, that he neither spared the female sex, nor the innocent age of children, but with savage cruelty put them to tormenting deaths, ravaging all their country for a long time, and resolving to cut off all the race of the English within the borders of Britain."* We see this change during this novel. Perhaps it is not to be seen as unusual. Alexander the Great was viewed in a similar way. Perhaps it is success which breeds such changes.

Osric, the King of Deira, did try to take a large walled town in which King Cadwallon waited. The army sortied and slaughtered all of them. Eanfrith did try to negotiate with King Cadwallon. It is said, by Bede, that he went to speak with King Cadwallon along with twelve warriors and he never returned. In many ways it was ironic for his successor, Oswald, fought and killed King Cadwallon at the battle of Heavenfield (Hexham) and then completely destroyed the Welsh army. King Cadwallon's reign as High King lasted less than two years and enabled the Angles, Jutes and Saxons to rule Britain until the Vikings arrived.

The bubonic plague was first brought to Britain in the sixth century. It was called Justinian's Plague. It devastated Wales on a number of occasions. Famously in 642, the year of the Battle of Maserfield, it is reputed to have taken King Cadafael although there were other rumours that he was murdered. King Penda did, indeed defeat and kill Oswald at Maserfield and he did it with an alliance of the Welsh and Brythionic people. It was the monk Bede who tells us of the events of this time and they should be taken with as much salt as possible! King Oswald was Christian and Penda was a pagan. Bede was an excellent propagandist!

King Penda invaded Northumbria some time in 636 or 637 and besieged Din Guardi. He was there for some months but he could not manage to break down the defenders' resistance. It proved too great a nut to crack and after laying waste to the land around the stronghold he eventually returned to Mercia. Oswald then spent the next few years building up his army before he and Eowa invaded Mercia in 642.

Oswald of Bernicia became king of Northumbria after his victory over Cadwallon at Heavenfield. Penda's status and activities during the years of Oswald's reign are obscure, and various interpretations of Penda's position during this period have been suggested. It has been presumed that Penda acknowledged Oswald's authority in some sense after Heavenfield, although Penda was probably an obstacle to Northumbrian supremacy south of the Humber. It has been suggested that Penda's strength during Oswald's reign could be exaggerated by the historical awareness of his later successes. Kirby says that, while Oswald was as powerful as Edwin had been, "he faced a more entrenched challenge in midland and eastern England from Penda".

At some point during Oswald's reign, Penda had Edwin's son Eadfrith killed, "contrary to his oath". The possibility that his killing was the result of pressure from Oswald—Eadfrith being a dynastic rival of Oswald—has been suggested. Since the potential existed for Eadfrith to be put to use in Mercia's favour in Northumbrian power struggles while he was alive, it would not have been to Penda's advantage to have him killed. On the other hand, Penda might have killed Eadfrith for his own reasons. It has been suggested that Penda was concerned that Eadfrith could be a threat to him because Eadfrith might seek vengeance for the deaths of his father and brother; it is also possible that Mercian dynastic rivalry played a part in the killing, since Eadfrith was a grandson of Penda's predecessor Cearl.

It was probably at some point during Oswald's reign that Penda fought with the East Angles and defeated them, killing their King Egric and the former king Sigebert, who had been brought out of retirement in a monastery against his will in the belief that his presence would motivate the soldiers. The time at which the battle occurred is uncertain; it may have been as early as 635, but there is also evidence to suggest it could not have been before 640 or 641. Presuming that this battle took place before the Battle of Maserfield, it may have been that such an expression of Penda's ambition and emerging power made Oswald feel that Penda had to be defeated for Northumbrian dominance of southern England to be secured or consolidated.

Penda's brother Eowa was also said by the Historia Brittonum and the Annales Cambriae to have been a king of the Mercians at the time of Maserfield. The question of what sort of relationship of power existed between the brothers before the battle is a matter of speculation. Eowa may have simply been a sub-king under Penda and it is also possible that Penda and Eowa ruled jointly during the 630s and early 640s: joint kingships were not uncommon among Anglo-Saxon kingdoms of the period. They may have ruled the southern and northern Mercians respectively. That Penda ruled the southern part is a possibility suggested by his early involvement in the area of the Hwicce, to the south of Mercia, as well as by the fact that, after Penda's death, his son Peada was allowed to rule southern Mercia while the northern part was placed under direct Northumbrian control.

Another possibility is that Penda might have lost power at some point after Heavenfield, and Eowa may have actually been ruling the Mercians for at least some of the period as a subject ally or puppet of Oswald. Brooks cited Bede's statement implying that Penda's fortunes were mixed during his 22 years in power and noted the possibility that Penda's fortunes were low at this time. Thus it may be that Penda was not consistently the dominant figure in Mercia during the years between Hatfield and Maserfield.

On 5 August 642, Penda defeated the Northumbrians at the Battle of Maserfield, which was fought near the lands of the Welsh, and Oswald was killed. Surviving Welsh poetry suggests that Penda fought in alliance with the men of Powys— apparently, he was consistently allied with some of the Welsh— perhaps including Cynddylan ap Cyndrwyn, of whom it was said that "when the son of Pyb desired, how ready he was", presumably meaning that he was an ally of Penda, the son of Pybba. If the traditional identification of the battle's location with Oswestry is correct, then this would indicate that it was Oswald who had taken the offensive against Penda. It has been suggested that he was acting against "a threat posed to his domination of Mercia by a hostile alliance of Penda and Powys." According to Reginald of Durham's 12th century Life of Saint Oswald, Penda fled into Wales before the battle, at which point Oswald felt secure and sent his army away. This explanation of events has been regarded as "plausible" but is not found in any other source, and may, therefore, have been Reginald's invention.

According to Bede, Penda had Oswald's body dismembered, with his head, hands and arms being placed onto stakes -this may have had a pagan religious significance; Oswald thereafter came to be revered as a saint, with his death in battle as a Christian king against pagans leading him to be regarded as a martyr.

Eowa was killed at Maserfield along with Oswald, although on which side he fought is unknown. It may well be that he fought as a dependent ally of Oswald against Penda. If Eowa was in fact dominant among the Mercians during the period leading up to the battle, then his death could have marked what the author of the Historia Brittonum regarded as the beginning of Penda's ten-year reign. Therefore it may be that Penda prevailed not only over the Northumbrians but also over his rivals among the Mercians.

The Historia Brittonum may also be referring to this battle when it says that Penda first freed (separavit) the Mercians from the Northumbrians. This may be an important clue to the relationship between the Mercians and the Northumbrians before and during Penda's time. There may have existed a "Humbrian confederacy" that included the Mercians until Penda broke free of it. On the other hand, it has been considered unlikely that this was truly the first instance of their separation: it is significant that Cearl had married his daughter to Edwin during Edwin's exile, when Edwin was an enemy of the Northumbrian king Æthelfrith. It would seem that if Cearl was able to do this, he was not subject to Æthelfrith; thus it may be that any subject relationship only developed after the time of this marriage.

The battle left Penda with a degree of power unprecedented for a Mercian king—Kirby called him "without question the most powerful Mercian ruler so far to have emerged in the midlands" after Maserfield and the prestige and status associated with defeating the powerful Oswald must have been very significant. Northumbria was greatly weakened as a consequence of the battle; the kingdom became fractured to some degree between Deira in its southern part and Bernicia in the north, with the Deirans acquiring a king of their own, Oswine, while in Bernicia, Oswald was succeeded by his brother, Oswiu. Mercia thus enjoyed a greatly enhanced position of strength relative to the surrounding kingdoms. Writers said that the battle left Penda as "the most formidable king in England", and observed that although "there is no evidence that he ever became, or even tried to become, the lord of all the other kings of southern England ... none of them can have been his equal in reputation".

I used many books to research the material. The first was the excellent Michael Wood's book "***In Search of the Dark Ages***" and the second was "***The Middle Ages***" Edited by Robert Fossier. The third was the Osprey Book- "***Saxon, Viking and Norman***" by Terence Wise. I also used Brian Sykes' book, "***Blood of the Isles***" for reference. "***Arthur and the Anglo-Saxon Wars***" by David Nicholle was useful. "***Anglo Saxon Thegn***" by Mark Harrison gave an insight into the way the minor chiefs ruled their lands. In addition, I searched online for more obscure information. All the place names are accurate, as far as I know, and I have researched the names of the characters to reflect the period. My apologies if I have made a mistake.

The battles at Oswestry and Winwaed did take place. The latter's site is open for debate. It is variously identified as Winwick in Cheshire, Leeds and Doncaster. Iedeu was the place where King Penda fought and defeated Oswiu. I have no idea why he did not kill him. He did take Oswiu's son as hostage and he received huge quantities of ransom from the Bernician King. It was as he was returning home that he was finally defeated. According to Bede, a biased and therefore suspect source, the Mercians and their allies lost more men in the flight back to Mercia than the battle. I have tried to reflect this in my account. Wherever the battle took place the result was still the same. King Penda was defeated and executed. King Oswiu and Northumbria became dominant. This was the end of Pagan England and the start of a Christian one. It remained the same until the Vikings came in a few years.

Although this is the last book in the series I have plans to write a standalone book about Arturus. It will bridge the Saxon and Viking series of my books.

Griff Hosker
June 2018

Other books by Griff Hosker

If you enjoyed reading this book, then why not read another one by the author?

Ancient History

The Sword of Cartimandua Series
(Germania and Britannia 50 A.D. – 128 A.D.)
Ulpius Felix- Roman Warrior (prequel)
The Sword of Cartimandua
The Horse Warriors
Invasion Caledonia
Roman Retreat
Revolt of the Red Witch
Druid's Gold
Trajan's Hunters
The Last Frontier
Hero of Rome
Roman Hawk
Roman Treachery
Roman Wall
Roman Courage

The Wolf Warrior series
(Britain in the late 6th Century)
Saxon Dawn
Saxon Revenge
Saxon England
Saxon Blood
Saxon Slayer
Saxon Slaughter
Saxon Bane
Saxon Fall: Rise of the Warlord
Saxon Throne

Saxon Sword

Saxon Sword

Medieval History

The Dragon Heart Series
Viking Slave
Viking Warrior
Viking Jarl
Viking Kingdom
Viking Wolf
Viking War
Viking Sword
Viking Wrath
Viking Raid
Viking Legend
Viking Vengeance
Viking Dragon
Viking Treasure
Viking Enemy
Viking Witch
Viking Blood
Viking Weregeld
Viking Storm
Viking Warband
Viking Shadow
Viking Legacy
Viking Clan
Viking Bravery

The Norman Genesis Series
Hrolf the Viking
Horseman
The Battle for a Home
Revenge of the Franks
The Land of the Northmen
Ragnvald Hrolfsson
Brothers in Blood
Lord of Rouen
Drekar in the Seine

Saxon Sword

Duke of Normandy
The Duke and the King

Danelaw
(England and Denmark in the 11th Century)
Dragon Sword
Oathsword
Bloodsword

New World Series
Blood on the Blade
Across the Seas
The Savage Wilderness
The Bear and the Wolf
Erik The Navigator
Erik's Clan

The Vengeance Trail

The Reconquista Chronicles
Castilian Knight
El Campeador
The Lord of Valencia

The Aelfraed Series
(Britain and Byzantium 1050 A.D. - 1085 A.D.)
Housecarl
Outlaw
Varangian

The Anarchy Series England 1120-1180
English Knight
Knight of the Empress
Northern Knight
Baron of the North
Earl
King Henry's Champion
The King is Dead

Saxon Sword

Warlord of the North
Enemy at the Gate
The Fallen Crown
Warlord's War
Kingmaker
Henry II
Crusader
The Welsh Marches
Irish War
Poisonous Plots
The Princes' Revolt
Earl Marshal
The Perfect Knight

**Border Knight
1182-1300**
Sword for Hire
Return of the Knight
Baron's War
Magna Carta
Welsh Wars
Henry III
The Bloody Border
Baron's Crusade
Sentinel of the North
War in the West
Debt of Honour
The Blood of the Warlord

**Sir John Hawkwood Series
France and Italy 1339- 1387**
Crécy: The Age of the Archer
Man At Arms
The White Company
Leader of Men

Lord Edward's Archer
Lord Edward's Archer
King in Waiting

Saxon Sword

An Archer's Crusade
Targets of Treachery
The Great Cause

Struggle for a Crown
1360- 1485
Blood on the Crown
To Murder a King
The Throne
King Henry IV
The Road to Agincourt
St Crispin's Day
The Battle for France
The Last Knight
Queen's Knight

Tales from the Sword I
(Short stories from the Medieval period)

Tudor Warrior series
England and Scotland in the late 14th and early 15th century
Tudor Warrior

Conquistador
England and America in the 16th Century
Conquistador

Modern History

The Napoleonic Horseman Series
Chasseur à Cheval
Napoleon's Guard
British Light Dragoon
Soldier Spy
1808: The Road to Coruña
Talavera
The Lines of Torres Vedras
Bloody Badajoz

Saxon Sword

The Road to France
Waterloo

The Lucky Jack American Civil War series
Rebel Raiders
Confederate Rangers
The Road to Gettysburg

Soldier of the Queen series
Soldier of the Queen

The British Ace Series
1914
1915 Fokker Scourge
1916 Angels over the Somme
1917 Eagles Fall
1918 We will remember them
From Arctic Snow to Desert Sand
Wings over Persia

Combined Operations series
1940-1945
Commando
Raider
Behind Enemy Lines
Dieppe
Toehold in Europe
Sword Beach
Breakout
The Battle for Antwerp
King Tiger
Beyond the Rhine
Korea
Korean Winter

Tales from the Sword II
(Short stories from the Modern period)

Other Books

Saxon Sword

Great Granny's Ghost (Aimed at 9-14-year-old young people)

For more information on all of the books then please visit the author's website at www.griffhosker.com where there is a link to contact him or visit his Facebook page: GriffHosker at Sword Books

Printed in Great Britain
by Amazon